Jack Dickey

A gallant group of courageous, audacious people caught in a life-and-death struggle for survival . . .

STORM WARNING
by Jack Higgins
Author of *The Eagle Has Landed*

JANET—She was a war-toughened nurse desperately in love with a Nazi officer.

GERICKE—He was the U-boat Commander willing to risk anything for victory.

LOTTE—She was a novice nun torn from her vows by a fierce, unyielding passion.

"THE WAVES CRASH ACROSS THE DECKS SO WILDLY YOU WILL FIND YOURSELF SINKING INTO YOUR ARMCHAIR FOR PROTECTION."

—*Philadelphia Bulletin*

"A TRUE SAGA OF THE SEA—THIS IS HIGGINS'S GREAT ACCOMPLISHMENT."

—*Washington Post*

STORM WARNING

JACK HIGGINS

BANTAM BOOKS · TORONTO · LONDON · NEW YORK

*This low-priced Bantam Book
has been completely reset in a type face
designed for easy reading, and was printed
from new plates. It contains the complete
text of the original hard-cover edition.*
NOT ONE WORD HAS BEEN OMITTED.

STORM WARNING

*A Bantam Book / published by arrangement with
Holt, Rinehart and Winston*

PRINTING HISTORY

Holt, Rinehart edition / August 1976
2nd printing .... August 1976   4th printing ... October 1976
3rd printing ... October 1976   5th printing .. November 1976
6th printing......November 1976
Literary Guild edition / September 1976
Playboy Book Club edition / January 1977
Condensations appeared in READER'S DIGEST *in November 1976
and East/West Network Publications of* CLIPPER *in December
1976 and* SKY *in January 1977.*
Bantam edition / June 1977

ISBN 0-553-10700-3

Published simultaneously in the United States and Canada.

*Bantam Books are published by Bantam Books, Inc. Its trade-
mark, consisting of the words "Bantam Books" and the por-
trayal of a bantam, is registered in the United States Patent
Office and in other countries. Marca Registrada. Bantam
Books, Inc., 666 Fifth Avenue, New York, New York 10019.*

PRINTED IN THE UNITED STATES OF AMERICA

For John Knowler—with Oak Leaves

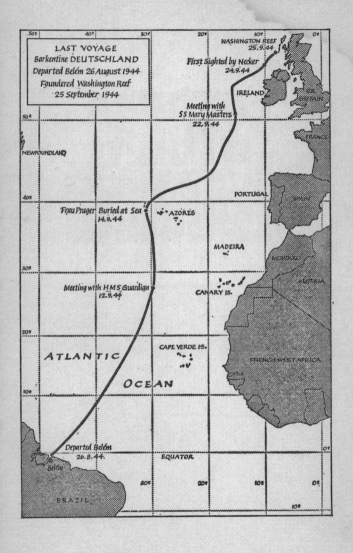

LAST VOYAGE
Barkentine DEUTSCHLAND
Departed Belém 26 August 1944
Foundered Washington Reef
25 September 1944

WASHINGTON REEF
25.9.44

First Sighted by Necker
24.9.44

IRELAND

GR.
BRITAIN

FRANCE

Meeting with
SS Mary Masters
22.9.44

NEWFOUNDLAND

PORTUGAL

SPAIN

Frau Prager Buried at Sea
14.9.44

AZORES

MADEIRA

MOROCCO

ALGERIA

Meeting with H.M.S. Guardian
12.9.44

CANARY IS.

ATLANTIC

CAPE VERDE IS.

FRENCH WEST AFRICA

OCEAN

Departed Belém
26.8.44.

Belém

EQUATOR

BRAZIL

STORM WARNING

FROM THE JOURNAL OF REAR ADMIRAL
CAREY REEVE, USN

*. . . and this, I find the greatest mystery of all—the
instinct in man to sacrifice himself that others might
live. But then, courage never goes out of fashion, and
at no other time in my life have I seen it better dis-
played than in the affair of the* Deutschland. *In the
midst of the greatest war history has known, people on
opposite sides in that conflict were able to come together for a time, take every risk, lay themselves on the
line, in an attempt to save a handful of human beings
from man's oldest and most implacable foe—the sea.
I have never seen the tragic futility of war better dem-
onstrated nor felt prouder of my fellow men than at
that time. . . .*

Barkentine Deutschland, *26 August 1944.*
Eleven days out of Rio de Janeiro. At an-
chorage in Belém. Begins hot. Moderate
trades. Last of the coal unloaded. No cargo
available. In ballast with sand for run to Rio.
Hatches battened down and ready to sail.
Rain toward evening.

One

*A*s Prager turned the corner, thunder rumbled far out to sea and lightning flashed across the sky, giving for one brief moment a clear view of the harbor. The usual assortment of small craft and three or four coastal steamers were moored at the main jetty. The *Deutschland* was anchored in midstream, distinctive if only for the fact that she was the one sailing ship in the harbor.

Rain came suddenly, warm and heavy, redolent with rotting vegetation from the jungle across the river. Prager turned up the collar of his jacket and, holding his old leather briefcase under one arm, hurried along the waterfront toward the Lights of Lisbon, the bar at the end of the fish pier.

There was the sound of music, muted yet plain

enough, a slow, sad samba with something of the night in it. As he went up the steps to the veranda he took off his spectacles and wiped rain from them with his handkerchief. He replaced them carefully and peered inside.

The place was empty, except for the bartender and Helmut Richter, the *Deutschland*'s bosun, who sat at the end of the bar with a bottle and a glass in front of him. He was a large, heavily built man in reefer jacket and denim cap with long, blond hair and a beard that made him look older than his twenty-eight years.

Prager stepped inside. The bartender, who was polishing a glass, looked up. Prager ignored him and moved along the bar, shaking the rain from his Panama. He dropped the briefcase on the floor at his feet.

"A good night for it, Helmut."

Richter nodded gravely and picked up the bottle. "A drink, Herr Prager?"

"I think not."

"A wise choice." Richter refilled his glass. *"Cachaca.* They say it rots the brain as well as the liver. A poor substitute for good schnapps, but they haven't seen any of that since '39."

"Is Kapitän Berger here?"

"Waiting for you on board."

Prager picked up his briefcase. "Then I suggest we get moving. There isn't much time. Has anyone been asking for me?"

Before Richter could reply a voice said in Portuguese, "Ah, Senhor Prager, a pleasant surprise."

Prager turned quickly as the curtain of one of the small booths behind him was pulled back. The man who sat there, a bottle of wine in front of him, was immensely fat, his crumpled khaki uniform stained with sweat and bursting at the seams.

Prager managed a smile. "Captain Mendoza. Don't you ever sleep?"

"Not very often. What is it this time, business or pleasure?"

"A little of both. As you know, the position of German nationals is a difficult one these days. Your government is more than ever insistent on a regular report."

"So, it is necessary that Berger and his men are seen by you personally?"

"On the first day of the last week in each month. Your people in Rio are most strict in this respect."

"And the good Senhora Prager? I am given to understand she was on the plane with you."

"I have a few days' leave due and she has never seen this part of the country. It seemed the ideal opportunity."

Richter slipped out without a word. Mendoza watched him go. "A nice lad," he said. "What was it he used to be? Chief helmsman on a U-boat. *Obersteuermann,* isn't that the word?"

"I believe so."

"You'll have a drink with me?"

Prager hesitated. "Just a quick one, if you don't mind. I have an appointment."

"With Berger?" Mendoza nodded to the barman who poured brandy into two glasses without a word. "When does he leave to go back to Rio? In the morning?"

"I believe so." Prager sipped the brandy, on dangerous ground now. He was sixty-five, an assistant consul at the German embassy in Rio until August 1942, when the Brazilians, enraged by the torpedoing of several of their merchant ships by U-boats, had declared war. Little more than a gesture, but it had presented the problem of what to do about German nationals—in particular the increasing number of sailors of the *Kriegsmarine* who found themselves washed up on her shores.

Prager, having spent twenty years in the country, and being acceptable in high places, had been left behind to cope with that. There were, after all, five thousand miles of ocean between Brazil and Germany, so no need to set up expensive internment camps. The Brazilian government was content with the monthly reports he presented on his fellow citizens. As long as they were gainfully employed and not a charge on the state, everyone was happy.

Mendoza said, "I've been harbor master here for two years now and for most of that time the *Deutschland* has been coming in regularly. Say every couple of months."

"So?"

"A boat of that size usually manages with a master, mate, bosun, probably six foremast hands, and a cook."

"That is correct."

Mendoza sipped a little of his brandy thoughtfully. "According to my information, Berger has a crew of something like twenty this trip."

He smiled genially, but the eyes in the fat face were sharp. Prager said carefully, "There are many German seamen in Rio."

"And more each day. The war, my friend, does not go well for you."

"Berger is probably trying to employ as many as possible."

Mendoza smiled beautifully. "But of course. That explanation had not occurred to me. But I mustn't keep you. Perhaps we'll have time for another drink tomorrow?"

"I hope so."

Prager went out quickly. Richter was waiting on the veranda by the steps. Beyond, the rain hammered relentlessly into the ground. "Everything all right?" he asked.

"Not really," Prager told him. "He knows something's going on. But how could he possibly suspect the truth? No one in his right mind would believe it." He clapped Richter on the shoulder. "Now let's get moving."

The bosun said, "I didn't get a chance to tell you inside, but there was someone asking for you."

There was a movement behind and, as Prager turned, a nun in white tropical habit stepped into the light. She was a small woman, not much over five feet tall, with clear, untroubled eyes and a calm, unlined face.

"Sister Angela," Richter said.

"Of the Sisters of Mercy from the mission station on the Río Negro. Introductions are not necessary, Helmut. Sister Angela and I are old acquaintances."

He took off his Panama and held out his hand, which she clasped briefly in a grasp of surprising strength.

"It's good to see you again, Sister."

"And you, Herr Prager. I think you know why I'm here."

"Why, yes, Sister." Otto Prager smiled warmly. "I believe I do."

An anchor light hung from the *Deutschland*'s forestay, as required by marine regulations, and this they saw first as Richter worked the dinghy across the harbor. Then suddenly she was very close, her masts and spars dark against the sky.

Prager looked up with conscious pleasure as he climbed the Jacob's ladder. She was a three-masted barkentine built by Hamish Campbell on the Clyde in 1881 and built with love and understanding and grace, with an elegant clipper bow to her and an extended jibboom.

She had spent a lifetime in trade: Newcastle upon Tyne with steam coal for Valparaíso; Chilean nitrates for America's west coast; lumber for Australia; wool for Britain . . . an endless circle, as sail died in a doomed attempt to combat steam, one owner after another through three changes of name until, finally, she had been bought by the Brazilian firm of Meyer Brothers, a

family of German extraction, who had rechristened her
Deutschland and put her to the coastal trade. Rio to
Belém and the mouth of the Amazon—just the craft
for such waters, having a draft of only eight feet fully
loaded.

Prager went over the bulwark and extended his
hand to Sister Angela. Richter was close behind on the
ladder. Three seamen by the mainmast gazed in astonishment as the little nun came over the side, and one of
them hurried forward to take her other hand.

She thanked him, and Prager said to her, "I think
it would be better if I spoke to Kapitän Berger alone to
start with."

"Whatever you think best, Herr Prager," she said,
tranquilly.

He turned to Richter. "Take the good sister down
to the saloon, then wait for me outside the Kapitän's
cabin."

Richter and Sister Angela descended the companionway and Prager went aft toward the quarterdeck.
Berger's cabin was underneath. He hesitated, then
braced himself, knocked on the door, and went in.

The cabin was small, spartan in its furnishings—
narrow bunk, three cupboards, and not much else except for the desk behind which Berger sat, making a
measurement with parallel rulers on the chart spread
before him.

He glanced up, and there was relief in his eyes.
"I was beginning to get worried."

He was at that time forty-eight years old, of medium height with good shoulders, his wiry, dark hair
and beard flecked with gray, and his face weathered by
sea and sun.

"I'm sorry," Prager said. "We ran into a bad electric storm on the flight from Rio. The pilot insisted on
touching down at Carolina until the weather cleared.
We were there for four hours."

Berger opened a sandalwood box and offered him
a cheroot. "What's the latest war news?"

"All bad." Prager sat in the chair opposite and accepted a light. "On the fifteenth of this month, American and French forces landed on the Mediterranean coast. Two days ago French tanks entered Paris."

Berger whistled softly. "Next stop the Rhine."

"I should imagine so."

"And then Germany." He stood up, crossed to one of the cupboards, opened it, and took out a bottle of rum and two glasses. "What about the Russians?"

"The Red Army is on the borders of East Prussia."

Berger poured rum into the glasses and pushed one across. "You know, Otto, we Germans haven't had to defend the soil of the fatherland since Napoleon. It should prove an interesting experience."

"Brazil might be the best place to be for the next year or two," Prager said. "A hell of a time to go home."

"Or the only time," Berger said. "It depends on your point of view. Have you got the papers?"

Prager put his briefcase on the desk. "Everything needed and I've checked again on the barkentine you mentioned when you first spoke of this crazy affair, the *Gudrid Andersen*. She's still in Göteborg harbor. Hasn't been to sea since the first year of the war."

"Excellent," Berger said. "Plain sailing from here on, then."

"You are fully prepared?"

Berger opened a cupboard and took out a life jacket which he dropped on the desk. The legend GUDRID ANDERSEN—GÖTEBORG was stenciled on the back.

"And this, of course." He produced next a Swedish ensign. "A most important item as I'm sure you'll agree." He smiled. "Everything is ready, believe me. The official change of name we'll make once clear of the coastal shipping lanes."

"And the log?"

"I've already prepared a false one in the name of

the *Gudrid Andersen* for use with our friends from the other side if we should be so unlucky as to run into them. The true log of the *Deutschland* I shall continue to keep privately. It would not be correct to do otherwise." He put the life jacket and ensign back in the cupboard. "As for you, old friend, what can I say? Without your hard work during these past few months, the information you have obtained, the forged papers, we could not have even begun to contemplate such an enterprise."

Prager said carefully, "There is just one more thing to discuss, Eric."

"What's that?"

Prager hesitated, then said, "Seven passengers."

Berger laughed harshly. "You must be joking."

"No, I'm perfectly serious. You've carried them before, haven't you?"

"You know damned well I have." There was something close to anger in Berger's voice. "I have accommodation for eight passengers. Two cabins on either side of the saloon, two bunks to each. I should also point out that this ship is amply crewed by ten men including myself. At the moment, we are twenty-two, as you very well know. Seven passengers would mean that the additional crew would have to bunk elsewhere. An impossible situation."

"But you'll be in ballast," Prager said. "No cargo, and surely genuine passengers would only strengthen your cover story?"

"Who are these passengers?"

"Germans, like you and your men, who want to go home." Prager took a deep breath and carried on, "All right, you might as well know the worst. They're nuns. Sisters of Mercy from a mission station on the Negro. I've been visiting them regularly for the past two years, just like all the other Germans on my list. Every three months; a special dispensation from the authorities as the place is so difficult to get to."

Berger stared at him in astonishment. "For God's sake, Otto, am I going out of my mind or are you?"

Prager got up without a word and opened the cabin door. Richter was standing outside smoking a cigarillo. Prager nodded and the bosun hurried away.

"Now what?" Berger demanded.

"I brought one of them on board with me. The others are waiting on shore. At least hear what she has to say."

"You must be out of your head. It's the only conceivable explanation."

There was a knock at the door. Prager opened it and Sister Angela stepped inside. He said, "Sister, I'd like you to meet Fregattenkapitän Eric Berger. Eric, this is Sister Angela of the Little Sisters of Mercy."

"Good evening, Kapitän," she said.

Berger looked down at the tiny nun for a moment, an expression of astonishment on his face, then he grabbed Prager by the arm and pushed him outside into the rain, pulling the cabin door behind him.

"What in the hell am I going to do? What am I supposed to say?"

"You're the Kapitän," Prager told him. "You make the decisions and no one else, or so I've always been given to understand. I'll wait for you here."

He walked to the mizzen shrouds on the port side. Berger cursed softly, hesitated, then went back in.

She was standing behind the desk, leaning over the chronometer in its box under a glass plate. She glanced up. "Beautiful, Kapitän. Quite beautiful. What is it?"

"The seaman's measure of the heavens, Sister, along with a sextant. If I can check the position of the sun, moon, and stars then I can discover my own exact position on the earth's surface—with the help of tables as well, of course."

She turned to the desk. "A British Admiralty chart. Why is that?"

"Because they're the best," Berger told her, feeling for some reason incredibly helpless.

"I see." She carried on in the same calm voice. "Are you going to take us with you?"

"Look, Sister," he said. "Sit down and let me explain." He pulled another chart forward. "Here we are at the mouth of the Amazon and this is the route home." He traced a finger up past the Azores and west of Ireland. "And if we get that far, there could be even greater hazards to face." He tapped at the chart. "We must pass close to the Outer Hebrides in Scotland, a graveyard for sailing ships, especially in bad weather —which is usually six days out of seven up there. And if we survive that, we only have the Orkneys passage, the run to Norway, then down through the Kattegat to Kiel," he added with heavy irony. "Five thousand miles, that's all."

"And how long will it take us?"

He actually found himself answering. "Impossible to say. Forty, maybe fifty days. So much depends on the weather."

"That seems very reasonable, under the circumstances."

Berger said, "Tell me something. When you first came out here, how did you make the trip?"

"A passenger liner. The *Bremen*. That was just before the war, of course."

"A fine ship. Comfortable cabins, hot and cold running water. Food that wouldn't disgrace a first-class hotel. Stewards to fetch and carry."

"What exactly are you trying to say, Kapitän?"

"That on this ship, life would be very different. Bad food, cramped quarters. A lavatory bucket to empty daily. Salt water only to wash in. And a blow— a real blow under sail—can be a frightening experience. In bad weather, we can spend a fortnight at a time without a dry spot in her from stem to stern. Have you ever strapped yourself into a bunk in wet blankets with a full gale trying to tear the sticks out of the deck above your head?" He rolled up the chart and said firmly, "I'm sorry. I can't see any point in prolonging this discussion."

She nodded thoughtfully. "Tell me something. How does a German naval officer come to command a Brazilian trading vessel?"

"I was Kapitän of a submarine supply ship, the *Essen,* camouflaged as the U.S. fuel ship *George Grant.* We were torpedoed in the South Atlantic on our third trip by a British submarine, which wasn't taken in by the disguise. You may consider that ironic in view of the fact that I intend to try and pass the *Deutschland* off as a similar ship of Swedish registration."

"And how did you manage to reach Brazil?"

"Picked up by a Portuguese cargo boat and handed over to the Brazilian authorities when we reached Rio. The Brazilians have been operating a kind of parole system for any of us who can find work. The Meyer brothers, who own the *Deutschland,* are coastal traders, Brazilian citizens but German by origin. They've helped a great many of us. We make the run from Rio to Belém and back once a month with general cargo."

"And you repay them now by stealing their boat?"

"A point of view, for which I can only hope they'll forgive me when they know the facts. But we don't really have any choice."

"Why not?"

"The Brazilians are starting to play a more active part in the war. Last month, they sent troops to Italy. I think things could get much more difficult for us here."

"And your other reason?"

"You think I have one?"

She waited, hands folded, saying nothing. Berger shrugged, opened the drawer of his desk, and took out a wallet. He extracted a snapshot and passed it across. It was badly creased and discolored by salt water, but the smiles on the faces of the three small girls were still clear enough.

"Your children?"

"Taken in '41. Heidi, on the left, will be ten now. Eva is eight, and Else will be six in October."

"And their mother?"

"Killed in a bombing raid on Hamburg three months ago."

She crossed herself automatically. "What happened to the children?"

"Herr Prager got word about them for me through our embassy in the Argentine. My mother has them in Bavaria."

"Thank God in His infinite mercy."

"Should I?" Berger's face was pale, jaw set. "Germany is going under, Sister, a matter of months only. Can you imagine how bad it's going to be? And my mother's an old woman. If anything happens to her . . ." A kind of shudder seemed to pass through his body and he leaned heavily on the desk. "I want to be with them because that's where I'm needed, not here on the edge of the world, so far off that the war has ceased to exist."

"And for that you'll dare anything?"

"Including five thousand miles of ocean dominated completely by the British and American navies, in a patched-up sailing ship that hasn't been out of sight of land in twenty years or more. An old tub that hasn't had a refit for longer than I care to remember. An impossible voyage."

"Which Mister Richter, your bosun, is apparently willing to make."

"Helmut is a special case. The finest sailor I've ever known. He has invaluable experience under sail. Served his time as a boy on Finnish windjammers on the Chilean nitrate run. That may not mean a lot to you, but to seamen anywhere . . ."

"But according to Herr Prager there are another

twenty men in your crew who are also willing to make this so-called impossible voyage."

"Most of them with a reason roughly similar to mine. I can think of at least seventy men in Rio who would gladly stand in their shoes. They held a lottery for the last ten places in a German bar on the Rio waterfront two weeks ago." He shook his head. "They want to go home, Sister, don't you see? And for that, to use your own words, they'll dare anything."

"And my friends and I are different, is that it? We, too, have families, Kapitän, as dear to us as yours. More than that, because of what lies ahead, home is where we are needed now."

Berger stood staring at her for a moment, then shook his head. "No. In any case, it's too late. You'd need Swedish papers; that's an essential part of the plan. Prager's arranged them for all of us."

She got to her feet, opened the cabin door and called, "Herr Prager!"

He moved in out of the rain. "What is it?"

"My papers, please. May I have them now?"

Prager opened his briefcase. He searched inside, then took out a passport which he dropped on the desk in front of Berger.

Berger frowned. "But this is Swedish." He opened it and Sister Angela stared out at him from the photo. He looked up. "I wonder if you'd be so kind as to step outside for a moment, Sister. I'd like a few words with my good friend here."

She hesitated, glanced briefly at Prager, then went out.

Prager said, "Look, Eric, let me explain."

Berger held up the passport. "Not something you can pick up at twenty-four hours' notice, so you must have known about this for quite some time. Why in the hell didn't you tell me?"

"Because I knew you'd react exactly as you are doing."

"So you thought you'd leave it until it was too late

for me to say no? Well, you made a mistake. I won't play. And what about this mission station they've been operating. Is it suddenly so unimportant?"

"The Brazilian Department of the Interior has changed its policy on the Indians in that area—moving them out and white settlers in. The mission was due to close anyway."

"They're a nursing order, aren't they? Surely there must be some other outlet for their talents up there."

"They are also Germans, Eric. What do you think it's going to be like when those first Brazilian casualty figures start filtering through from Italy?"

There was a long pause. Berger picked up the Swedish passport, opened it, and examined the photo again. "She looks like trouble to me. She's been used to getting her own way for too long."

"Nonsense," Prager said. "I knew her family from the old days. Good Prussian stock. Her father was an infantry general. She was a nurse on the western front in 1918."

Berger's astonishment showed. "A hell of a background for a Little Sister of Mercy. What went wrong? Was there some sort of scandal?"

"Not at all. There *was* a young man, I believe. A flier."

"Who didn't come back one fine morning so she sought refuge in a life of good works." Berger shook his head. "It's beginning to sound like a very bad play."

"The way I heard it, he simply let her think he was dead. She had a breakdown that almost cost her her life and was just coming out of it nicely when she met him walking along the Unter den Linden one day with another girl on his arm."

Berger held up both hands. "No more. I know when I'm beaten. Bring her back in."

Prager went to the door quickly and opened it. She was standing outside talking to the bosun.

Berger said, "You win, Sister. Tell Richter to have you taken ashore to collect the rest of your friends.

Be back here by two A.M. because that's when we leave, and if you aren't here, we go without you."

"God bless you, Kapitän."

"I think He's got enough on his plate at the moment without me." As she moved to the door, he added, "Just one thing. Try not to let the crew know before they have to."

"Are they likely to be disturbed by our presence?"

"Very much so. Sailors are superstitious by nature. Among other things, sailing on a Friday is asking for trouble. Taking any kind of a minister along as a passenger, the same. We should certainly pick up all the bad luck in the world with seven nuns sailing with us."

"Five, Kapitän. Only five," she said and went out.

Berger frowned and turned to Prager. "You said seven passengers."

"So I did." Prager rummaged in the briefcase and produced two more Swedish passports which he pushed across the desk. "One for Gertrude and one for me. She, too, is waiting on shore with our baggage which includes, I might add, that wireless transmitter you asked me to try and get you."

Berger gazed at him in stupefaction. "You and your wife?" he said hoarsely. "Good God, Otto, you're sixty-five if you're a day. And what will your masters in Berlin say?"

"From what I hear, the Russians are far more likely to get there before I do, so it doesn't really matter." Prager smiled gently. "You see, Eric, we want to go home, too."

When Berger went up to the quarterdeck just before two it was raining harder than ever. The entire crew was assembled on the deck below, faces pale, oilskins glistening in the dim glow of the deck lights.

He gripped the rail, leaned forward, and spoke in a low voice. "I won't say much. You all know the score. It's one hell of a trip, I'm not going to pretend any different, but if you do as I tell you, we'll make it, you and I and the old *Deutschland* together."

There was a stirring among them, no more than that, and he carried on, a touch of iron in his voice now. "One more thing. As most of you will have observed, we're carrying passengers. Herr Prager, once assistant consul at our embassy in Rio and his wife, and five nuns from a mission station on the Negro."

He paused. There was only the hissing of the rain as they all waited. "Nuns," he said, "but still women and it's a long journey home, so let me make myself plain. The first man to step over the line, I'll shoot, and so enter it in the log." He straightened. "Now everyone to his station."

As he turned from the rail his second-in-command moved out of the darkness to join him. Lieutenant Johann Sturmm, a tall, fair youth from Menden in Westphalia, had celebrated his twentieth birthday only three days earlier. Like Richter, he was a submariner and had served in a U-boat as second watch officer.

"Everything under control, Mister Sturmm?" Berger inquired in a low voice.

"I think so, Kapitän." Sturmm's voice was surprisingly calm. "I've stowed the wireless transmitter Herr Prager brought with him from Rio in my cabin, as you ordered. It's not much, I'm afraid, sir. A limited range at the best."

"Better than nothing," Berger told him. "And the passengers? Are they safely stowed away also?"

"Oh, yes, sir." There was a hint of laughter in the boy's voice. "I think you could say that."

A white figure appeared out of the darkness and materialized as Sister Angela. Berger swallowed hard and said in a low, dangerous voice, "Could you now, Mister Sturmm?"

Sister Angela said brightly, "Are we leaving, Kapitän? Is it all right if I watch?"

Berger glared at her helplessly, rain dripping from

the peak of his cap, then turned to Sturmm and said, "Haul up the spanker and outer jib only, Mister Sturmm, and let the anchor chain go."

Sturmm repeated the order and there was a sudden flurry of activity. One seaman dropped down the fore-peak hatch. Four others hauled briskly on the halyard and the spanker rose slowly. A moment later there was a rattle as the anchor chain slithered across the deck, then a heavy splash.

Richter was at the wheel but, for the moment, nothing seemed to happen. Then Sister Angela, glancing up, saw, through a gap in the curtain of rain, stars pass across the jib.

"We're moving, Kapitän! We're moving!" she cried as excitedly as any child.

"So I've observed," Berger told her. "Now will you kindly oblige me by going below?"

She went reluctantly, and he sighed and turned to the bosun. "Steady as she goes, Richter. She's all yours."

And Richter took her out through the harbor entrance, drifting along like some pale ghost, barely moving, leaving a slight swirl of phosphorescence in her wake.

Fifteen minutes later, as Captain Mendoza sat playing whist in his booth at the Lights of Lisbon with a young lady from the establishment next door, the man he had assigned to keep watch on the fish pier burst in on him.

"What is it?" Mendoza demanded mildly.

"The *Deutschland,* Senhor Capitain," the watchman whispered. "She is gone."

"Indeed." Mendoza laid his cards face down on the table and stood up. "Watch her, José," he called to the barman. He picked up his cap and oilskin coat and went out.

When he reached the end of the fish pier, the rain

was falling harder than ever in a dark, impenetrable curtain. He lit a cigar in cupped hands and stared into the night.

"Will you notify the authorities, senhor?" the watchman inquired.

Mendoza shrugged. "What is there to notify? Undoubtedly Captain Berger wished an early start for the return trip to Rio, where he is due in eight days from now, although it would not be uncommon for him to be perhaps one week overdue, the weather at this time of the year being so unpredictable. Time enough for any official inquiry needed to be made then."

The watchman glanced at him uncertainly, then bobbed his head. "As you say, Senhor Capitain."

He moved away and Mendoza looked out over the river toward the mouth of the Amazon and the sea. How far to Germany? Nearly five thousand miles, across an ocean that was now hopelessly in the grip of the American and British navies. And in what? A three-masted barkentine long past her prime.

"Fools," he said softly. "Poor, stupid, magnificent fools." And he turned and went back along the fish pier through the rain.

Barkentine Deutschland. *9 September 1944.
Lat. 25° 01′N, long. 30° 46′W. Fourteen
days out of Belém. Wind NW 6–8. Hove the
log and found we were going 12 knots. In
the past twenty-four hours we have run 228
miles. Frau Prager still confined to her bunk
with the seasickness that has plagued her
since leaving Belém. Her increasing weakness
gives us all cause for concern. Heavy rain
toward evening.*

Two

*T*he morning weather forecast for sea area Hebrides had been far from promising: winds five-
to-six with rain squalls. Off the northwest coast of Skye,
things were about as dirty as they could be—heavy,
dark clouds swollen with rain, merging with the horizon.

Except for the occasional seabird, the only living
thing in that desolation was the motor gunboat making
southwest for Barra, her Stars and Stripes ensign the
one splash of color in the gray morning.

Dawn was at six-fifteen, but at nine-thirty visibility was still bad enough to keep the RAF grounded. No

one on board the gunboat could have been blamed for failing to spot the lone Junkers 88S coming in low off the sea astern. The first burst of cannon shell kicked fountains of water high into the air ten or fifteen yards to port. As the plane banked for a second run, the 13 mm machine gun, firing from the rear of the cockpit canopy, loosed off a long burst that ripped into the deck aft of the wheelhouse.

Harry Jago, in his bunk below trying to snatch an hour's sleep, was awake in an instant and making for the companionway. As he reached the deck, the gun crew were already running for the twin 20 mm antiaircraft cannon. Jago beat them into the bucket seat, hands clamping around the trigger handles.

Suddenly, as the Junkers came in off the water for the second time, heavy, black smoke swirled across the deck. Jago started to fire as its cannon punched holes in the deck beside him.

The Junkers was making its pass at close to four hundred miles an hour. He swung to follow it, aware of Jansen on the bridge above him working the Browning. But it was all to no purpose, and the Junkers curved away to port through puff-balls of black smoke and fled into the morning.

Jago stayed where he was for a moment, hands still gripping the handles. Then he got out of the seat and turned to Seaman Harvey Gould, who was in charge of the antiaircraft cannon.

"You were five seconds too late, you and your boys."

The men of the gun crew shuffled uneasily. "It won't happen again, Lieutenant," Gould said.

"See that it doesn't." Jago produced a crumpled pack of cigarettes from his shirt pocket and stuck one in his mouth. "Having survived the Solomons, D day, and the worst those E-boat flotillas in the English Channel could offer, it would look kind of silly to die in the Hebrides."

The pilot of the Junkers, Captain Horst Necker, logged his attack as having taken place at 0935 hours precisely. A hit-and-run affair of no particular importance, which had served to enliven an otherwise boring routine patrol, especially for a pilot who in the spring of that year, during the renewed night attacks on London, had been employed by the elite pathfinder *Gruppe* 1./K.G.66 with the kind of success that had earned him the Knight's Cross only two months previously.

It had been something of a comedown to be transferred to K.G.40 based at Trondheim, a unit specializing in shipping and weather reconnaissance, although the JU 88S they had given him to fly was certainly a superb plane—an all-weather machine capable of a top speed of around four hundred miles per hour.

His mission that morning had one purpose: to look for signs of a convoy expected to leave Liverpool for Russia that week, although the exact day of departure was unknown. He had crossed Scotland at 30,000 feet to spend a totally abortive couple of hours west of the Outer Hebrides.

The sighting of the gunboat had been purest chance, following an impulse to go down to see just how low the cloud base was. The target, once seen, was too tempting to pass up.

As he climbed steeply after the second attack, Rudi Hubner, the navigator, laughed excitedly. "I think we got her, Herr Hauptmann. Lots of smoke back there."

"What do you think, Kranz?" Necker called to the rear gunner.

"Looks to me like they made it themselves, Herr Hauptmann," Kranz replied. "Somebody down there knows his business, and they weren't Tommies either. I saw the Stars and Stripes as we crossed over the second time. Probably my brother Ernst," he added gloomily. "He's in the American navy. Did I ever tell you that?"

Schmidt, the wireless operator, laughed. "The first time over London with the port engines on fire, and you've mentioned it on at least fifty-seven different occasions since. I suppose it shows that at least one person in your family has brains."

Hubner ignored him. "A probable then, Herr Hauptmann?" he suggested.

Necker was going to say no, then saw the hope in the boy's eyes and changed his mind. "I don't see why not. Now let's get out of here."

When Jago went up to the bridge, there was no sign of Jansen. He leaned against the Browning and looked down. The smoke had almost cleared and Gould was kicking the burned-out flare under the rail into the sea. The deck was a mess by the port rail beside the antiaircraft gun, but otherwise things didn't look too bad.

Jansen came up the ladder behind him. He was a tall, heavily built man and, in spite of the tangled black beard, the knitted cap, and faded reefer coat with no rank badges, was a chief petty officer. A lecturer in moral philosophy at Harvard before the war and a fanatical weekend yachtsman, he had resolutely defeated every attempt to elevate him to commissioned rank.

"A lone wolf, Lieutenant."

"You can say that again," Jago told him. "A JU Eighty-eight in the Hebrides."

"And one of the Reichmarschall's later models to judge by his turn of speed."

"But what in hell was he doing here?"

"I know, Lieutenant," Jansen said soothingly. "It's getting so you can't depend on anyone these days. I've already checked below, by the way. Superficial damage. No casualties."

"Thanks," Jago said. "And that smoke flare was quick thinking."

He found that his right hand was trembling slightly and held it out. "Would you look at that. Wasn't it yesterday I was complaining that the only thing we got to fight up here was the weather?"

"Well, you know what Heidegger had to say on that subject, Lieutenant."

"No, I don't, Jansen, but I'm sure you're going to tell me."

"He argued that for authentic living what is necessary is the resolute confrontation of death."

Jago said patiently, "Which is exactly what I've been doing for two years now and you've usually been about a yard behind me. Under the circumstances, I'll tell you what you can do with Heidegger, Jansen. You can put him where Grandma had the pain. And try to rustle up some coffee while I check over the course again."

"As the Lieutenant pleases."

Jago went into the wheelhouse and slumped into the chart-table chair. Petersen had the wheel—a seaman with ten years in the merchant service before the war, including two voyages to Antarctica in whalers.

"You okay?" Jago demanded.

"Fine, Lieutenant."

Jago pulled out British Admiralty chart 1796. BARRA HEAD TO SKYE. South Uist, Barra, and a scattering of islands below it, with Fhada, their destination, at the southern end of the chain. The door was kicked open and Jansen came in with a mug of coffee, which he put on the table.

"What a bloody place," Jago said, tapping the chart. "Magnetic anomalies reported throughout the entire area."

"Well, that's helpful," Jansen said. "Just the thing when you're working out a course in dirty weather."

"Those islands south of Uist are a graveyard," Jago went on. "Everywhere you look on the damned chart it says HEAVY BREAKERS or DANGEROUS SEAS. One hazard after another."

Jansen unfolded a yellow oilskin tobacco pouch, produced a pipe, and started to fill it, leaning against the door. "I was talking to some fishermen in Mallaig before we left. They were telling me that sometimes the weather out there is so bad, Fhada's cut off for weeks at a time."

"The worst weather in the world when those Atlantic storms start moving in," Jago said. "God knows what it must be like in the winter."

"Then what in the hell is Admiral Reeve doing in a place like that?"

"Search me. I didn't even know he was up here till I was told to pick up that dispatch for him in Mallaig and deliver it. Last I heard of him was D day. He was deputy director of operations for naval intelligence and got himself a free trip on the Norwegian destroyer *Svenner* that was sunk by three Mowe-class torpedo boats. He lost his right eye and they tell me his left arm's only good for show."

"A hell of a man," Jansen said. "He got out of Corregidor after MacArthur left. Sailed a lugger nearly six hundred miles to Cagayan and came out on one of the last planes. As I remember, he went down in a destroyer at Midway, was taken aboard the *Yorktown*, and ended up in the water again."

"Careful, Jansen. Your enthusiasm is showing and I didn't think that was possible where top brass was concerned."

"But this isn't just another admiral we're talking about, Lieutenant. He's responsible for an excellent history of naval warfare and probably the best biography of John Paul Jones in print. Good God, sir, the man can actually read and write." Jansen put a match to the bowl of his pipe and added out of the side of his mouth, "Quite an accomplishment for any naval officer, as the Lieutenant will be the first to agree?"

"Jansen," Jago said, "get the hell out of here."

Jansen withdrew, and Jago swung around to find Petersen grinning hugely. "Go on. You, too! I'll take over."

"Sure thing, Lieutenant."

Petersen went out and Jago reached for another cigarette. His fingers had stopped trembling. Rain spattered against the window as the MGB lifted over another wave and it came to him, with a kind of wonder, that he was actually enjoying himself, in spite of the aching back, the constant fatigue that must be taking years off his life.

Harry Jago was twenty-five and looked ten years older, even on a good day, which was hardly surprising when one considered his war record.

He'd dropped out of law school at Yale in March 1941 to join the navy and was assigned to PT boats, joining Squadron Two in time for the Solomons campaign. The battle for Guadalcanal lasted six months. Jago went in at one end a crisp, clean, twenty-two-year-old ensign and emerged a lieutenant, junior grade, with a Navy Cross and two boats shot from under him.

Afterward, Squadron Two was recommissioned and sent to England, at the urgent request of the Office of Strategic Services, to land and pick up American agents on the French coast. Again Jago survived, this time the Channel and the constant head-on clashes with German E-boats out of Cherbourg. He even survived the hell of Omaha Beach on D day.

His luck finally ran out on June 28, when E-boats attacked a convoy of American landing craft waiting in Lyme Bay to cross the Channel. Jago arrived with dispatches from Portsmouth to find himself facing six of the best that the *Kriegsmarine* could supply. In a memorable ten-minute engagement, he sank one, damaged another, lost five of his crew, and ended up in the water with shrapnel in his left thigh, the right cheek laid open to the bone.

When he finally came out of the hospital in August they gave him what was left of his old crew, nine of them, and a new job and the rest that he so badly needed: playing postman in the Hebrides to the various American and British weather stations and similar establishments in the islands in a prewar MGB, courtesy of the Royal Navy, that started to shake herself to pieces if he attempted to take her above twenty knots. Some previous owner had painted the legend DEAD END underneath the bridge rail, a sentiment capable of several interpretations.

"Just for a month or two," the squadron commander had told Jago. "Look on it as a kind of holiday. I mean to say, nothing ever happens up there, Harry."

Jago grinned in spite of himself and, as a rain squall hurled itself against the window, he increased speed, the wheel kicking in his hands. The sea was his life now. Meat and drink to him, more important than any woman. It was the circumstance of war that had given him this, but the war wouldn't last forever.

He said softly, "What in the hell am I going to do when it's all over?"

There were times when Rear Admiral Carey Reeve definitely wondered what life was all about. Times when the vacuum of his days seemed unbearable, and the island that he loved with such a deep and unswerving passion, a prison.

On such occasions he usually made for the same spot, a hill called in the Gaelic *Dun Bhuide,* the yellow fort, above Telegraph Bay on the southwest tip of Fhada, and so named because of an abortive attempt to set up a Marconi station at the turn of the century. The bay lay at the bottom of four-hundred-foot cliffs, a strip of white sand slipping into gray water with Labrador almost three thousand miles away to the west and nothing in between.

The path below was no place for the fainthearted, zigzagging across the face of the granite cliffs, splashed with lime, seabirds crying, wheeling in great clouds, razorbills, shags, gulls, shearwaters, and gannets—gannets everywhere. He considered it all morosely for a while through his one good eye, then turned to survey the rest of the island.

The ground sloped steeply to the southwest. On

the other side of the point from Telegraph were South Inlet and the lifeboat station, the boathouse, its slipway, and Murdoch Macleod's cottage, nothing more. On his left was the rest of the island. A scattering of crofts, mostly ruined, peat bog, sheep grazing the sparse turf, the whole crossed by the twin lines of the narrow-gauge railway track running northwest to Mary's Town.

Reeve took an old brass telescope from his pocket and focused it on the lifeboat station. No sign of life. Murdoch would probably be working on that damned boat of his, but the kettle would be gently steaming on the hob above the peat fire and a mug of hot tea generously laced with illegal whisky of Murdoch's own distilling would not come amiss on such a morning.

The admiral replaced the telescope in his pocket and started down the slope as rain drove across the island in a gray curtain.

There was no sign of Murdoch when he went into the boathouse by the small rear door. The forty-one-foot Watson-type motor lifeboat, *Morag Sinclair,* waited in its carriage at the head of the slipway. She was trim and beautiful in her blue-and-white paint, showing every sign of the care Murdoch lavished on her. Reeve ran a hand along her counter with a conscious pleasure.

Behind him the door swung open in a flurry of rain and a soft Highland voice said, "I was in the outhouse, stacking peat."

Reeve turned to find Murdoch standing in the doorway, and in the same moment an enormous Irish wolfhound squeezed past him and bore down on the admiral.

His hand fastened on the beast's ginger ruff. "Rory, you old devil. I might have known." He glanced up at Murdoch. "Mrs. Sinclair's been looking for him this morning. He was wandering last night."

"I intended bringing him in myself later," Murdoch said. "Are you in health, Admiral?"

He was himself seventy years old, of immense stature, dressed in thigh boots and guernsey sweater, his eyes gray, water over stone, his face seamed and shaped by a lifetime of the sea.

"Murdoch," Admiral Reeve said. "Has it ever occurred to you that life is a tale told by an idiot, full of sound and fury, and signifying precisely nothing?"

"So it's that kind of a morning?" Murdoch wiped peat from his hands onto his thighs and produced his tobacco pouch. "Will you take tea with me, Admiral?" he inquired with grave Highland courtesy.

"And a little something extra?" Reeve suggested hopefully.

"Uisgebeatha?" Murdoch said in Gaelic. "The water of life. Why not indeed, for it is life you need this morning, I am thinking." He smiled gravely. "I'll be ten minutes. Time for you to take a turn along the shore with the hound to blow the cobwebs away."

The mouth of the inlet was a maelstrom of white water, waves smashing in across the reef beyond with a thunderous roaring, hurling spray a hundred feet into the air.

Reeve trudged along in the wolfhound's wake at the water's edge, thinking about Murdoch Macleod. Thirty-two years coxswain of the Fhada lifeboat, legend in his own time—during which he had been awarded the BEM by old King George and five silver and two gold medals for gallantry in sea rescue by the Lifeboat Institution. He had retired in 1938, when his son Donald had taken over as coxswain in his place, and had returned a year later when Donald was called to active service with the Royal Naval Reserve. A remarkable man by any standards.

The wolfhound was barking furiously. Reeve looked up across the great bank of sand that was known as *Traig Mhoire*—Mary's Strand. A man in a yellow life jacket lay face down on the shore twenty yards away, water slopping over him as one wave crashed in after another.

The admiral ran forward, dropped to one knee, and turned him over, with some difficulty for his left arm was virtually useless now. He was quite dead, a boy of eighteen or nineteen, in denim overalls, eyes closed as if in sleep, fair hair plastered to his skull, not a mark on him.

Reeve started to search the body. There was a leather wallet in the left breast pocket. As he opened it, Murdoch arrived on the run, dropping on his knees beside him.

"Came to see what was keeping you." He touched the pale face with the back of his hand.

"How long?" Reeve asked.

"Ten or twelve hours, no more. Who was he?"

"Off a German U-boat from the look of those overalls." Reeve opened the wallet and examined the contents. There was a photo of a young girl, a couple of letters, and a leave pass so soaked in seawater that it started to fall to pieces as he opened it gingerly.

"A wee lad, that's all," Murdoch said. "Couldn't they do better than schoolboys?"

"Probably as short of men by now as the rest of us," Reeve told him. "His name was Hans Bleichrodt and he celebrated his eighteenth birthday while on leave in Brunswick three weeks ago. He was *Funkgefreiter*, telegraphist to you, on U-743." He replaced the papers in the wallet. "If she bought it this morning, we might get more like this coming in for the rest of the week."

"You could be right." Murdoch crouched down and, with an easy strength that never ceased to amaze Reeve, hoisted the body over one shoulder. "Better get him into Mary's Town then, Admiral."

Reeve nodded. "Yes, my house will do. Mrs. Sinclair can see him this afternoon and sign the death certificate. We'll bury him tomorrow."

"I am thinking that the kirk might be more fitting."

"I'm not certain that's such a good idea," Reeve said. "There are eleven men from this island dead at sea owing to enemy action during this war. I would have thought their families might not be too happy to see a German lying in state in their own place of worship."

The old man's eyes were fierce. "And you would agree with them?"

"Oh, no," Reeve said hurriedly. "Don't draw me into this. You put the boy where you like. I don't think it will bother him too much."

"But it might well bother God," Murdoch said gently. There was no reproof in his voice, in spite of the fact that, as a certified lay preacher of the Church of Scotland, he was the nearest thing to a minister on the island.

There was no road from that end of Fhada, had never been any need for one, but during the two abortive years that the Marconi station had existed the telegraph company had laid the narrow-gauge railway line. The lifeboat crew, mostly fishermen from Mary's Town, traveled on it by trolley when called out in an emergency, pumping it by hand or hoisting a sail when the wind was favorable.

That morning Murdoch and the admiral coasted along at a brisk five knots, the triangular strip of canvas billowing out to one side. The dead body lay in the center of the trolley and Rory squatted beside him.

Two miles, then three, and the track started to slope down and the wind tore a hole in the curtain of rain, revealing Mary's Town, a couple of miles farther on in the northwest corner of the island, a scattering of granite houses, four or five streets sloping to the harbor. There were half a dozen fishing boats anchored in the lee of the breakwater.

Murdoch was standing, one hand on the mast, staring out to sea. "Would you look at that now, Admiral? There's some sort of craft coming in toward the harbor out there, and I could have sworn that was the Stars and Stripes she's flying. I must be getting old."

Reeve had the telescope out of his pocket and focused in an instant. "You're damned right it is," he said as the *Dead End* jumped into view, Harry Jago on the bridge.

His hand was shaking with excitement as he pushed the telescope back into his pocket. "You know something, Murdoch? This might just turn out to be my day after all."

When the MGB eased into the landing stage, a woman was sitting on the upper jetty under an umbrella, painting at an easel. She was in her early forties, with calm blue eyes in a face that was strong and pleasant rather than handsome. She wore a head scarf, an old naval officer's coat that carried the bars of a full captain on the epaulets, and slacks.

She stood up, moved to the edge of the jetty, holding the umbrella, and smiled down. "Hello, there, America. That makes a change."

Jago went over the rail and up the steps to the jetty quickly. "Harry Jago, ma'am."

"Jean Sinclair." She held out her hand. "I'm bailie here, Lieutenant, so if there's anything I can do."

"Bailie?" Jago said blankly.

"What you'd call a magistrate."

Jago grinned. "I see. You mean you're the law around here."

"And coroner and harbor master. This is a small island. We have to do the best we can."

"I'm here with dispatches for Rear Admiral Reeve, ma'am. Have you any idea where I might locate him?"

She smiled. "We have a saying in these islands, Lieutenant. Speak of the devil and you'll find he's right behind you."

Jago turned quickly and got a shock. When he'd

received his Navy Cross from Nimitz at Pearl, Admiral Reeve had been one of those on the platform, resplendent in full uniform with three rows of medal ribbons. There was no echo of him at all in the small, dark man with the black eye patch who hurried toward him now, wearing an old reefer coat and seaboots. It was only when he spoke that Jago knew beyond a doubt who he was.

"You looking for me, Lieutenant?"

"Admiral Reeve?" Jago got his heels together and saluted. "I've got a dispatch for you, sir. Handed to me by the Royal Naval officer in command at Mallaig. If you'd care to come aboard."

"Lead me to it, Lieutenant," the admiral said eagerly, then paused and turned to Jean Sinclair. "I found Rory. He was with Murdoch at the lifeboat station."

Her eyes were lively now and there was a slightly amused smile on her mouth. "Why, Carey, I thought you were going to ignore me altogether."

He said gravely, "I found something else down there on *Traig Mhoire*. A body on the beach. A German boy off a U-boat."

Her smile died. "Where is he now?"

"I left him at the church with Murdoch."

"I'd better get up there then. I'll pick up a couple of women on the way. See the lad's decently laid out."

"I'll be along myself later."

She walked away quickly, her umbrella tilted to take the force of the rain. "Quite a lady," Jago remarked.

The admiral nodded. "And then some. As a matter of interest, she owns the whole damned island. Left it by her father. He was a kind of feudal lord around here."

"What about that naval greatcoat, sir?" Jago asked, as they descended the ladder.

"Her husband's. Went down in the *Prince of Wales* back in '41. He was a Sinclair, too, like her. A second cousin, I believe." He laughed. "It's an old island custom to keep the name in the family."

The crew were assembled on deck, and as the admiral went over the rail, Jansen piped him on board. Reeve looked them over in amazement and said to Jago, "Where did this lot spring from? A banana boat?"

"Chief Petty Officer Jansen, sir," Jago said weakly.

Reeve examined Jansen, taking in the reefer, the tangled beard, and knitted cap. He turned away with a shudder. "I've seen enough. Just take me to my dispatch, will you?"

"If you'll follow me, Admiral."

Jago led the way down the companionway to his cabin. He took a briefcase from under the mattress on his bunk, unlocked it, and produced a buff envelope, seals still intact, which he passed across. As Reeve took it from him, there was a knock at the door and Jansen entered with a tray.

"Coffee, gentlemen?"

Reeve curbed the impulse to tear the envelope open and said to Jago as he accepted a cup, "How's the war going then?"

It was Jansen who answered. "The undertakers are doing well, Admiral."

Reeve turned to stare at him in a kind of fascination. "You did say chief petty officer?"

"The best, sir," Jago said gamely.

"And where, may I ask, did you find him?"

"Harvard, sir," Jansen said politely, and withdrew.

Reeve said in wonderment, "He's joking, isn't he?"

"I'm afraid not, Admiral."

"No wonder the war wasn't over by Christmas."

Reeve sat on the edge of the bunk, tore open the package, and took out two envelopes. He opened the smaller first. There was a photo inside and a letter that he read quickly, a smile on his face. He passed the photo to Jago.

"My niece, Janet. She's a doctor at Guy's Hospital in London. Been there since 1940. Worked right through the blitz."

She had grave, steady eyes, high cheekbones, a mouth that was too wide. There was something in her expression that got through to Jago.

He handed the photo back reluctantly. "Very nice, sir."

"You could say that and it would be the understatement of the year."

Reeve opened the second envelope and started to read the letter it contained eagerly. Gradually the smile died on his face, his eyes grew dark, his mouth tightened. He folded the letter and slipped it into his pocket.

"Bad news, sir?"

"Now that, son, depends entirely on your point of view. The powers-that-be are of the opinion that the war can get on without me. That, to use a favorite phrase of our British allies, I've done my bit."

Jago opened a cupboard behind him and took out a bottle of Scotch and a glass that he held out to the admiral. "Most people I know wouldn't find much to quarrel with in that sentiment, sir."

He poured a generous measure of whisky into the glass. Reeve said, "Something else that's strictly against regulations, Lieutenant." He frowned. "What is your name, anyway?"

"Jago, sir. Harry Jago."

Reeve swallowed some of the whisky. "What kind of deal are you on here? This old tub looks as if it might be left over from the Crimea."

"Not quite, sir. Courtesy of the Royal Navy. We're only playing postman, you see. I suppose they didn't think the job was worth much more."

"What were you doing before?"

"PT boats, sir. Squadron Two, working the Channel."

"Jago?" Reeve said and his face brightened. "You lost an Elco in Lyme Bay."

"I suppose you could put it that way, sir."

Reeve smiled and held out his hand. "Nice to meet you, son. And those boys up top? They're your original crew?"

"What's left of them."

"Well, now I'm here, you might as well show me over this pig boat."

Which Jago did from stem to stern. They ended up in the wheelhouse, where they found Jansen at the chart table.

"And what might you be about?" Reeve demanded.

"Our next stop is a weather station on the southwest corner of Harris, Admiral. I was just plotting our course."

"Show me." Jansen ran a finger out through the Sound into the Atlantic and Reeve said, "Watch it out there, especially if visibility is reduced in the slightest. Here, three miles to the northwest." He tapped the chart. "Washington Reef. Doesn't it make you feel at home, the sound of that name?"

"And presumably it shouldn't?" Jago asked.

"A death trap. The greatest single hazard to shipping on the entire west coast of Scotland. Two galleons from the Spanish Armada went to hell together on those rocks four hundred years ago and they've been tearing ships apart ever since. One of the main reasons there's a lifeboat here on Fhada."

"Maybe we'd be better taking the other route north through the Little Minch, sir."

Reeve smiled. "I know—it's a hell of a war, Lieutenant, but it's the only one we've got."

Jansen said solemnly, " 'As long as war is regarded

as wicked it will always have its fascination. When it is looked upon as vulgar, it will cease to be popular.' Oscar Wilde said that, sir," he said helpfully.

"Dear God, restore me to sanity." Reeve shook his head and turned to Jago. "Let me get off this hooker before I go over the edge entirely."

"Just one thing, sir. Do you know a Mr. Murdoch Macleod?"

"He's coxswain of the lifeboat here and a good friend of mine. Why do you ask?"

Jago unbuttoned his shirt pocket and took out an orange envelope. "The Royal Naval officer in command at Mallaig asked me to deliver this telegram to him, sir, there being no telephone or telegraph service to the island at the moment, I understand."

"That's right," Reeve said. "The cable parted in a storm last month and they haven't gotten around to doing anything about it yet. In fact, at the moment the island's only link with the outside world is my personal radio."

He held out his hand for the envelope, which he saw was open. "It's from the Admiralty, sir."

"Bad news?"

"He has a son, sir. Lieutenant Donald Macleod."

"That's right. Commanding an armed trawler doing escort duty on east-coast convoys in the North Sea. Newcastle to London."

"Torpedoed off the Humber yesterday, with all hands."

Reeve's voice dropped to a whisper. "No one was saved at all? You're certain of that?"

"I'm afraid not, Admiral."

Reeve seemed to age before Jago's eyes. "One thing they obviously didn't tell you, Lieutenant, was that although Donald Macleod was master of that trawler, there were four other men from Fhada in the crew." He passed the envelope back to Jago. "I think the sooner we get this over with, the better."

The Church of St. Mungo was a tiny, weather-beaten building with a squat tower, constructed of blocks of heavy granite on a hillside above the town.

Reeve, Jago, and Frank Jansen went in through the lych-gate and followed a path through a churchyard scattered with gravestones to the porch at the west end. Reeve opened the massive oaken door and led the way in.

The dead boy lay on a trestle table in a tiny side chapel to one side of the altar. Two middle-aged women were arranging the body while Murdoch and Jean Sinclair stood close by, talking in subdued tones. They turned and looked down the aisle as the door opened. The three men moved toward them, caps in hand. They paused, then Reeve held the orange envelope out to Jean Sinclair.

"I think you'd better read this."

She took it from him, extracted the telegram. Her face turned ashen; she was wordless. In a moment of insight, Reeve realized that she was reliving her own tragedy. She turned to Murdoch, but the admiral stepped in quickly, holding her back.

Murdoch said calmly, "It is bad news you have for me there, I am thinking, Carey Reeve."

"Donald's ship was torpedoed off the Humber yesterday," Reeve said. "Went down with all hands."

A tremor seemed to pass through the old man's entire frame. He staggered momentarily, then took a deep breath and straightened. "The Lord disposes."

The two women working on the body stopped to stare at him, faces frozen in horror. Between them, as Reeve well knew, they had just lost a husband and brother. Murdoch moved past and stood looking down at the German boy, pale in death, the face somehow very peaceful now.

He reached down and took one of the cold hands in his. "Poor lad," he said. "Poor wee lad!" His shoulders shook and he started to weep softly.

Barkentine Deutschland, *12 September
1944. Lat. 26°11'N, long. 30°26'W. Wind
NW 2–3. Overcast. Poor visibility. A bad
squall last night during the middle watch and
the flying jib split.*

Three

Some five hundred miles south of the Azores, Eric
Berger sat at the desk in his cabin entering his
personal journal.

*. . . our general progress has, of course, been
far better than I could ever have hoped and
yet our passengers find the experience tedious
in the extreme. For most of the time, bad
weather keeps them below, the skylight leaks,
and the saloon is constantly damp.*

*The loss of the chickens and two goats
kept for milk, all swept overboard in a bad
squall three days out of Belém, has had an
unfortunate effect on our diet, although here
again, it has been most noticeable in the nuns.
Frau Prager is still my main worry, and her*

condition, as far as I may judge, continues to decline.

As for the prospect of a meeting with an enemy ship, we are as ready in that respect as can reasonably be expected. The Deutschland *is now the* Gudrid Andersen *to the last detail, including the library of Swedish books in my cabin.*

The plan of campaign, if boarded at any time, is simple. The additional men carried beyond normal crew requirements will secrete themselves in the bilges. A simple device admittedly, and one easily discovered by any kind of a thorough search, but we have little choice in the matter.

The Deutschland *stands up well so far to all the Atlantic can offer, although there is not a day passes that shrouds do not part or sails split and, this morning, Mister Sturmm reported twelve inches of water in the bilges. But, as yet, there is no cause for alarm. We all get old and the* Deutschland *is older than most. . . .*

The whole ship lurched drunkenly and Berger was thrown from his chair as the cabin tilted. He scrambled to his feet, got the door open, and ran out on deck.

The *Deutschland* was plunging forward through heavy seas, the deck awash with spray. Lieutenant Sturmm and Leading Seaman Kluth had the wheel between them and it was taking all their strength to hold it.

High above the deck, the main gaff topsail fluttered free in the wind. The noise was tremendous and could be heard even above the roaring of the wind, and the topmast was whipping backward and forward. A matter of moments only before it snapped. But already Richter was at the rail, the sea washing over him as he pulled on the downhaul to collapse the sail.

Berger ran to join him, losing his footing and rolling into the scuppers as another great sea floated in across the deck, but somehow he was on his feet and lending his weight to the downhaul with Richter.

The sail came down, the *Deutschland* righted herself perceptibly, the continual drumming ceased. Richter shouted, "I'd better get up there and see to a new outhaul."

Berger cried above the wind, "You wouldn't last five minutes out there on that gaff in this weather. It'll have to wait till the wind eases."

"But that sail will tear herself to pieces, sir."

"A gasket should hold her for the time being. I'll see to it."

Berger sprang into the ratlines and started to climb, aware of the wind tearing at his body like some living thing. When he paused fifty feet up and glanced down, Richter was right behind him.

There was a foot of water in the saloon, a sea having smashed the skylight and flooded in. Sister Angela went from cabin to cabin, doing her best to calm her alarmed companions.

When she went into the Pragers, she found the old man on his knees at his wife's bunk. Frau Prager was deathly pale, eyes closed, little sign of life there at all.

"What is it?" Otto Prager demanded in alarm.

She ignored him for the moment and took his wife's pulse. It was still there, however irregular.

Prager tugged at her sleeve. "What happened?"

"I'll find out," she said calmly. "You stay with your wife."

She went out on deck to find the *Deutschland* racing north, every fore and aft sail drawing well, yards braced as she plunged into the waves. Sturmm and Kluth were still at the wheel. The young lieutenant called to her, but his words were snatched away by the wind.

She made it to the mizzen shrouds on the port

side, the wind tearing at her black habit, and she looked up at the ballooning sails. The sky was a uniform gray, the whole world alive with the sound of the ship, a thousand creaks and groans. And then, a hundred feet up, she saw Berger and Richter swaying backward and forward on the end of the gaff as they secured the sail.

It was perhaps the most incredible thing she had ever seen in her life and she was seized by a tremendous feeling of exhilaration. A sea slopped in over the rail in a green curtain that bowled her over, sending her skidding across the deck on her hands and knees.

She crouched against the bulwark and, as she tried to get up, Berger dropped out of the shrouds beside her and got a hand under her arm.

"Bloody fool!" he shouted. "Why can't you stay below?"

He ran her across the deck and into his cabin before she had a chance to reply. Sister Angela collapsed into the chair behind the desk and Berger got the door shut and leaned against it. "What in the hell am I going to do with you?"

"I'm sorry," she said. "There was panic down below. I simply wanted to know what had happened."

He picked up a towel from his bunk and tossed it across to her. "A line parted, a sail broke free. It could have snapped the topmast like a matchstick, only Richter was too quick for it." He opened a cupboard and reached for the bottle. "A drink, Sister? Purely medicinal, of course. Rum is all I can offer, I'm afraid."

"I don't think so." Berger poured himself a large one and she wiped her face and regarded him curiously. "It was incredible what you were doing out there. You and Mister Richter, so high up and in such weather."

"Not really," he said indifferently. "Not to anyone who's reefed main t'gallants on a fully rigged clipper in a Cape Horn storm."

She nodded slowly. "Tell me, do you still think we're bad luck? A positive guarantee of contrary winds, wasn't that what you said at our first meeting? And yet we've made good progress, wouldn't you agree?"

"Oh, we're making time all right," Berger admitted. "Although she shakes herself to pieces around us just a little bit more each day."

"You speak of her, the *Deutschland,* as if she is a living thing. As if she has an existence of her own."

"I wouldn't quarrel with that. Although I suppose your church would. A ship doesn't have one voice, she has many. You can hear them calling to each other out there, especially at night."

"The wind in the rigging?" There was something close to mockery in her voice.

"There are other possibilities. Old-timers will tell you that the ghost of anyone killed falling from the rigging remains with the ship."

"And you believe that?"

"Obligatory in the *Kriegsmarine.*" There was an ironic smile on his face now. "Imagine the shades who infest this old girl. Next time something brushes past you in the dark on the companionway, you'll know what it is. One Our Father and two Hail Marys should keep you safe."

Her cheeks flushed, but before she could reply, the door was flung open and Sister Else appeared. "Please, Sister, come quickly. Frau Prager seems to be worse."

Sister Angela jumped to her feet and moved out. Berger closed the door behind her, then picked up the towel she dropped and wiped his face. Strange how she seemed to bring out the worst in him. A constant source of irritation, but then perhaps it was simply that they'd all been together for too long in such a confined space. And yet . . .

For most of the afternoon, HMS *Guardian,* a "T" class submarine of the British Home Fleet, en route to

Trinidad for special orders, had proceeded submerged, but at 1600 hours she surfaced.

It was the throb of the diesels that brought her captain, Lieutenant Commander George Harvey, awake. He lay there for a moment on the bunk, staring up at the steel bulkhead, aware of the taste in his mouth, the smell of submarine, and then the green curtain was pulled aside and Petty Officer Swallow came in with tea in a chipped enamel mug.

"Just surfaced, sir."

The tea was foul, but at least there was real sugar in it, which was something.

"What's it like up there?"

"Overcast. Wind northwest. Two to three. Visibility poor, sir. Slight sea mist and drizzling."

"Succinct as always, coxswain," Harvey told him.

"Beg pardon, sir?"

"Never mind. Just tell Mr. Edge I'll join him on the bridge in five minutes."

"Sir."

Swallow withdrew and Harvey swung his legs to the floor and sat there, yawning. Then he moved to the small desk bolted to the bulkhead, opened the *Guardian*'s war diary, and in cold, precise naval language started to insert the daily entry.

There were three men on the bridge. Sublieutenant Edge, who was officer of the watch, a signalman, and an able seaman for lookout. The sea was surprisingly calm and there was none of the usual corkscrewing or pitching that a submarine frequently experiences when traveling on the surface in any kind of rough weather.

Edge was thoroughly enjoying himself. The rain in his face was quite refreshing, and the salt air felt sweet and clean in his lungs after the hours spent below.

Swallow came up the ladder, a mug of tea in one hand. "Thought you might like a wet, sir. Captain's compliments and he'll join you on the bridge in five minutes."

"Good show," Edge said cheerfully. "Not that there's anything to report."

Swallow started to reply and then his eyes widened and an expression of incredulity appeared on his face. "Good God Almighty!" he said. "I don't believe it."

In the same instant, the lookout cried out, pointing, and Edge turned to see a three-masted barkentine, all sails set, emerge from a fogbank a quarter of a mile to port.

On board the *Deutschland* there was no panic, for the plan to be followed in such an eventuality had been gone over so many times that everyone knew exactly what to do.

Berger was on the quarterdeck, Sturmm and Richter beside him at the rail. The bosun was holding a signaling lamp. The captain spoke without lowering his glasses. "A British submarine. 'T' class."

"Is this it, sir?" Sturmm asked. "Are we finished?"

"Perhaps."

The *Guardian*'s gun crew poured out of her conning tower and manned their positions. For a moment, there was considerable activity, then a signal lamp flashed.

" 'Heave to or I fire,' " Richter translated.

"Plain enough. Reply: 'As a neutral ship I comply under protest.' "

The shutter on the signal lamp in the bosun's hands clattered. A moment later, the reply came: "I intend to board you. Stand by."

Berger lowered his glasses. "Very well, gentlemen. Action stations, if you please. Take in all sail, Mister Sturmm. You, Richter, will see the rest of the crew into the bilges and I will attend to the passengers."

There was a flurry of activity as Sturmm turned to bark orders to the watch on deck. Richter went down the quarterdeck ladder quickly. Berger followed him, descending the companionway.

When he entered the saloon, four of the nuns were seated around the table listening to a Bible reading from Sister Lotte.

"Where is Sister Angela?" Berger demanded.

Sister Lotte paused. "With Frau Prager."

The door of the consul's cabin opened and Prager emerged. He seemed haggard and drawn, and had lost weight since that first night in Belém, so that his tropical linen suit seemed a size too large.

"How are things?" Berger asked.

"Bad," Prager said. "She gets weaker by the hour."

"I'm sorry." Berger addressed his next remark to all of them. "There's a British submarine on the surface about a quarter of a mile off our port beam and moving in. They intend to board."

Sister Kathë crossed herself quickly and Sister Angela came out of Prager's cabin clutching an enamel bucket, her white apron soiled.

When Berger next spoke, it was to no one but her. "You heard?"

"Yes."

"We had a bad night of it, Sister—a hell of a night. You understand me?"

"Perfectly, Kapitän." Her face was pale, but the eyes sparkled. "We won't let you down."

Berger picked up a broom that leaned against the bulkhead, reached up, and jabbed at the skylight again and again, glass showering across the table so that the nuns scattered with cries of alarm.

He tossed the broom into the corner. "See that you don't," he said and went back up the companionway.

There was total silence, the nuns staring at Sister Angela expectantly. With a violent gesture she raised the bucket in her hands and emptied the contents across the floor. There was the immediate all-pervading stench of vomit and Sister Brigitte turned away, stomach heaving.

"Excellent," Sister Angela said. "Now you, Lotte, go to the lavatory and fetch a bucket of slops. I want conditions down here to be so revolting those Tommies will be back up that companionway in two minutes flat."

She had changed completely, the voice clipped, incisive, totally in command. "As for the rest of you, complete disorder in the cabins. Soak your bedding in seawater."

Prager tugged at her sleeve. "What about me, Sister? What shall I do?"

"Kneel, Herr Prager," she said. "At your wife's bedside—and pray."

As the *Guardian* moved in, Harvey observed the activity on the deck of the *Deutschland* closely through his glasses.

Edge came up the ladder behind him. "I've checked Lloyd's Register, sir. It seems to be her all right. *Gudrid Andersen,* three-masted barkentine, registered Göteborg."

"But what in the hell is she doing here?"

Harvey frowned, trying to work out the best way of handling the situation. His first officer, Gregson, lay in his bunk with a fractured left ankle. In such circumstances to leave the *Guardian* himself, however temporarily, was unthinkable. Which left Edge, a nineteen-year-old boy on his first operational patrol—hardly an ideal choice.

On the other hand, there was Swallow. His eyes met the chief petty officer's briefly. Not a word spoken, and yet he knew that the coxswain read his thoughts perfectly.

"Tell me, Coxswain, does anyone on board speak Swedish?"

"Not to my knowledge, sir."

"We must hope they run to enough English over there to get us by, then. Lieutenant Edge will lead the boarding party. Pick him two good men—sidearms only. And I think you might as well go along for the ride."

"Sir."

Swallow turned, and at his shouted command, the forward hatch was opened and a rubber dinghy broken out. Edge went below and reappeared a few moments later buckling a webbing belt around his waist, from which hung a holstered Webley revolver. He was excited and showed it.

"Think you can handle it?" Harvey asked.

"I believe so, sir."

"Good. A thorough inspection of ship's papers and identity documents of everyone on board."

"Am I looking for anything special, sir?"

"Hardly," Harvey said dryly. "The Germans last used a sailing ship as a surface raider in 1917, if I remember my naval history correctly, and times have changed. No, we're entitled to check her credentials, and I'm consumed with curiosity as to the nature of her business, so off you go."

Sturmm waited at the rail as the dinghy coasted in. Edge went up the Jacob's ladder first, followed by one of the ratings and Swallow, who carried a Thompson gun. The other rating stayed with the dinghy. Of Berger, there was no sign.

Sturmm, who spoke excellent English, pointed to the ensign, which fluttered at the masthead. "I must protest, sir. As you can see, this is a Swedish vessel."

"Ah, good, you speak English," Edge said with a certain relief. "Lieutenant Philip Edge of his Brittanic Majesty's submarine *Guardian*. Are you the master of this vessel?"

"No, my name is Larsen. First mate. Captain Nillsen is in his cabin getting out the ship's papers for you. I'm afraid things are in a bit of a mess. We had a bad night of it. Almost turned turtle when a squall hit us during the middle watch. It caused considerable damage."

Edge said to Swallow, "You handle things here, Coxswain, while I have a word with the captain."

"Shall we take a look below, sir?" Swallow suggested.

Edge turned, taking in the watchful gun crew on the *Guardian,* and the Browning machine gun that had been mounted on the rail beside Harvey.

"Yes, why not?" he said and followed Sturmm toward the quarterdeck.

The young German opened the door to the captain's cabin and stood politely to one side. Edge paused on the threshold, taking in the shambles before him. A porthole was smashed, the carpet soaked, the whole place littered with books and personal belongings.

Berger stood behind the desk, face stern, the ship's log and other papers ready on the desk before him.

"I'm afraid Captain Nillsen doesn't speak English, so I'll have to interpret for you." Which was far from the truth, for Berger's English, though modest, was adequate. "The captain," Sturmm added, "is not pleased at this forcible boarding of a neutral vessel about her lawful business."

"I'm sorry," Edge said, considerably intimidated by the stern expression on Berger's face, "but I'm afraid I must insist on seeing your ship's papers and log, also your cargo manifest."

Berger turned away as if angry. Sturmm said, "But we carry no cargo, Lieutenant, only passengers." He picked up the ship's log, soaked in seawater, its pages sticking together. "Perhaps you would care to examine the log? You will find all other relevant papers here also."

Edge took it from him, sat down in Berger's chair, and tried to separate the first two water-soaked pages, which promptly tore away in his hand. And at that precise moment, Richter and the eleven other members of the crew secreted in the bilges with him, were lying in several inches of stinking water, aware of Swallow's heavy footsteps in the hold above their heads.

Edge left the cabin fifteen minutes later, having examined as thoroughly as he could an assortment of papers, and clutching the Swedish passports offered for his inspection.

Swallow emerged from the companionway looking ill. Edge said, "Are the passengers down there, Coxswain?"

"Yes, sir." Swallow was taking in deep breaths of salt air rapidly. "Five nuns, sir, and an old gentleman and his wife—and she doesn't look too healthy."

Edge advanced to the top of the companionway and Swallow said hastily, "I wouldn't bother, sir. Not unless you feel you have to. They've obviously had a rotten time of it in last night's storm. Still cleaning up."

Edge hesitated, turned to glanced at Sturmm, Berger glowering behind, then started down.

The stink was appalling, the stench of human excrement and vomit turning his stomach. The first thing he saw in the shambles of the saloon below was four nuns on their knees in the filth with buckets and brushes, scrubbing the floor. Edge got a handkerchief to his mouth as Sister Angela appeared in the doorway of the Pragers' cabin.

"Can I help you?" she asked in good English.

"Sorry to trouble you, ma'am. My duty—you understand?" He held out the passports. "International law in time of war. I'm entitled to inspect the passenger list."

He glanced past her at Prager, who knelt beside his wife. Her face was deathly pale, shining with sweat, and she was breathing incredibly slowly.

"And this lady and gentleman?" He started to sort through the passports.

"Mr. Ternström and his wife. As you can see, she is very ill."

Prager turned to look at him, the agony on his face totally genuine, and Edge took an involuntary step back. Lotte chose that exact moment to be sick, crouching there on the floor like some animal. It was enough.

Edge turned hastily, brushed past Sturmm, and went back up the companionway. He leaned on the starboard rail, breathing deeply, and Swallow moved beside him.

"You all right, sir?"

"God, what a pesthole. Those women—they've been through hell." He pulled himself together. "You've checked the holds thoroughly, Coxswain?"

"Clean as a whistle, sir. She's in ballast with sand."

Edge turned to Sturmm who stood waiting, Berger a pace or two behind. "I don't understand."

"For many months we work the coastal trade in Brazil," Sturmm told him. "Then we decide to come home. As you may imagine, no one seemed anxious to risk a cargo with us."

"And the passengers?"

"The good sisters have been stranded in Brazil for more than a year now. We are the first Swedish ship to leave Brazil during that time. They were grateful for the opportunity for any kind of passage."

"But the old lady," Edge said, "Mrs. Ternström. She looks in a bad way."

"And anxious to see her family again while there is still time." Sturmm smiled bitterly. "There's a war on, or hadn't you noticed? It makes things difficult for us neutrals when we want to travel from one place to another."

Edge made his decision and handed the passports back. "You'll want these. My apologies to your captain. I'll have to confirm it with my commanding officer, but I see no reason why you shouldn't be allowed to proceed." He moved to the head of the Jacob's ladder and paused. "Those ladies down there . . ."

"Will be fine, Lieutenant. We'll soon have things shipshape again."

"Anything else we can do for you?"

Sturmm smiled. "Bring us up to date on the war, if you would. How are things going?"

"All *our* way now, no doubt about that," Edge said. "Though they do seem to be slowing down rather in Europe. I don't think we're going to see Berlin by Christmas after all. The Germans are making one hell of a fight of it in the low countries."

He went down the ladder quickly followed by Swallow and the other rating and they cast off. "Well, Coxswain?" he asked as they pulled away.

"I know one thing, sir. I'll never complain about serving in submarines again."

On the quarterdeck, Berger smoked a cigar and waited, Sturmm at his side.

"What do you think, Herr Kapitän?" Sturmm asked. "Has it worked?"

At the same moment, the signal lamp on the bridge of the *Guardian* started to flash.

" 'You may proceed,' " Berger spelled out. " 'Happy voyage and good luck.' " He turned to Sturmm, his face calm. "My maternal grandmother was English, did I ever tell you that?"

"No, sir."

Berger tossed his cigar over the side. "She's all yours, Mister Sturmm. Let's get under way again as soon as possible."

"Aye, aye, sir."

Sturmm turned, raising his voice to call to the men below, and Berger descended to the deck. He stood in the entrance to the companionway, aware of the stench, of Sister Angela's pale face peering up at him.

"Did it work?" she called softly.

"Remind me, when I have the time, to tell you what a very remarkable woman you are, Sister."

"At the appropriate moment, I shall, Kapitän. You may be certain of that," she said serenely.

Berger turned away. The *Guardian* was already departing toward the southwest. He watched her go, and behind him Helmut Richter emerged from the forward hatch and came aft. His body was streaked with filth, but he was smiling.

"Can the lads come on deck and wash off under the pump? They smell pretty high after those bilges."

"So I observe." Berger wrinkled his nose. "Give it another twenty minutes until our British friends are really on their way, Helmut, then turn them loose."

He went into his cabin and Richter stripped his shirt from his body, worked the deck pump with one hand, and turned the hose on himself. As he did so, Sister Lotte came out on deck clutching a full pail of slops in both hands. She got as far as the starboard rail and was about to empty it when Richter reached her.

"Never into the wind," he said. "That way you get the contents back in your face." He peered down in disgust. "And that, you can definitely do without."

He carried the pail to the port rail, emptied it over the side, then flushed it out under the pump. She stood watching him calmly.

She was small and very slightly built, a lawyer's daughter from Munich who looked younger than her twenty-three years. Unlike the other nuns, she was still a novice, and had been transferred to Brazil, by way of Portugal, the previous year only because she was a trained nurse and there was a shortage of people with her qualifications.

She picked up his shirt. "I'll wash this for you."

"No need."

"And the seam is splitting on one shoulder. I'll mend it." When she looked up, he saw that her eyes were a startling cornflower blue. "It must have been horrible down there."

"For you also."

He handed her the pail, she took it, and for a brief

moment they held it together. Sister Angela said quietly, "Lotte, I need you."

She was standing in the entrance to the companionway, her face calm as always, but there was a new wariness in her eyes when she looked at Richter. The girl smiled briefly and joined her and they went below. Richter started to pump water over his head vigorously.

Berger sat behind the desk, surveying the wreckage of his cabin—not that it mattered. It could soon be put straight again. He was filled with a tremendous sense of elation and opened his personal journal. He picked up his pen, thought for a moment, then wrote:

> *I am now more than ever convinced that we shall reach Kiel in safety. . . .*

Barkentine Deutschland, *14 September*
1944. Lat. 28°16′N, long. 30°50′W. Frau
Prager died at three bells of the midwatch.
We delivered her body to the sea shortly af-
ter dawn, Sister Angela taking the service.
Ship's company much affected by this calami-
tous event. A light breeze sprang up during
the afternoon watch, increasing to fresh in
squalls. I estimate that we are 1,170 miles
from Queenstown in Ireland this day.

Four

Night was falling fast as Jago and Petty Officer
Jansen went up the hill to St. Mungo's. They
found the burial party in the cemetery at the
back of the church. There were twenty or so islanders
there, men and women, Jean Sinclair and Reeve standing together, the admiral in full uniform. Murdoch
Macleod, in his best blue serge suit, stood at the head of
the open grave, a prayer book in his hands.

The two Americans paused some little distance
away and removed their caps. It was very quiet except
for the incessant calling of the birds, and Jago looked

down across Mary's Town to the horseshoe of the harbor where the MGB was tied up at the jetty.

The sun was setting in a sky the color of brass, splashed with scarlet, thin mackerel clouds high above. Beyond Barra Head, the islands marched north to Barra, Mingulay, Pabbay, Sandray, rearing out of a perfectly calm sea, black against flame.

Reeve glanced over his shoulder, murmured something to Jean Sinclair, then moved toward the men through the gravestones. "Thanks for coming so promptly, Lieutenant."

"No trouble, sir. We were on our way to Mallaig from Stornoway when they relayed your message." Jago nodded toward the grave into which half a dozen fishermen were lowering the coffin. "Another one from U-743?"

Reeve nodded. "That makes eight in the past three days." He hesitated. "When you were last here you said you were going to London on leave this week."

"That's right, Admiral. If I can get to Mallaig on time I intend to catch the night train for Glasgow. Is there something I can do for you, sir?"

"There certainly is." Reeve took a couple of envelopes from his pocket. "This first one is for my niece. Her apartment's in Westminster, not far from the Houses of Parliament."

"And the other, sir?"

Reeve handed it over. "If you would see that gets to SHAEF headquarters personally. It would save time."

Jago looked at the address on the envelope and swallowed hard. "My God!"

Reeve smiled. "See that it's handed to one of his aides personally. No one else."

"Yes, sir."

"You'd better move out then. I'll expect to hear from you as soon as you get back. As I told you, I have a radio at the cottage, one of the few courtesies the navy still extends me. They'll brief you at Mallaig on the times during the day I sit at the damned thing hoping someone will take notice."

Jago saluted, nodded to Jansen, and then moved away. As the admiral rejoined the funeral party, Murdoch Macleod started to read aloud in a firm, clear voice, ". . . man that is born of woman hath but a short time to live, and is full of misery. He cometh up and is cut down like a flower . . ."

Suddenly it was very dark, with only the burned-out fire of day on the horizon as they went out through the lych-gate.

Jansen said, "Who's the letter for, Lieutenant?"

"General Eisenhower," Jago said simply.

In Brest, they were shooting again across the river as Paul Gericke turned the corner, the rattle of small-arms fire drifting across the water. Somewhere on the far horizon rockets arched through the night, and in spite of the heavy rain considerable portions of the city appeared to be on fire. Most of the warehouses that had once lined the street had been demolished by bombing, the pavement was littered with rubble and broken glass, but the small hotel on the corner that served as naval headquarters still seemed to be intact. Gericke ran up the steps quickly, showed his pass to the sentry at the door, and went inside.

He was a small man, no more than five feet five or six, with fair hair and a pale face that seemed untouched by wind and weather. His eyes were very dark, with no light in them at all, contrasting strangely with the good-humored, rather lazy smile that seemed to permanently touch his mouth.

His white-topped naval cap had seen much service and he was hardly a prepossessing figure in his old leather jerkin, leather trousers, and seaboots. But the young lieutenant sitting at his desk in the foyer saw only the Knight's Cross, with Oak Leaves for a second award, at the throat and was on his feet in an instant.

"I was asked to report to the commodore of submarines as soon as I arrive," Gericke told him. "Korvettenkapitän Gericke. U-235."

"He's expecting you, sir," the lieutenant said. "If you'd follow me."

They went up the curving staircase. A petty officer, a pistol at his belt, stood guard outside one of the hotel bedrooms. The handwritten notice on the door said KAPITÄN ZUR SEE OTTO FRIEMEL, FÜHRER DER UNTERSEE-BOOT WEST.

The lieutenant knocked and went in. "Korvettenkapitän Gericke, sir."

The room was in half darkness, the only light the reading lamp on Friemel's desk. He was in shirtsleeves, working his way through a pile of correspondence, steel-rimmed reading glasses perched on the end of his nose, and an ivory cigarette holder jutting from the left corner of his mouth.

He came around the desk smiling, hand outstretched. "My dear Paul. Good to see you. How was the West Indies?"

"A long haul," Gericke said. "Especially when it was time to come home."

Friemel produced a bottle of schnapps and two glasses. "We're out of champagne. Not like the old days."

"What, no flowers on the dock?" Gericke said. "Don't tell me we're losing the war?"

"My dear Paul, in Brest we don't even have a dock any longer. If you'd arrived in daylight you'd have noticed the rather unhappy state of those impregnable U-boat pens of ours. Five meters of reinforced concrete pulverized by a little item the RAF call the earthquake bomb." He raised his glass. "To you, Paul. A successful trip, I hear?"

"Not bad."

"Come now. A Canadian corvette, a tanker, and three merchant ships? Thirty-one thousand tons, and you call that not bad? I'd term it a rather large miracle. These days two out of three U-boats that go out never return." He shook his head. "It isn't 1940 any longer. No more Happy Time. These days they send out half-trained boys. You're one of the few old-timers left."

Gericke helped himself to a cigarette from a box on the table. It was French and of the cheapest variety, for when he lit it and inhaled, the smoke bit at the back of his throat, sending him into a paroxysm of coughing.

"My God! Now I know things are bad."

"You've no idea how bad," Friemel told him. "Brest has been besieged by the American Eighth Army Corps since the ninth of August. The only reason we're still here is because of the quite incredible defense put up by General Ramcke and the Second Airborne Division. Those paratroopers of his are without a doubt the finest fighting men I've ever seen in action, and that includes the *Waffen* SS." He reached for the schnapps bottle again. "Of course, they were pulled out of the Ukraine to come here. It could be they are still euphoric at such good fortune. An American prison camp, after all, is infinitely to be preferred to the Russian variety."

"And what's the U-boat position?"

"There isn't one. The Ninth Flotilla is no more. U-256 was the last to leave. That was eleven days ago. Orders are to regroup in Bergen."

"Then what about me?" Gericke asked. "I could have made for Norway by way of the Irish Sea and the North Channel."

"Your orders, Paul, are quite explicit. You will make for Bergen via the English Channel as the rest of the flotilla has done, only in your case someone at High Command has provided you with what one might term a slight detour."

Gericke, who had long since passed being surprised at anything, smiled. "Where to, exactly?"

"It's really quite simple." Friemel turned to the table behind, rummaged among a pile of charts, found the one he was looking for, and opened it across the desk.

Gericke leaned over. "Falmouth?"

"That's right. The Royal Navy's Fifteenth MGB Flotilla operating out of Falmouth has been causing havoc on this entire coast recently. To be perfectly honest, it's made any kind of naval activity impossible."

"And what am I supposed to do about it?"

"According to your orders, go into Falmouth and lay mines."

"They're joking, of course."

Friemel held up a typed order. "Dönitz himself."

Gericke laughed out loud. "But this is really beautiful, Otto. Quite superb in its idiocy, even for those chair-bound bastards in Kiel. What on earth am I supposed to do, win the war in a single bold stroke?" He shook his head. "They must believe in fairy stories. Someone should tell them that when the tailor boasted he could kill seven at one blow he meant flies on a slice of bread and jam."

"I don't know," Friemel said. "It could be worse. There's a protecting curtain of mines plus a blockship here between Pendennis Point and Blackrock and a temporary net boom from Blackrock to St. Anthony Head. That's supposed to be highly secret, by the way, but it seems the *Abwehr* still have an agent operational in the Falmouth area."

"He must feel lonely."

"Ships in and out all the time. Go in with a few when the net opens. Drop your eggs, up here in Carrick Roads and across the inner harbor and out again."

Gericke shook his head. "I'm afraid not."

"Why?"

"We may get in, but we certainly won't get out."

Friemel sighed. "A pity, as I'll be going with you. Not out of any sense of adventure, I assure you. I have orders to report to Kiel, and as the land routes to Germany are cut, my only way would seem to be with you to Bergen."

Gericke shrugged. "So, in the end, all roads lead to hell."

Friemel helped himself to one of the French cigarettes and inserted it in his holder. "What shape are you in?"

"We were strafed by a Liberator in Biscay. Superficial damage only, but my engines need a complete overhaul. New bearings for a start."

"Not possible. I can give you four or five days. We must leave on the nineteenth. Ramcke tells me he can hold out for another week at the most. No more."

The door opened and the young lieutenant entered. "Signal from Kiel, sir. Marked most urgent."

Friemel took the flimsy from him and adjusted his spectacles. A slight, ironic smile touched his mouth. "Would you believe it, Paul, but this confirms my promotion as Konteradmiral in command of all naval forces in the Brest area. One can only imagine it has been delayed in channels."

The lieutenant passed across another flimsy. Friemel read it, his face grave, then handed it to Gericke. It said: CONGRATULATIONS ON YOUR PROMOTION IN THE FULL AND CERTAIN KNOWLEDGE THAT YOU AND YOUR MEN WILL DIE RATHER THAN YIELD ONE INCH OF SOIL TO THE ENEMY. ADOLF HITLER.

Gericke passed it back. "Congratulations, Herr Konteradmiral," he said formally.

Without a flicker of emotion, Friemel said to the lieutenant, "Send this message to Berlin. 'Will fight to the last. Long live the Führer.' That's all. Dismiss!"

The young lieutenant withdrew. Friemel said, "You approve?"

"Wasn't that Lütjens's last message before the *Bismarck* went down?"

"Exactly," Rear Admiral Otto Friemel said. "Another drink, my friend?" He reached for the bottle, then sighed. "What a pity. We appear to have finished the last of the schnapps."

It was still raining heavily in London at eight-thirty on the following evening when JU 88 pathfinders of *Gruppe* 1/K.G.66, operating out of Chartres and Rennes in France, made their first strike. By nine-fifteen, the casualty department of Guy's Hospital was working at full stretch.

Janet Munro, in the end cubicle, curtain drawn, carefully inserted twenty-seven stitches into the right thigh of a young auxiliary fireman. He seemed dazed and lay there, staring blankly at the ceiling, an unlit cigarette hanging from the corner of his mouth.

Janet was being assisted by a male nurse named Callaghan, a white-haired man in his late fifties who had served on the western front as a medical corps sergeant in the First World War. He strongly approved of the young American doctor in every possible way, and made it his business to look out for her welfare, something she seemed quite incapable of doing for herself. Just now he was particularly concerned about the fact that she had been on duty for twelve hours, and it was beginning to show.

"You going off after this one, miss?"

"How can I, Joey?" she said. "They'll be coming in all night."

Bombs had been falling for some time on the other side of the Thames but now there was an explosion close at hand. The whole building shook and there was a crash of breaking glass. The lights dimmed for a moment and somewhere a child started to wail.

"My God, Jerry certainly picks his time," Callaghan remarked.

"What do you mean?" she said, still concentrating on the task in hand.

He seemed surprised. "Don't you know who's here tonight, miss? Eisenhower himself. Turned up an hour ago just before the bombing started."

She paused and looked at him blankly. "General Eisenhower? Here?"

"Visiting those Yank paratroopers in ward seventy-three. The lads they brought over from Paris last week. Decorating some of them, that's what I heard."

She was unable to take it in, suddenly very tired. She turned back to her patient and inserted the last couple of stitches.

"I'll dress it for you," Callaghan said. "You get yourself a cup of tea."

As she stripped the rubber gloves from her fingers, the young fireman turned his head and looked at her. "You a Yank then, Doctor?"

"That's right."

"Got any gum, chum?"

She smiled and took a cigarette lighter from her pocket. "No, but I can manage a light."

She took the cigarette from his mouth, lit it, and gave it back to him. "You'll be fine now."

He grinned. "Can you cook as well, Doc?"

"When I get the time."

Suddenly, the effort of keeping her smile in place was too much and she turned and went into the corridor quickly. Callaghan was right. She needed that cup of tea very badly indeed. And about fifteen hours' sleep to follow—but that, of course, was quite impossible.

As she started along the corridor, the curtain of a cubicle was snatched back and a young nurse emerged. She was obviously panic-stricken, blood on her hands. Turning wildly she saw Janet and called out—soundlessly, because at that moment another heavy bomb fell close enough to shake the walls and bring plaster from the ceiling.

Janet caught her by the shoulders. "What is it?"

The girl tried to speak, pointing wildly at the cubicle as another bomb fell, and Janet pushed her to one side and entered. The woman who lay on the padded operating table, covered with a sheet, was obviously very much in labor. The young man who leaned over her was a corporal in the commandos, his uniform torn and streaked with dust.

"Who are you?" The tiredness had left her now, as if it had never been.

"Her husband, miss. She's having a baby." He plucked at her sleeve. "For God's sake do something."

Janet pulled back the sheet. "When did she start?"

"Half an hour, maybe longer. We was in the High Street when the siren went, so I took her into the underground. Borough Station. When she started feeling bad I thought I'd better get her to hospital, but it was hell out there. Bombs falling all over the place."

Another landed very close to the hospital now, followed by a second. For a moment, the lights went out. The woman on the table cried out in fear and pain. Her eyes started from her head as the lights came on again and she tried to sit up.

Janet pushed her down and turned to the young nurse. "You know what's wrong here?"

"I'm not sure," the girl said. "I'm only a probationer." She looked at her hands. "There was a lot of blood."

The young commando pulled at Janet's sleeve. "What's going on? What's up?"

"A baby is usually delivered head first," Janet said calmly. "This is what's known as a breech. That means it's presenting its backside."

"Can you handle it?"

"I should imagine so, but we haven't got much time. I want you to stand over your wife, hold her hand, and talk to her. Anything you like, only don't stop."

"Shall I get Sister Johnson?" the young nurse asked.

"No time," Janet said. "I need you here."

Bombs were falling steadily now, and from the sound of it, panic had broken out among the crowd that waited in general casualty for treatment. She took a deep breath, tried to ignore that nightmare world outside, and concentrated on the task in hand.

The first problem was to deliver the legs. She probed gently inside until she managed to get a finger up against the back of one of the child's knees. The leg flexed instantly and so did the other when she repeated the performance.

The woman cried out and Janet said to the husband, "Tell her to push. Push hard."

A moment later, the legs delivered themselves. She held out her hands for the young nurse to wipe away the blood, then grasped the legs, fingers beneath the thighs, and pulled down firmly until the shoulders were in sight.

Now the arms were extended. She twisted the child to the left until the shoulder flexed, hooked a finger under the elbow and delivered the left arm. Bombs were still falling, but farther away now, as she repeated the performance with the right.

There was a tremendous hubbub outside, people running up and down the corridor, and a smell of burning. She whispered to the young nurse, "So far so good. Now for the head."

She put her right arm beneath the child and got her forefinger into its mouth, then probed with her left hand for a grip on the shoulders and started to pull. Slowly, very slowly, it moved, and yet the strength required was so considerable that sweat sprung to her forehead.

And then it was clear and safe in her hands. But it was obvious at once that it wasn't breathing and the whole body was deep purple.

"Cotton wool, quickly!" The young nurse passed some across and Janet cleared the mouth and nostrils. "Now you can get Sister Johnson, if she's available, or Callaghan. Anybody, only hurry."

The girl went out on the run and Janet blew into

the tiny mouth. Quite suddenly the child shuddered, gave an audible gasp, and started to cry.

Janet looked up and found the young commando staring at her wildly. "A daughter," she said. "If you're interested."

His wife gave a stifled moan and fainted. At the same moment the curtain was jerked back and Sister Johnson rushed in. Janet handed her the baby. "This one's yours, Sister," she said. "I'll see to the mother." And she elbowed the young commando out of the way and leaned over his wife.

It was later, when the bombing had stopped and she had moved out onto the porch to smoke a cigarette, that the tiredness hit her again.

"Oh, God," she said softly. "Isn't it ever going to end, this war?"

There were fires on the other side of the Thames toward Westminster and the acrid smell of smoke filled the air. Behind her the blackout curtain opened briefly and Callaghan appeared, an American officer in raincoat and peaked cap with him.

"Oh, there you are, Doctor," Callaghan said. "Been looking all over for you. This gentleman would like a word with you."

"Colonel Brisingham, ma'am." He saluted punctiliously.

Callaghan withdrew, leaving them alone on the dimly lit porch. "What can I do for you, Colonel?" Janet asked.

"General Eisenhower would appreciate a word, ma'am, if you could spare him a few minutes of your time."

He delivered the words gravely and courteously and yet, for Janet, the walls of the porch seemed to move in and out again, very slowly. She fell against the colonel who caught hold of her arms.

"Are you all right?"

"It's been a long day." She took a deep breath. "Where is the general?"

"Just across the yard, ma'am, in his staff car. If you'd follow me. We haven't much time, I'm afraid. He has to be back in Paris by tomorrow morning."

The car was parked in a corner by the main gate. She was aware of the jeeps surrounding it, the helmets of the military police, then Brisingham had the rear door open.

"Dr. Munro, General."

Janet hesitated, then climbed inside, and Brisingham closed the door. In the faint light from the dashboard she could only get the briefest impression. He was wearing a trench coat, a forage cap, she could see that, but not much of his face except for the brief gleam of teeth that went with the inimitable smile.

"Would it surprise you if I said I felt as if I already knew you?" Eisenhower said.

She frowned and then saw the solution. "Uncle Carey?"

He chuckled. "You were all he used to talk about over the coffee at SHAEF when we were putting Overlord together. But I knew him from long before then. Panama—1922, '23. I was a major and he, as I recall, was a lieutenant commander with a reputation for being difficult to handle."

"He hasn't changed."

"Not in the slightest." He hesitated. "When he went down in that Norwegian destroyer on D day, for example. He should never have been there. A direct contravention of his orders."

"Which cost him an eye and most of one arm."

"I know. Tell me. This place Fhada? This Scottish island he's staying on at the moment? What's he doing there?"

"His father's family came from there originally. He was left a cottage by a cousin just before the war. He wanted somewhere to hide for a while and I suppose it seemed as good as any. It's a strange place."

"You think he was looking for something?"

"Perhaps."

The general nodded. "Did you know he's been trying to get back into action?"

"No, but it doesn't surprise me."

"Me either. He couldn't change his nature this late in the day, but it just isn't possible, you must see that. One eye, an apology for an arm. He's given as much as any man could . . ."

"Except his life."

"Damn it!" Eisenhower said. "The Navy Department won't budge. They want him on the retired list now."

"And you?"

He sighed heavily. "He sent me a letter by hand, delivered by some young naval officer on leave. Lucky I happened to be in London today."

"He asked for your help? Carey Reeve?" She smiled. "Now that, General, is really something."

"The same thought *had* occurred to me," Eisenhower said.

"And can you help?"

"I've a job in Paris for him, starting the first of October. Supply and personnel coordination. Deputy director."

"A desk job?" Janet shook her head. "It's action he's after."

"Those days are over. If he wants a job, there's one for him. Otherwise it's the boneyard. He must understand that."

"But will he?" she said softly and almost to herself.

Eisenhower said, "Look, is there any chance you could get a few days off and go and see him?"

She hesitated. "I suppose so. I haven't had more than a weekend in the past six months."

"Wonderful," he said. "Naturally I'll have someone on my staff make all the necessary travel arrangements for you. I'll give you a letter, making clear the terms of my offer. But the real pressure must come from you."

There was a tap on the window. Eisenhower lowered it and Brisingham leaned in. "We'll have to get moving if we're to make that plane, General."

Eisenhower nodded impatiently and wound up the window again. "They won't leave me alone for a minute. A hell of a war, even for generals, believe me."

Far out in the Atlantic, the horizon crackled with sheet lightning and rain started to fall heavily. The wind was force eight on the Beaufort scale, a mountainous sea running, and the *Deutschland* fled under staysails only, Richter and Sturmm at the wheel.

At four bells in the first watch a sudden vicious squall struck from the southeast with incredible force, driving hail before it like bullets. The *Deutschland* lurched to one side, swinging nearly five points off course. Sturmm lost his balance and was swept into the scuppers by a cascade of water, leaving Richter to struggle desperately with the spinning wheel. The *Deutschland* staggered as the wind dealt her another savage blow and started to heel over.

Berger, unable to sleep, had been lying in his bunk for the best part of an hour, smoking a cigar and listening to the music of the gale. Every part of the ship creaked and groaned, and the wind whistled through the rigging with a hundred separate voices. He was wearing foul-weather gear, seaboots, and oilskin coat, ready for any emergency.

The crisis, when it came, was so unexpected that he was thrown from his bunk before he knew what was happening and rolled across the cabin, fetching up against the desk.

The floor continued to incline as he tried to get up. "Oh, dear God, she's going!" he said aloud. Then the tilting ceased. He scrambled across to the door, got it open, and went outside.

The lightning that flickered constantly in the sky above illuminated an extraordinary scene. The *Deutschland* was lying over, almost on her beam-ends, with her lee rail under and lower yardarm dipping into broken water.

Richter and Sturmm were wrestling with the wheel and several members of the crew lurched and slithered across the sloping deck in complete panic.

"She's going! She's going!" one man screamed. Berger punched him in the jaw, sending him flat on his back.

He cried, "Bring her around, for God's sake. Bring her around!"

Gradually, and with considerable difficulty, the *Deutschland* started to turn into the wind, as Richter and Sturmm got the helm up, but the deck remained at such a slope that no one could stand without hanging on to something.

Berger yelled at the two nearest men, "Take the wheel and tell Richter and Mister Sturmm to come to me."

He managed to make it to the aft cargo hatch on his hands and knees and was wrestling with the ropes of the canvas cover when Sturmm and Richter arrived. "What do you think?" Sturmm cried above the roaring of the sea.

"The ballast's moved, that's obvious," Berger replied. "But how much is the important thing. Let's have this hatch cover open and see the state of the game."

Below, for the passengers, there was total confusion. When the squall struck, Sister Angela and Sister Else had been sitting together on the bottom bunk in their cabin, discussing a passage of the Scriptures, the usual evening task before bed. They were both thrown to the floor, and the oil lamp fell from its hook in the ceiling to smash beside them. The spreading pool of oil flared, but was almost immediately extinguished as the cabin tilted, the door burst open, and water poured in.

Sister Angela started to make a final act of contrition. "Oh, my God, who art infinitely good in thyself . . ." But she choked on the words, every instinct rebelling against such a calm acceptance of death. She crawled to the door, calling to Sister Else to follow her.

The saloon was in total darkness, water pouring in through the shattered skylight. It was a nightmare world. Voices called hysterically. Someone lurched into her; she reached out and touched a face as an arm fastened about her in panic. And then a cabin door opened and light flooded out as Otto Prager appeared with a lantern in one hand.

The floor of the saloon was tilted at an angle of forty-five degrees, the dining table and chairs, all bolted to the floor, still in place, but on the port side at the bottom of the slope water had gathered to a depth of three feet. Each time the *Deutschland* rolled, more came in through the broken skylight, newly repaired only the previous day after the *Guardian* episode.

Sister Angela found herself held by Sister Lotte, the youngest of the nuns. The girl was out of her mind with fear, and Sister Angela had to struggle to tear herself free.

She shook the younger woman vigorously and slapped her face. "Pull yourself together, Sister. Remember what you are."

Sister Else managed to get to her feet beside her, waist deep in water, the skirt of her black robe floating around her, and at that moment, the cabin door next to Prager's opened and Sisters Kathë and Brigitte peered through.

Prager, who seemed remarkably calm, said, "Everything will be fine, Sisters, no need to panic. Make for the companionway."

Sister Angela got there first, an arm around Sister Lotte. Prager handed her the lantern and assisted the others, one by one, until they were all on the tilting companionway.

As he moved up to join Sister Angela, the door at the head of the companionway opened and Berger peered in, a storm lantern in one hand. "Everyone all right?"

"I think so," Sister Angela said.

He crouched down to speak to her. "No point in putting you into one of the boats. It wouldn't last five minutes in this sea. You understand me, Sister?"

"What must we do then, Kapitän?"

"Stay here for the moment."

"What's gone wrong, Eric?" Prager demanded.

"The ballast has shifted into the lee bow. Most of the crew are down there now trying to do something about it. We need you, too, Otto. If another squall hits while we're in this state she'll turn turtle."

Prager moved out into the night without a word. Sister Angela said, "Is there anything we can do, Kapitän?"

"Pray," Eric Berger told her. "Very hard." And he slammed the door shut and disappeared.

When Otto Prager went down the ladder into the cargo hold it was like a descent into hell. The crew worked in the light of a couple of storm lanterns, furiously shoveling sand to windward. Each time the ship rolled, men stumbled into each other and went down.

Prager stepped off the ladder and fell to one knee. Someone cried out in fear, but otherwise everyone shoveled away with a grim frenzy, the only sound the creaking of the ship's timbers and the gale outside.

A strong arm hoisted Prager to his feet and Helmut Richter grinned down at him. "Just think, Herr Prager, you could have been safe in Rio at this very moment enjoying a drink before a late dinner, looking out from the terrace of the Copacabana at the lights in the bay . . ."

"Well, I'm not," Prager told him, "so just give me a bloody shovel and let's get to it."

For some time now it had been obvious that the *Deutschland* was tilting to windward, but on the companionway in the half darkness it seemed an eternity before the door opened again and Berger peered in. He managed a smile, but only just.

"Did you pray, Sister?"

"We did."

"Well, for what it's worth, your prayers were answered. Somebody on this tub must live right. It isn't me, so it must be you."

"I'm willing to admit that possibility, Kapitän."

"Excellent. We'll have the pump working as soon as we can, but it may not be possible to light a fire in the galley again before morning. I'm afraid you're going to find it rather uncomfortable down there for the rest of the night."

"We'll manage."

In a sudden outburst, he added roughly, "Damn it, Sister, it was you who insisted on coming. I warned you."

"Yes, Kapitän, I believe you did," she said. "And for that I thank you, among other things." She looked down at the faces of the others, upturned in the dim light of the lamp. "Shall we pray, my beloved sisters?"

She began to recite aloud the prayers for thanksgiving after a storm. "So they cried unto the Lord in their trouble; and he delivered them from their distress."

Berger shut the companionway door and turned toward Prager who leaned wearily on the hatch beside him. "What a woman," he said. "What a bloody infuriating—"

"Wonderful woman," Prager finished.

Berger laughed, then turned to look up at the quarterdeck where Richter had the wheel on his own now, for the wind had dropped a little, although there was still a heavy sea running.

Sturmm came down the ladder to join him. "I've got a party on the pump, sir. Any further orders?"

"Yes," Berger said. "Wood, Mister Sturmm. Every plank you can find. Gut the ship if needs be. Every cabin and locker, but I want that sand decked off within twenty-four hours so it can't damn well move again, whatever happens."

"Aye, aye, sir." Sturmm hesitated. "A close one, Kapitän."

"Too close," Eric Berger said. "Let's try not to make a habit of it," and he turned and walked toward his cabin.

Barkentine Deutschland, *17 September 1944. Lat. 38°56′N, long. 30°50′W. Wind hauled into the west during the middle watch and we braced the yards forward. Hove the log and found we were going 10 knots. Over-cast cleared just before noon and allowed the sun to come through, the wind dropping to a flat calm.*

Five

*T*he *Deutschland* seemed to float in space, completely still, every sail set, yards braced, perfectly reflected in a sea of green glass.

It was hot and airless. Conditions below were unbearable and, on the captain's orders, a canvas awning had been rigged aft of the mainmast so that the sisters might be protected to some degree from the fierceness of the sun.

Most of the crew and passengers were suffering from sea boils now, a product not only of the unsatisfactory diet but of the constant action of salt water on the skin. One of the men, a brawny Hamburger named Schirmer, was virtually crippled by a whole crop of them on his left leg. He leaned back groaning in a canvas chair while Sister Angela went to work with a lancet.

Forward from the mainmast, under the supervision of Sturmm, four of the crew worked the heavy metal bar of the ship's two suction pumps and water gushed across the deck in a brown stream.

Richter, who had just finished a thirty-minute stint himself, dipped a pannier into the water bucket, wrinkling his nose in disgust. "Have you seen this, Herr Leutnant?" he asked Sturmm, and poured the contents of the pannier back into the bucket. The water was dark red.

"Rust from the tanks, I expect." Sturmm grinned. "On this ship we think of everything, Helmut. You don't just get a drink of water. We throw in an iron tonic as well. Good for the constitution."

"My belly doesn't agree." Richter ran a hand across his stomach. "Sometimes the cramps are terrible. Most of the lads will tell you the same."

Sister Lotte was standing by the mizzen shrouds on the port side. Like the other nuns she had put on her white tropical habit again, because of the heat. And, as always, Richter wondered how on earth she managed to keep it so clean. She made a rather appealing figure as she stood there, one hand on a rope, gazing out to sea.

Walz, the cook, came out of the galley and emptied a pail of garbage over the rail beside her. She moved back hastily.

"Sorry, Sister," he said, with total insincerity.

"That's all right, Herr Walz," she answered in a low, sweet voice.

He looked her over boldly and grinned, showing bad teeth. The lust in his eyes was plain: her smile faded and she reached for the shrouds as if to support herself.

Walz turned back to the galley and found Richter leaning against the entrance. He was stripped to the waist, his muscular body burned brown by the sun, the long, blond hair and beard bleached white, a black Brazilian cigarillo between his teeth. A match flared in the bosun's cupped hands. As he leaned down to it, he said softly, "Manners, you bastard. That isn't some San Pauli whore you're talking to."

"So, you fancy her, too?" Walz grinned again. "I don't blame you. It's a long trip home and women are women, as the captain said, whatever they choose to wear. It's what's between the legs that counts."

He was hurled into the shadows of the galley, found himself back across the table, a hand of iron at his throat. There was a sharp click as the blade of the Finnish gutting knife in the bosun's right hand sprang into view.

"One wrong word, you lump of dung," Richter said calmly, "try even looking at her again as you did now and you go over the side—and I wouldn't like to guarantee it'll be in one piece."

Walz almost fainted with terror, felt his bowels move. The bosun patted his face. "That's it, Ernst. That's exactly the way I like you. Frightened to death."

He snapped the blade of the gutting knife back into place and went outside.

Sister Lotte was still standing by the mizzen shrouds and, at that moment, an albatross swooped down to where the garbage floated, motionless as the ship itself.

She turned, as if by instinct, and became aware that Richter was watching her. She smiled and he crossed the deck to join her.

"Mister Richter." There was no attempt to conceal the pleasure in her eyes. "That bird—what was it?"

"An albatross, Sister. King of the scavengers. There'll be more around soon, when they get wind of our garbage."

"So beautiful." She shaded her eyes against the sun and watched it go.

And so are you, by God, Richter thought. "They say an albatross is probably the ghost of a dead sailor."

"And you believe that?"

Her eyes were very blue, her face a perfect oval framed by the white coif. Richter's throat was suddenly dry. He said, "Of course not, Sister. Superstitious nonsense." He took a deep breath. "Now, if you'll excuse me, I must see the Kapitän."

He had a rope burn on his right wrist. She reached for his hand and frowned. "That's nasty. It could get worse. You must let me see to it for you."

Her fingers were cool. There was sweat on his brow and then, across her shoulder, he saw that Sister Angela, seated under the awning, her medical case open beside her as she treated one of the seamen, was watching him gravely.

Richter pulled his hand away. "No need, Sister. It's nothing, believe me."

Berger, seated at the desk in his cabin, was entering the log.

> *18 September 1944. A bad night. Rain and heavy seas. Lower t'gallant split during a sudden squall at six bells in the midwatch. Weather changes again to flat calm in the forenoon. Mister Sturmm reports sixteen inches of water in the bilges.*

He put down his pen and sat back, aware of the dull monotonous thumping of the pump. Not good. Not good at all for her to be taking so much water. Although he had said nothing to Sturmm and Richter about it, he knew that the seriousness of the situation must be as apparent to them as it was to him.

There was a knock on the door and Richter entered. "Mister Sturmm's compliments, sir. From the sound of things, she's just about dry again."

Berger nodded. "What do you think, Helmut?"

Richter shrugged. "She's old, sir. Too old, and I shouldn't think the copper's been off her in years.

God knows what state her timbers are in." He hesitated. "And when that squall struck the other night, when she nearly turned turtle . . ."

"You think she took some damage that we weren't aware of?"

Before Richter could reply, there was a confused shouting on deck, mixed with cheering. And a strange drumming. Berger was on his feet in an instant, got the door open, and rushed outside with Richter at his heels.

It was raining, a freak tropical downpour. Most of the crew were running about the deck like madmen, those who had been able to find buckets holding them up to catch the sweet water. The nuns, sheltering under the awning, were laughing like children as water poured from it in a torrent. Sturmm stood underneath the impromptu shower, water cascading over his head. He turned and, seeing Berger, moved aside hurriedly.

"Sorry, Kapitän. Collective madness."

He stood mopping his face with his neckerchief, like a schoolboy caught out. The rain ceased as suddenly as it had started, and steam began to rise from the decks.

Berger said, "How's the pumping?"

"Sucked dry, sir." Sturmm hesitated. "For the moment."

Berger nodded, aware that most of the crew were hanging around, intent on picking up any information that was going. He made his judgment and acted on it. There was, after all, little point in pretending the situation didn't exist.

"Not good, Mister Sturmm. Sixteen inches today. The same yesterday. Fourteen the day before. There has to be a reason."

There was a heavy silence, broken only by the creaking of the rigging and the slapping of the empty sails.

Richter spoke first. "Maybe I should go down and take a look, Kapitän."

He was an excellent swimmer, and strong as a bull. With the ship totally becalmed, there was little danger. Berger nodded. "All right." He took a key from his pocket and handed it to Sturmm. "Get a rifle from the gun locker, just in case."

As Richter pulled off his canvas, rope-soled shoes, Sister Angela moved to Berger's side. "Why the rifle, Kapitän?"

Berger shrugged. "Sharks. No sign now, but amazing how they appear with a man in the water, and all that garbage doesn't help."

Sister Lotte turned pale. She moved to Richter's side where he stood at the rail, tightening his belt. "It's —it's very deep, isn't it, Mister Richter?"

Richter laughed out loud. "A thousand fathoms, at least. But don't worry, I'm not going all the way down."

Berger, listening to this exchange, frowned, but the time was hardly appropriate to make any comment. Instead he said, "You want a line, Helmut?"

Richter shook his head. "Why bother? There isn't an inch of movement in her." He put one foot on the rail, sprang up, and dived cleanly into the water.

A shoal of small fish scattered before him, disintegrating in a silver cloud. He went down fast, through water that was like green glass, pale with sunlight. The planks of the hull of the *Deutschland* were coated with barnacles, and sea grass sprouted everywhere in a gaudy carpet.

Years since her bottom's been scraped, he thought, and he swam down to the keel, hanging on to it for a moment, then started to work his way along toward the prow.

On deck, they waited in silence. Richter surfaced once for air, waved, and went under again. Sister Lotte gripped the rail tightly, her knuckles white as she stared down into the water. Berger, watching her closely, glanced up and found Sister Angela looking at him. Her face was calm but there was something close to pain in her eyes. He took out his pipe and started to fill it from the worn oilskin pouch. More problems. As if he didn't have enough on his plate. And why did it have to be Richter, the finest seaman in the crew?

At that moment the bosun surfaced and floated at the port rail, coughing, his hair plastered to his skull. Someone tossed him a line and he was hauled over the rail.

He squatted on the deck for a moment, shivering. Berger said, "How was it? You can speak up. Let everyone hear."

"Nothing marked, Kapitän," Richter said. "No sign of any real damage. It's as we thought: she's a very old lady. In places there are gaps between her planks where you can stick two fingers. I'd say she needed recaulking ten years ago."

Berger turned to address the men. "You heard him. Nothing we can't handle. And with double the normal crew there won't be any difficulties in manning the pump."

The faces around him were still filled with uncertainty, but at that moment the mainsail flapped as a tiny wind rippled the water from the southeast.

Berger looked up as the sails started to fill, and laughed. "There you are—a good omen. We're on the move again. Back to work, Mister Sturmm, if you please."

Sturmm barked orders and the crew broke away. Sister Angela said, "If you have a moment, Kapitän, I'd like a word with you."

Berger glanced from her to Lotte who, with the other nuns, was clearing away her belongings from under the awning. "All right, Sister."

In his cabin, she faced him across the desk, perfectly composed, hands folded. "Lotte is the most vulnerable of those among my charges, Kapitän. It is my sworn duty to see that nothing interferes with the path she has chosen."

"What you're trying to say is that she isn't a

proper nun yet," Berger said. "Not like the rest of you?" He shook his head. "It doesn't make any kind of difference to me, I assure you. My orders to the crew are plain where you and your friends are concerned."

"And Mister Richter?"

He leaned back and looked up at her. "All right, so you've caught him looking at the girl a few times. What do you expect me to do about that?"

"She was afraid for him when he went over the side and she allowed it to show."

"He's a good-looking boy."

"Which is exactly what's worrying me."

Berger said, "Helmut Richter was Obersteuermann on a U-boat before he fetched up in Brazil like the rest of us. Chief helmsman, to you. Iron Cross, Second and First Class. The finest seaman I've ever known and a remarkable young man in every way. You've nothing to worry about, believe me."

"I have your assurance in this matter, then?"

"Yes, damn it." He was unable to contain his exasperation, went to the door, opened it, and called to Sturmm, "Send Richter in here."

As he went back to his desk, Sister Angela made a move toward the door. Berger said, "No, don't go. You might as well hear this."

She hesitated, and at that moment there was a knock on the door and Richter entered. He had put on a heavy sweater and reefer, but still looked pale.

"You wanted me, Herr Kapitän?"

Berger produced a bottle and a glass from his desk cupboard. "Scotch whisky. Haig and Haig. The very best. You've earned it."

"It was colder than I thought down there."

Richter drank some of the whisky and Berger sat down. "How long have we known each other, Helmut?"

"A year, Kapitän. Fourteen months to be precise. Why do you ask?"

"The young nun," Berger told him. "Sister Lotte." He hesitated, choosing his words. "She was worried about you?"

Richter glanced at Sister Angela, his face paler than ever now, then placed his glass on the desk carefully. "My affair, Herr Kapitän."

"Don't play the fool with me, Helmut," Berger snapped. "The girl is still a novice. Do you know what that means to these people?"

"That she hasn't made up her mind yet," Richter said evenly.

"And you'd like to make it up for her, is that it?"

Richter glanced at Sister Angela, then turned back to Berger. "You don't understand, either of you, so let me make it plain." He held up his left hand. "Before I would see harm come to her from any man, I would cut this off."

"I believe you, boy. And what happens when we reach Kiel and dry land again will be none of my concern, but for the present, you'll stay away from her. I could make it an order, but I won't. I'll simply ask for your word instead."

For a moment he thought that Richter was going to argue, but the bosun's hesitation was only fractional. He braced himself, heels together. "You have it, sir."

"That's all right, then."

Richter went out quickly and Berger said to Sister Angela, "Was there anything else?"

"No, I don't think so. I appear to anger you at times, Kapitän. I wonder why?"

"God knows, Sister. I wish *I* did. I've experienced a few hard cases in my time; you get them in every crew. They can be handled well enough. With boot and fist if necessary, but you . . ."

She said gently, "Poor Kapitän Berger. If only everything in life were capable of such a simple solution."

She went out. Berger sat there, thinking about it,

realizing suddenly that it was the first time he'd seen her smile.

Like many a distinguished sailor before him, seasickness was an old story to Rear Admiral Otto Friemel, and the foul weather that had allowed U-235 to make such an excellent surface run from Brest had had an unfortunate effect on his stomach. On arrival off the mouth of the Fal, he had accepted the offer of the bunk in Gericke's cabin on which to recover.

He slept surprisingly well and drifted up from darkness into a word of total silence. For a moment he could not remember where he was and lay there frowning in the dim light. Then the curtain was pulled back and Gericke entered with a pot of coffee and two cups on a tray.

Friemel swung his legs to the floor. "Things were a total blank. Does that ever happen to you?"

"Frequently."

"A nasty feeling. Perhaps I'm getting too old. For this sort of thing certainly."

Gericke said, "It's the war, that's all. It's gone on too long."

He took a chart from the shelf above the bunk and opened it out across the small table. Friemel said, "It's damned quiet."

"And so it should be. Most of the crew are lying down. Those who have to move are walking with rags around their boots."

"How are they taking it?"

"The prospect of imminent death, you mean?" Gericke shrugged. "They're good lads, and we've been together a long time. But they've been to Japan and back, remember, so there's a distinct feeling that we could be taking our pitcher to the well once too often." He lit a cigarette and picked up a slide rule. "Of course, it hasn't helped that I've taken the coding machine to pieces and distributed them around the crew in case the worst comes to the worst."

"And you share their pessimism?"

"Not entirely." Gericke traced a pencil across the mouth of the Fal from Blackrock Beacon to St. Anthony's Head. "According to the *Abwehr*'s friendly local agent the boom is positioned here. Getting in is no problem. There have been several ships in and out since we arrived, but so far they've always been singles. I'd rather follow a small convoy if possible. It would give us better cover."

Friemel inserted a cigarette in his holder. "Another point in your favor, as I see it, is that at this stage in the war the Tommies are hardly likely to expect a German U-boat to attempt to penetrate a major naval installation."

"A comforting thought. But I'd rather not rely on it. Once in, we drop the mines through the stern tubes. Here in Carrick Roads, across the mouth of the inner harbor, what's left across the entrance to St. Mawes . . ."

"And out again."

"You forget the boom. We'll need a ship coming in or out for it to open again. We'll have to wait. And if anyone's unfortunate enough to touch off one of those mines in the meantime, the door, I assure you, will remain very tightly shut."

"And what do we do then—scuttle?"

"There is another possibility. Not much of a one, but it's there." Gericke ran his pencil across to Pendennis Point. "Here, between the Point and Blackrock Beacon."

"The minefield?" Friemel said. "A death trap, surely."

"Not the inshore run. South Passage, they call it. According to the *Abwehr* report, they haven't bothered to mine it. Simply stopped the hole by sinking an old merchant ship."

Friemel looked at the map. "In six meters. It would surprise me if a mackerel could find room to squeeze past."

"Six meters now," Gericke said, "but at high tide, which tonight is at twenty-three-hundred hours, nine meters at least in that slot."

Friemel examined the map again. "Sorry, Paul, but I just don't see it. Barely room to submerge, even at high water. And the navigation would be impossible."

"But I wasn't thinking of submerging," Gericke said. "Not completely. I'd stay on the bridge and give steering directions. I've memorized the chart."

"God in heaven!" Friemel whispered.

The green curtain was pulled aside and Lieutenant Karl Engel, the first watch officer, appeared. "Contact, sir. Ships moving in from the east, line astern. Three, possibly four."

Gericke glanced at his watch. It was a few minutes past nine. "Sounds like exactly what we've been waiting for. You know what to do. Ready to move out in five minutes from now. We follow them in blind. I'll take the helm myself."

"No periscope?" Friemel said.

"Not until we're well into Carrick Roads."

Engel disappeared and the curtain dropped back into place. Gericke opened a cupboard under the bunk and took out a bottle and a couple of tin mugs.

"Schnapps?" Friemel asked.

"The best." Gericke poured a generous tot into each mug. "It's been to Japan and back, this bottle. The one I keep only for the most special occasions."

"And to what shall we drink, my dear Paul?" asked Rear Admiral Otto Friemel.

"Why, to the game," Gericke said. "That would seem appropriate. To the bloody stupid and imbecilic game we've all been playing for five years now, which would once more appear, as they say, to be afoot."

Janet Munro came awake reluctantly to the persistent buzzing of the front doorbell. She had a splitting headache; her mouth was dry. She lay staring up at the

ceiling through the darkness, trying to pull herself together, hoping that damn noise would cease. But it
didn't. Suddenly angry, she flung the bedclothes aside
and reached for her bathrobe.

When she opened the front door, a tall, slightly
built young naval officer in reefer coat and peaked cap
was reaching for the bell again. He had stooped shoulders and seemed tired, particularly around the eyes,
and a bad scar ran down the left side of the face.

She glanced at her watch. It was just after ten.
She'd had three hours sleep. Under the circumstances
she found considerable difficulty in keeping her temper.

"Yes, what is it?"

"Dr. Munro? My name's Jago. Harry Jago."

"I'm afraid you've chosen the wrong night. I don't
know who sent you, but I have to sleep. Maybe some
other time."

Jago's smile faded. He suddenly looked very
young. "You don't understand." He produced a letter
from his pocket and held it out to her. "Your uncle
asked me to deliver this."

She frowned. "Uncle Carey? I thought he was
still in the Hebrides."

"That's right. I spoke with him on Fhada the day
before yesterday."

She took the letter from him and nodded slowly as
if still having difficulty in taking it all in. "And what
are you doing up there, Lieutenant?"

"Oh, I run a kind of postal service around the
islands," Jago said cheerfully.

"Hardly the dead center of the only war we've
got."

"While good men and true are fighting and dying
elsewhere? It's a point of view." He was no longer
smiling. "Anyway, you've got your letter, Doctor, and
if you're interested, the admiral was in good health
when I last saw him."

She regretted the sarcasm instantly. She had become increasingly prone to such cruel remarks of late.

"Just a minute," she said. Jago turned. She smiled. "You'd better come in and have a drink while I read this."

The living room was small and untidy. She switched on the electric fire and sat down. "Take off your coat and help yourself to a drink. You'll find some Scotch in the corner cupboard. No ice, I'm afraid. Something you learn to live without over here."

"What about you?"

"A small one would be fine. Nice and straight."

He took off his coat and cap and moved to the cupboard, and while he busied himself getting the drinks she read the letter. It told her nothing she had not already learned from General Eisenhower, and was mainly concerned with her uncle's desperate need to get back into the war again. Talking it out, she thought, just as if I were sitting in front of him, that's all he's doing.

She looked up as Jago came back with a couple of glasses, and the first thing she noticed was the Navy Cross ribbon. She took the drink automatically, without even saying thank you.

"Sorry about the delay," Jago said. "The letter, I mean. I tried here yesterday evening but you were out, and when I called at the hospital today, they said you were too busy to see anyone."

"You could have left it."

"The admiral asked me to see that you got it personally."

"You're a rotten liar, you know that?"

"I'm afraid so."

"Why was it so important?"

"He showed me a photo of you."

She laughed again. "And what is that supposed to do—sweep me off my feet?"

"No, ma'am," Jago said. "You asked me, I told you, that's all." He stood up and reached for his reefer. "I'd better be moving."

"Oh, be your age, for God's sake." She was suddenly angry again. "Let me tell you something, Lieutenant. Tonight, I feel not only totally exhausted but old enough to be your mother."

"You're twenty-seven," he said. "Birthday, November ninth. That's Scorpio, and I can certainly see why."

"Did you get that out of Uncle Carey, too? All right, I surrender. What is it you do in the navy in those circumstances?"

"Strike your flag."

"I've had a rather heavy afternoon," she said. "Fourteen flying bombs hit London today. Maybe you heard the bangs but I saw the results. I fell into bed exactly three hours ago. Then you arrived."

He was on his feet again in a moment. "I'm sorry. I just didn't realize."

"You brought a letter for Ike as well, didn't you?" He hesitated and she carried on. "Don't worry, you aren't giving away state secrets. He spoke to me about it last night. My uncle's trying to get back into the glorious fight."

Jago didn't know what to say. He was fascinated by this strange, abrasive girl, by her wide, almost ugly mouth, and her harsh, distinctive voice.

She said, "When are you going back? The weekend?"

"That's right."

"Me, too. I mean, I'm going to see my uncle, courtesy of the supreme commander, but they haven't given me a date yet."

"Maybe we'll be on the same train."

She took an English cigarette from a packet on the mantelpiece and he lit it for her. "And the rest of your leave? What do you plan to do with that?"

"I don't really know." Jago shrugged. "There doesn't seem to be too much fun in this town these days."

"Oh, I don't know," she said. "You Yanks seem to do all right, with your cigarettes and whisky. Why, you can even get a cab when you need one, which is more than the locals can, believe me."

"Is that how you see yourself? A kind of American Cockney?"

"I came out of Paris in 1940. I've been here ever since."

There was a hiatus and Jago couldn't think of anything to say. Janet said, "Where are you going now? Out on the town?"

"I don't think so. I've got a bed in one of the officers' clubs."

"And just think—you could be walking along the Embankment with me."

He stared at her. "The Embankment?"

"Sure, why not? I could do with the air. Give me three minutes to throw something on." She crossed to the bedroom door and paused to look back at him. "You don't mind, do you?"

In Falmouth, coasting along at periscope depth, U-235 discharged the last of her mines across the entrance to St. Mawes harbor and started to turn away. Gericke was at the periscope, Admiral Friemel and Engel beside him, and the chief helmsman, Willie Carlsen, at the helm. The tension had been incredible, the crew padding about like ghosts, no one speaking above a whisper.

There was sweat on Engel's face. He said eagerly, "And now we go home?"

"Bergen is home?" Gericke said as he started his sweep, checking the situation in the harbor.

But at that moment a tug, emerging from Carrick Roads, struck one of the mines. There was an instant searing explosion, a tongue of flame that illuminated the entire harbor area. The concussion drummed on the hull of the submarine.

"Oh, my God," Engel moaned.

Friemel, face ashen, plucked at Gericke's shoulder. "A mine?"

"I'm afraid so. Strike one." And then he seemed to go rigid, his shoulders hunched. He turned to look at them. "There are two river-class frigates moored almost side by side just north of the inner harbor."

"Not even you could be crazy enough for such a thing," Engel said desperately. "We wouldn't stand a chance."

"And what chance do we stand now?" Gericke demanded. "Frigates, Karl. Two of them."

He seemed to crackle with electricity, his face very white, his mad, dark eyes blazing. It was as if he had been sleeping and was now awake.

He turned on Friemel. "Konteradmiral?"

Friemel found himself shaking, not with fear, but with a kind of fierce joy. "Why not, by God? A hell of a way to go, Paul."

And Engel, touched now by the same madness, all fear leaving him, saluted, heels together. "At your orders, Herr Kapitän."

"Good man," Gericke clapped him on the shoulder. "Take her up. We'll have to do this the hard way. Prepare tubes one to four for surface firing." He turned to Carlsen. "You take the helm, Willie, and make it good."

There was a sudden bustle of activity, the klaxon sounding battle stations. As Gericke moved toward the ladder he added almost casually, over his shoulder, "Perhaps you'd care to join me on the bridge, Herr Konteradmiral?"

At the top of the ladder he waited. There was a hiss of compressed air, a rushing of water, and then Engel called, "The hatch is above water."

Gericke unclipped it and scrambled out onto the bridge of the conning tower. Heavy rain smacked solidly into his face and the waters of the harbor heaved in turmoil. The tug was almost under now but the oil around it was on fire, and when he focused his night glasses, men jumped into view, hurling themselves into the icy water.

In the forward torpedo compartment the crew worked frantically to make ready. Engel was already aligning the attack periscope as Gericke swung his glasses to focus on the two frigates.

Beside him, Friemel said, "A lot of activity on deck. I'd say you've got three minutes before they chop those anchors and get out of there."

Alarm klaxons echoed stridently across the water. There was considerable movement now on the harbor wall. Suddenly, there was a hollow staccato booming and brilliant balls of fire seemed to cascade toward them in a great curve, falling into the water to port.

"That's it," Friemel said grimly. "They know we're here."

U-235 surged forward. Gericke said calmly, "Tubes one to four prepare for surface firing."

Engel called into the voice pipe. There was the briefest of pauses before he looked up. "One to four ready, sir."

"Six meters," Gericke said. "Line of sight. One and two on the starboard frigate, three and four take care of the gentleman to port. Distance one thousand meters, speed thirty-five. Director angle blue four."

Engel relayed the orders through the voice pipe to Leading Seaman Pich, who manned the TDC, the complicated electrical device linking gyro compass, attack periscope, and torpedo circuits, which from now on would, in effect, be responsible for the success or failure of the operation.

He made the final connection. Engel guided the aiming cross of the attack periscope onto the starboard frigate which, relieved of its anchor, was starting to swerve to port.

"Blue four, ready to fire, sir!"

"Fire," Gericke called.

"Tube one fire. Tube two fire!"

The U-boat staggered as the torpedoes broke free and raced toward the target at thirty-five knots. The port frigate was moving now, surging forward as her captain gave her everything she had, the bow wave rising.

"She'll make it, Paul. She'll make it," Friemel cried, his binoculars glued to his eyes.

"Oh, no, she won't," Gericke said calmly. "This is my night. Hard starboard," he called. "It's all yours, Karl. Fire at will."

Machine-gun bullets rattled against the conning tower, and several shells landed close enough on the port side to cause the U-boat to roll violently. But it was Karl Engel's night, too—calm, detached, cooler than he had ever been, as the captain of the frigate made his one mistake, turning to starboard to bring all guns to bear, momentarily exposing his entire port side, a perfect target.

As the torpedoes were released, the U-boat corkscrewed in the heavy seas. "Hard port," Gericke called. "And tell Deetz to give me everything he's got."

There was a muffled explosion, followed by another, as the first two torpedoes struck home. A cheer drifted up from the control room. Across the water, orange fire erupted from the first frigate and black smoke billowed into the night. The second was turning frantically now, as if her captain already sensed that the ax was about to fall, her guns still firing.

A moment later, number three torpedo hit, closely followed by the fourth. The frigate staggered drunkenly, her prow seemed to lift high into the air, then plunged. There was a further great explosion and flames towered into the night.

"That's it," Gericke said. "The magazine. It has to be." He called to Engel. "I said speed, damn you! Speed! Let's get out of here."

All hell had broken loose now, guns firing across the harbor from the shore installations. Friemel, ducking between the steel canopy as a bullet ricocheted close to his head, said, "Gun crew, Paul?"

"No," Gericke said. "We'd only give them a better target. We'll be out of it soon, believe me. They won't be expecting us to try the South Passage run. It isn't supposed to exist, remember."

The wind rolled thick, oily smoke in a black pall across the harbor, blanketing the entire scene, and U-235, hidden from view, made toward Pendennis Point at full speed.

The tide was running fast under the Point as they turned into the channel. In the control room, Engel had the helm, Friemel at his shoulder. Everyone seemed to have crowded in—Deetz, the chief engineering officer, young Heini Roth, the second watch officer.

The diesels had stopped and the propellers were being driven by the electric motors. It seemed very still, and when Gericke's voice crackled over the tannoy, Roth gave a startled gasp.

"We haven't got too much time to spare. The tide's beginning to ebb and there's a five- or six-knot current running, so let's get it right first time."

His voice, clearly audible to every man on board, was properly calm. Engel, speaking into the microphone box above his head, barely managed to keep his voice steady as he replied, "Aye, aye, sir. Ready when you are."

Gericke, on the bridge, was colder than he'd ever been in his life before. Reaction, he told himself, to all that action and passion. He managed a smile. He wore a life jacket, headphones, and a throat microphone, and was up to his chest in water.

It was not totally dark for an eerie phosphorescence and considerable broken water gave him a far better view of the general situation than he had expected. The hubbub on the far side of the harbor seemed muffled and far away, without reality.

"Course one-eight-two," he said.

Engel's voice crackled in his ears. "Seven meters under the keel . . . six meters under the keel."

They surged on, caught by the current, white water all around, and somewhere high above in the night, the turret on Pendennis Point lifted into the darkness. Gericke could hear traffic, and wondered briefly whether there might be searchlights mounted.

There was sudden panic in Engel's voice. "Two meters, sir. Only two meters under the keel . . . one meter."

Gericke said calmly, "Steady as she goes, Karl. Nice and easy. Half ahead."

"We would appear to have run out of water, my dear Paul," Friemel's voice sounded equally calm.

U-235 seemed to shudder, there was a crunch, a long-drawn-out grating that set on edge the teeth of every man on board.

"Oh, God, that's it," Heini Roth said aloud in the control room.

And yet they were still moving, a long, continuous grating that suddenly ceased as Gericke's voice called, "Full ahead."

There was a ragged cheer through the entire boat. "He's done it!" Deetz said excitedly. "As usual," he added.

Gericke's voice sounded again. "If you think we're out of the woods yet, forget it. We haven't passed the blockship. A hundred meters to go. I can see her plain. Half engines and make ready to give me everything you've got when I give the word."

On the bridge he faced the last obstacle. U-235 drifted forward in the grip of the current that coursed through South Passage as the tide started to ebb. The blockship was an old coaster, her single stack clear against the night sky, deck awash.

"Hard starboard," Gericke said.

The slot between the rocks and the blockship

seemed inconceivably narrow, but it was too late to turn back now. Again there was a grating under the keel.

Engel's voice was frantic. "There should be six meters, sir. Six meters."

The grating stopped as the U-boat slid on. "Probably a chain," Gericke said. "Keep going, Karl. Not long now."

Somewhere behind him, beyond the smoke on the other side of the harbor, there was a muffled explosion. He paid no heed, and gave all his concentration to the task in hand, gripping the rail with numbed fingers.

And then the boat seemed to be caught in a giant hand and pushed forward by a sudden fierce current. The blockship was alongside—the stack looming above him, rusting plates, bridge windows smashed, a ghost ship.

He leaned over the rail. This was the moment of maximum danger, the time for jagged metal or protruding girders to open them up like a sardine can.

There was a grating on the starboard side, the cliff seemed very close, too close, and then, as they swung to port in the current, the blockship seemed to drift away into the night, was suddenly abeam.

Gericke said hoarsely, "We're into clear water. Heavy seas. Wind force six by my estimation. Full ahead; diesels, too, if you please."

The scene in the control room was incredible. Deetz burst into tears and Friemel, in an excess of emotion, grabbed Heini Roth and hugged him.

"Remarkable," the admiral said. "There I was, lying in my coffin ready to go. Now I've just been told it was all a mistake."

On the bridge, Gericke hung on tight as U-235 rode into the full force of the wind sweeping in from the Channel. It was very dark now, with no landmarks to guide him, as one great wave after another slapped over him. Only the roaring of the sea was in his ears. Better to get out of it now. "All right, Karl," he said. "Bring her up and let me get dry, then we'll submerge till we're in midchannel."

And suddenly, the roaring was louder and it was no longer the sea. He became conscious of an enormous, white bow wave to starboard. There was a tremendous crash, the tearing of metal, as a dark, greyhound shape plowed right across the U-boat's forecastle and plunged on into the night.

The U-boat rolled, the conning tower swung to port, and Gericke was tossed over the side.

"My night," he thought, for some inane reason clutching at his cap. "Wasn't that what I said?" And then he hit the water and the first wave rolled over him.

The dim shape Gericke had glimpsed momentarily as she plowed across the U-boat's forecastle was a Vospar MTB of the Royal Navy's Fifteenth Flotilla, racing home from patrol at thirty-five knots, on receipt of the news from Falmouth over the radio.

Now she drifted helplessly, making water, all engines stopped. On the bridge, her commander, an RNVR lieutenant named Drummond, was taking the damage report from the boat's chief petty officer.

"How long have we got, Chief?"

"In this sea, an hour at the most, sir. If they want to save her they'd better get a tug out here fast."

"You're certain it was a submarine?"

"Definite, sir. Leading Seaman Cooper saw it, too." He hesitated. "But whether one of ours or theirs, I couldn't be sure."

"My God," Drummond said softly.

There was an excited cry aft of the bridge. "Someone in the water, sir, off the port rail."

"Searchlight," Drummond said. "Quickly now!"

The beam sliced across the broken water and picked out Gericke in his yellow life jacket, his cap pulled down over his ears. He waved as he was swept in under the rail.

"Quickly!" Drummond called. "He must be frozen half to death in there."

Bell, the petty officer, ran down from the bridge to supervise. There was a flurry of activity at the rail and Gericke was hauled aboard. Drummond leaned over the bridge rail, watching anxiously, training the searchlight on them, and then Bell looked up.

"Good God, sir, we've got ourselves a Jerry."

In London it was raining hard, and fog crouched at the ends of the streets. Janet Munro's trench coat was soaked through as was the scarf bound around her hair.

They had walked for several miles in the pouring rain—Birdcage Walk, the Palace, St. James's Park, and Downing Street, although Jago hadn't been able to see very much. Not that he cared.

"Sure you haven't had enough?" he asked, as they moved down toward Westminster Bridge.

"Not yet. I promised you something special, remember?"

"Did you?" Jago looked puzzled.

They came to the bridge and she turned onto the Embankment. "Well, this is it," she said. "The most romantic place in town. Every American in London should walk along the Embankment at least once, preferably after midnight."

"It's almost that now," Jago said.

"Good, we'll have another cigarette and wait for the witching hour."

They leaned on the parapet and listened to the lapping of the water. "Have you enjoyed it, your guided tour?" she asked.

"Oh, yes, ma'am, you could say that," Jago told her. "I was a stranger in your city, but not anymore."

"I like that," she said. "You're a poet, too."

"Not me," Jago said. "Thank the Gershwins." He

leaned over the parapet beside her. "You really like this old town, don't you?"

"We have a special relationship. I've seen her through good times and bad, often burning like hell, and we're still here, both of us."

"But you don't like people much?"

Her chin tilted. He could sense anger in her, barely contained. "Should I, darling? I wish you could give me a good reason."

"What is it, Doctor? Don't you think you're up to the snuff? Do you have to let too many people die?"

"Damn you to hell, Jago." Her hand went up as if she would strike him. Big Ben chimed the first stroke of midnight.

Jago put up his arms defensively. "The witching hour—remember. And this is the Embankment, the most romantic place in London."

She reached out to touch his face. "Tell me, Jago, did they cut you up badly back there? Did they take a few years off your life?"

"Too many," he said.

The last stroke of midnight boomed out. The rain increased into a drenching downpour and she seemed to be standing very close. Tentatively he put his hands on her shoulders. She ran a hand up behind his head and kissed him passionately on the mouth.

"Take me home, Jago," she whispered.

Barkentine Deutschland, *19 September 1944.*
Lat. 43°4′N, long. 20°55′W. Last night in
the middle watch, fore upper topsail split
during a bad blow. Weather continues to
deteriorate. Full gale in the morning watch
with big sea running.

Six

I spite of the fact that it was only two bells of the
afternoon watch, it was so dark in the saloon that
Sister Angela had to light the lamp. She sat at the table which, like the chairs, was bolted to the floor. Her
Bible was open in front of her. Lotte sat opposite, busy
with needle and thread as she mended a denim shirt.

Outside, the wind howled and the *Deutschland*
rolled heavily to port taking her own time to come
back again, an event that would once have caused
them both considerable alarm, but not now. Water
trickled down the companionway steps and slopped
across the floor. It was cold and damp—everything
was damp—even the blanket that she had draped
around her shoulders.

Lotte, concentrating on her task in the poor light,
smiled briefly, as if at some private thought. Sister

Angela had seen that smile often of late, knew only too well what it meant. It was as if the girl was slipping away from her, from everything that had once seemed so important—and for what?

She was aware of anger rising inside as old wounds opened, but she resolutely held it in check. It was an unworthy emotion and solved nothing.

She said to Lotte, "That shirt—isn't it Mister Richter's?"

Lotte looked up. "Why, yes, Sister."

Before the conversation could be taken any further, there was a clatter on the companionway and the bosun appeared, a billycan in one hand. His head was bare, the blond hair and beard beaded with rain, and his yellow oilskin ran with water.

He smiled as he placed the can on the table. "Hot tea, ladies. All the galley can manage at the moment."

"Is it bad up there, Mister Richter?" Sister Angela asked.

"Just another Atlantic gale, Sister," he replied. "Nothing special to an old hand like you."

She smiled, in spite of herself, for it was hard not to.

Lotte said, "Your shirt, Mister Richter, will be ready for you this evening."

"You'll spoil me, Fräulein." The *Deutschland* lurched so that he had to brace himself against the table. "I'd better get back up there. That wasn't too good."

He mounted the companionway and Lotte paused in her sewing. "He never stops. One would think at times that he was the only man in the crew."

"The finest sailor, certainly," Sister Angela said. She paused, then carried on, "A fine young man altogether. Has he told you much about himself?" Lotte glanced up, her face coloring. "I only ask because Sister Kathë mentioned that she had noticed you and Mister

Richter enjoying a lengthy conversation on deck yesterday evening."

Before the girl could reply, the ship staggered under another mighty blow, swinging off course. There was a cry of alarm on deck, the doors at the head of the companionway burst open, and water cascaded in.

Berger had the wheel with two seamen to help him as the *Deutschland* plowed on through a wilderness of white foam. In spite of their combined efforts, the ship was swinging a couple of points on each side of her course.

Sturmm and Leading Seaman Knorr were attempting to reef the fore staysail and were having a hard time of it, for the sea constantly poured over the weather bulwark, covering the hatches, swirling waist deep, so that again and yet again they had to stop work and simply hang on to prevent themselves from being swept away.

Richter emerged from the companionway, closed the doors behind him, and turned to move toward the quarterdeck ladder. An enormous wave raced in astern, towering into the rain as if intent on engulfing them. He cried a warning to Berger, pointing, but the wave broke full upon the poop, knocking the captain's two companions from their feet.

Richter grabbed for the weather-jigger rigging and held on. Water boiled around him as the wave passed, taking all before it, so that for a moment he believed she must certainly founder under all that weight.

Slowly, the *Deutschland* started to rise and, as the water receded, he saw that there was now only Sturmm up there in the weather rigging by the fore staysail.

Knorr floundered in the lee scuppers, trying to get to his feet. Richter started toward him as the *Deutschland* continued to climb, and then another great sea rolled in and knocked him off his feet again. He grabbed for the edge of the main hatch cover and held on tight, but the same sea lifted Knorr over the rail. As Richter struggled to his feet, he caught a single flash of yellow out there that as quickly was gone.

Sturmm started to work his way along the deck using the weather lines. Berger and his two companions were winning in their battle to control the wheel. Richter saw that the doors at the head of the companionway swung open. He stepped inside, closed them behind him, and went down.

There was a foot of water in the saloon, and the other nuns had emerged from their cabins in some alarm to join Sister Angela and Lotte.

"It's all right, ladies," Richter assured them. "Everything is under control, but I would suggest you return to your cabins and strap yourselves into those bunks until the gale blows itself out."

There was a certain hesitation, but Sister Angela said briskly, "Mister Richter is right. We must all do as he says at once."

The other nuns retreated to their cabins, ankle-deep in water, skirts raised, but Lotte stayed, reaching up to touch the smear of blood on Richter's right cheek.

"You are hurt, Mister Richter."

"Nothing," he said. "A scratch only. Please do as I say." He turned to Sister Angela. "We lost a man overboard just now. Knorr. You can tell the others in your own good time. I didn't want to alarm them unnecessarily."

She crossed herself. "Was there nothing to be done?"

"In these seas? He was swallowed whole."

The ship staggered again and he turned, swearing, brushed past Lotte, and went up the companionway fast. She reached out as if she would hold him back.

"Helmut," she whispered.

She stood there, her skirts dragging in the water that slopped around her feet, something close to despair on her face. "He'll kill himself, I know it."

Sister Angela said gently, "You like him, don't you? Like him a great deal, I mean?"

"Yes, Sister," Lotte replied in a low voice.

Sister Angela sat down at the table, her hands gripping the edge of the table. "My child, you must remember that we are members of an order whose vows urge us to love all our fellow creatures equally. The danger for us, in any kind of personal relationship, is that it detracts from what one is able to give to others. Our vow is to be servant to humanity, Lotte."

"I have taken no such vow, Sister."

Sister Angela braced herself against the table as the floor tilted again. She was slightly breathless now and not from any physical exertion.

"Do you know what you are saying?"

"Yes," Lotte replied, a new firmness in her voice. "That I am no longer certain of my vocation."

Sister Angela reached out, grasping the girl's hands tightly. "Think well, Lotte," she said urgently. "To give up God's love for . . ."

"A man?" Lotte asked. "Is it not possible then to have both?"

Sister Angela tried to stay calm, and yet that ancient bitterness floated up again like bile. "Things are not always what they seem. Human beings are frail. Once, when I was even younger than you, I loved a man, gave him my heart, and, God help me, gave him my body also—and in return—" She choked on the words. "And in return . . ."

Lotte said gently, "And because one man acted so, all men are tainted? Is this what you would have me believe, Sister?"

"No," Sister Angela whispered. "Of course not." She squeezed Lotte's hand. "We've talked enough for the moment. Go and lie down as Mister Richter ordered. He knows what is best for us."

Lotte hesitated, but did as she was told. The door to her cabin clicked shut behind her. Sister Angela sat there at the table, her eyes vacant, staring into space.

"Why, Karl?" she whispered. "Why?"

And then, as hot tears stung her eyes, the iron discipline of the years came to her aid as always. She took a deep breath to steady herself, folded her hands, and started to pray for the repose of Leading Seaman Peter Knorr's soul, for all sinners everywhere whose actions only cut them off from the infinite blessing of God's love.

Toward evening the gale abated, but it was still blowing very hard and, high above the deck, Helmut Richter, Sturmm, and Leading Seaman Kluth balanced on the yardarm, struggling to refit the freshly mended fore upper topsail. The rain, sweeping in from the southeast, was like bullets and bitterly cold as they punched the wet canvas, cursing as blood spurted from torn fingers.

Berger stood gazing up at the men aloft, Otto Prager at his side in black oilskin and sou'wester.

"It frightens me just to watch," the consul said. "I'd never get used to it, not if we sailed around the world and took a year over it."

"It certainly separates the men from the boys," Berger told him as Sturmm and the others started to come down.

The young lieutenant mounted to the quarterdeck. "All square up there now, Kapitän." His face was pale and drawn, the memory of Knorr still with him.

Berger said, "Don't blame yourself, boy. There was nothing to be done."

"I almost had him," Sturmm said. "Then he slipped from my grasp."

Berger put a hand on his shoulder, "Get yourself some coffee."

Sturmm went down the ladder. Berger looked over the rail and saw Richter stanching blood with a handkerchief. "Bad?" he called.

"Fingertip, that's all."

"See Sister Angela. She'll fix you up."

When the bosun went down the companionway, the saloon was deserted except for Lotte, who sat at the table, a book open before her. She glanced up at the sound of his foot on the stair and she smiled.

"Mister Richter."

"Fräulein." For some reason lately he found it impossible to call her Sister. "You should be in your bunk."

She reached for his damaged hand and started to unwrap the handkerchief. "What have you done?"

"It's nothing," he said. "A split finger, that's all. Punching canvas. It happens all the time."

The end of the middle finger was open to the bone. "You must let me do something."

"I'll see to it." Sister Angela spoke from behind. "Please return to your devotions and the task I set you. In your cabin," she added.

Lotte colored, picked up her book, and went out quickly. It was very quiet in the saloon, the voice of the wind outside subdued, far away. Richter and Sister Angela confronted each other.

"I'll get my medical case."

He sat at the table and lit a cigarette. "You don't mind?" he asked when she returned.

"Your smoking? Oh, no, Mister Richter. My father used to say a man should have some vices. Of the right kind, that is."

"A short leash, you mean?"

"Do I?" She examined the finger. "This will need two stitches. You'd better look the other way."

He drew on his cigarette, watching the door to Lotte's cabin, grunting a little as the needle entered the flesh.

"Where are you from, Mister Richter?"

"Vienna."

She was surprised. "A Viennese sailor? I didn't know there were such things. What did you do, run away to sea?"

"Strangely enough, that's exactly what I did,"

Richter told her. "My father, if you are interested, was a surgeon, and had a similar career mapped out for me."

"And you had other ideas. Are you married?"

"No," he said evenly.

The needle was inserted again. "You should be. It's good for the soul, Mister Richter. There, I've finished."

"How strange," he said. "I'd always understood it was good for the flesh."

She kept her temper and contented herself with saying calmly, "Leave her alone. She has better things to do with her life."

"Why, because that was the way it worked out for you?"

She stood abruptly, picked up the medical case, and went into her cabin. Richter sat there for a moment longer. As he got up, Lotte's door clicked open. "Are you all right now, Mister Richter?" she whispered.

"Fine," he said. "In fact, I've never felt better, Fräulein."

"That's all right, then."

She smiled again and withdrew. Richter went up the companionway steps two at a time.

For Paul Gericke things progressed with extraordinary rapidity. A preliminary interrogation at Falmouth during which his own clothes had been dried, then returned to him. He had then been moved by road to Portsmouth, where he had found himself in the hands of naval intelligence.

They had treated him with respect. He was, after all, something of a catch for them—the most important U-boat commander to be captured since Kretschmer.

For five straight hours they had interrogated him in shifts, but with a total lack of success. Gericke had resolutely stuck to the personal information required under the Geneva Convention, and nothing more.

Just after noon he was informed that he was to

be moved to London. He was transferred in a naval police van, handcuffed and escorted by a petty officer, two ratings, and a sublieutenant, all armed.

And so it was that at four-thirty in the afternoon he was in the London District POW Cage, a requisitioned house in Kensington Palace Gardens. This time the treatment wasn't so good, particularly from the chief petty officer who took charge of him on arrival, a massively built man of forty-six named Carver, with the broken nose of a boxer.

"If I had my way, son," he informed Gericke, "there's nothing I'd fancy more than getting you inside a ring for six straight rounds, and I'd make sure you'd last right up to the final bell."

"Oh, I don't know, Chief," Gericke told him calmly. "I should have thought you would have been at your best up a dark alley with a bottle in your hand."

For a moment he thought Carver was going to strike him, but there were two ratings present in reception. The chief petty officer, shaking with rage, contented himself with stripping Gericke of his decorations.

The room to which he was finally taken was pleasant enough. More like a study than an office, books lining the wall, a fire in the grate, and, although the tall window was heavily barred, there was a view of the garden outside. He was placed in a chair on one side of a wide desk, still handcuffed, and waited impassively for whatever was to come, an armed rating on either side of him.

After a while, the door opened. The man who walked around to the other side of the desk was a full captain in the Royal Navy. He had a DSO and ribbons for the First World War—Gericke took that in automatically, along with the iron-gray hair and pale aesthetic face. He had a bad limp and leaned heavily on an ebony walking stick.

He placed a couple of manila folders on the desk and said rather formally, "Commander Gericke—my name is Vaughan."

"I wish I could say I was happy to meet you."

Vaughan nodded to one of the ratings. "You can take the handcuffs off now, then wait outside."

He waited for them to comply with his order and only sat down as the door clicked shut behind them. Gericke eased his cramped wrists. "Thank you. They were beginning to be rather uncomfortable."

"Cigarette?" Vaughan pushed a box across the table. "Your English is really quite excellent, but then you did live over here for a couple of years, didn't you?" He opened one of the folders and put on a pair of half-moon reading glasses. "Nineteen twenty-six to twenty-eight. Hull. You went to grammar school there."

"You seem to know."

"Yes, I do, Commander," Vaughan told him, in the same calm, neutral voice. "Everything about you. An excellent record by the way. I congratulate you."

Gericke restrained an impulse to laugh. "Of course."

"Not only the Knight's Cross, but the Oak Leaves to go with it. A rare distinction."

"It *was*."

"Why do you say that?"

Gericke opened his leather jerkin to indicate the tunic underneath, bare of decorations. "The spoils of war."

For the first time, Vaughan showed emotion. A tiny muscle twitched in his right cheek. "Your decorations were taken from you?"

"Yes."

"In this establishment? You will be good enough to tell me by whom."

"The chief petty officer in charge of reception," Gericke said, and added maliciously, "I had assumed it to be the normal run of things."

"Not while I am in charge here, I can assure you, Commander." Vaughan's face was white and pinched around the mouth as he picked up the telephone on the desk. "Send Chief Petty Officer Carver up to twenty-two at once."

He got to his feet and stumped across to the window, leaning on his cane. There was a knock at the door a moment later and Carver entered.

"You wanted me, sir?"

Vaughan spoke without turning around. "Carver, I understand you have in your possession certain decorations belonging to this officer."

"Sir?" Carver started to bluster.

Vaughan swung around to face him. "Damn your eyes, man, get them out on the table. Now!"

Carver hurriedly produced Gericke's Knight's Cross, Iron Cross First Class, and wound badge and laid them on the desk. "Is that the lot?" Vaughan asked Gericke.

Gericke nodded.

Vaughan said to Carver harshly, "I'll deal with you later. Get out."

As the door closed behind Carver, Gericke picked up the medals and put them in his pocket.

Vaughan sat down, took a cigarette from the box on the desk, and examined the file again. "As I was saying, quite a record. Let's see now. You joined the Tenth Flotilla at Brest after your return from the Far East, didn't you?"

"I've told you who I am; that's all that's required of me. I'm sorry, Captain Vaughan, I have nothing else to say."

"All right," Vaughan said. "You compel me to become unpleasant. You really leave me no other choice."

"Bring on the rubber hoses by all means. But it won't change anything."

Vaughan was annoyed. "We're not the Gestapo. We don't operate that way."

"Then I shall be even more fascinated to hear your proposal," Gericke assured him.

Vaughan opened the second folder. "On the fifth of April, 1942, you sank, in American waters near Rhode Island, an oil tanker named the *San Cristobál*."

"Perfectly correct."

"You are aware, of course, that this ship was a Spanish vessel registered in Bilbao and that to torpedo and sink her was contrary to the articles of war?"

"You don't say."

"But I do, and what is more to the point, our American friends intend to make you answer for it. As a courtesy, American Naval Intelligence was informed of your capture this morning. Within two hours they'd made a formal application to take you into custody. From what I hear, they intend to ship you to the United States to stand trial."

Gericke laughed. "What nonsense. The *San Cristobál* was under charter to carry oil for the American War Department."

"There's no mention of that fact here."

"Strange—the rest of your information seems to have been so uniformly accurate."

Vaughan shrugged. "The Americans have asked for you, Gericke; that is fact, and the consequences if they do try you for this business could be most unpleasant."

"But you could save me from all that?"

"If you were willing to cooperate."

Gericke sighed. "Sorry, but you really are wasting your time."

Vaughan nodded calmly, put the manila folder under his arm, got up, and limped out without another word.

Left alone, Gericke, on impulse, pinned the Iron Cross and wound badge to his tunic and hung the Knight's Cross around his neck. Then he stood at the window and looked out through the bars. The garden was enclosed by a high wall and was badly overgrown. Rain drifted down through the branches of a large beech tree into a wilderness of rhododendrons. It was a melancholy sight.

The door opened behind him and Carver entered, followed by a rating carrying a covered tray. "Put it down there, lad," Carver ordered and added to Gericke, "Something to eat, Commander?"

The rating withdrew and Gericke walked to the desk. Carver leaned across and grabbed him by the front of the tunic. The eyes were cold.

"I'm going to have you, you German bastard, you see if I don't," he whispered. He hurled Gericke back into Vaughan's chair and hurriedly left the room.

Just after seven on the same evening, Janet Munro and Harry Jago arrived by taxi at the house in Kensington Palace Gardens. They went up the steps to the front door, which was guarded by two sentries, and into the entrance hall, where an Army Intelligence Corps sergeant sat at a trestle table.

Jago produced his pass. "Lieutenant Jago. I'm supposed to report to a Captain Vaughan."

"Oh, yes, sir, he's expecting you. I'll get someone to take you up."

The sergeant pressed a buzzer and Jago said, "Okay if the lady waits for me here?"

"I don't see why not, sir."

Jago turned to Janet. "Sorry about this. Why the hell I'm supposed to report to a Royal Naval captain in the first place, God only knows. Let's hope it doesn't take long and we can get straight to the theater."

She patted his cheek. "How could this mighty war machine of ours roll on without you?"

Before Jago could think of a suitable reply, a young ATS corporal appeared to escort him to Vaughan. Janet sat on a chair by the window, crossing one leg over the other in a manner that filled the intelligence sergeant at his desk with admiration.

"Not too bad today then, miss," he ventured.

"Three in Hackney, two down Poplar way, and one in Golders Green."

"And that's good?" she said.

The flying bombs, the V-1 variety, had been bad enough, the grating roar of their engines growing steadily louder as they approached, but at least you knew they were coming. With the V-2 rockets, on the other hand, there was no warning: a supersonic bang, the roar of an explosion, and total devastation.

A door on the far side of the hall opened and Gericke came through, flanked by two armed ratings. His hands were handcuffed in front of him, but he made a striking figure in the white naval cap with the Iron Cross on his tunic, the Knight's Cross around his neck.

He didn't appear to notice Janet, his head half turned, laughing at something one of the guards had said, and they went up the stairs and disappeared from view.

The desk sergeant said, "Jerry prisoner, miss. Naval officer. We get a lot of them through here."

"Oh, I see."

She stood up, crossed the hall, and stood in the porch at the top of the steps. There was a staccato roaring high above in the darkness, and she glanced up to see a V-1 passing across the night sky, a short jet of flame sprouting from its tail.

"I wonder where that bastard will come down," the sentry said beside her.

Death and destruction. She'd just seen one of the men responsible. *The enemy.* It was the closest she'd been to a German since before the war. For a moment, she saw Gericke again, laughing as he went up the stairs between the guards, and was conscious of a kind of anger.

Jago emerged behind her and took her arm. "Okay, let's get out of here."

They went down the steps and turned along the pavement. "And what was all that about?"

"Well, I don't see why I shouldn't tell you. The British picked up a German U-boat commander last night, one of the really top boys. A guy named Paul Gericke. They've had him in here for interrogation. It seems they're giving him to us. He's being sent up to Glasgow on the night express tomorrow evening. He'll be handed over to our people and shipped out on a convoy leaving for the States three or four days from now."

"And where do you come into it?"

"Well, he'll have a British escort, but some bright boy at naval headquarters remembered I was traveling on that train and decided it would be a good idea if I kept an eye out for our interests."

"Did you meet him?"

"Just now."

"Was he medium height—pale face, dark eyes, Iron Cross on his tunic?"

"That's our boy."

"He was laughing as he went up the stairs," she said. At that moment they were passing behind a row of half-demolished houses. "He was laughing. He and his kind caused all this."

"They tell me Berlin doesn't look too hot these days."

She slipped an arm through his. "You're not for real, Harry Jago. By the way, I didn't get a chance to tell you, but Colonel Brisingham turned up at the hospital this afternoon with my travel warrant for tomorrow night's train."

Jago was over the moon with delight. "That means we can be together all the way to Mallaig."

"I'm not so sure," she said. "Actually they've provided me with a sleeping compartment. A single berth all to myself."

"They've what?" Jago said in astonishment. "Have you any idea what it takes to get one of those things these days?"

"Yes," she said. "Eisenhower."

Jago laughed. The rain increased, and they ran across to the corner of the main road. She sheltered under a tree while he tried to whistle up a cab.

And as she waited, for some reason, she kept seeing Gericke's face, laughing as he went upstairs.

The clock in the chart house chimed seven bells of the first watch. Seated at his desk in the cabin, a cigar between his teeth, Eric Berger paused to listen and then returned to his journal, the scratching of his pen sounding unnaturally loud in the silence.

> . . . *the loneliest sound in the world, a ship's bell at sea by night, or is it that it simply accentuates for me the loneliness of command? I think to be a ship's master no simple task, especially in the conditions under which I find myself at the moment. . . .*

There was a knock on the door and Sturmm entered in a flurry of rain. He wore black oilskins and a sou'wester, and water glistened on him in the light of the oil lamp.

"Well, Mister Sturmm?" Berger said.

Sturmm saluted. "I've just made the rounds, sir. Everything nice and tight. Kluth and Weber have the wheel at present. Heading northwest by west at ten knots by estimation."

"Full sail?"

"Every stitch she can carry."

"And what about the weather?"

"Wind force five with heavy rain, but it's surprisingly warm."

"Excellent." Berger went to the cupboard and found the rum bottle and two glasses. "How long were you operating the radio yesterday?"

Sturmm accepted the glass gratefully. "An hour and a half exactly."

"What about the batteries?"

"Not too good, sir, but then they never were. It's not much of a set. The best Herr Prager could manage at short notice I know. Still!" He hesitated. "Do you want me to stop listening in, sir?"

"No, I don't think so. Those British and American weather reports are too useful, and the war news. But it's when we're close to home and wanting to transmit that we're going to need the power. I want to be sure we have enough in reserve."

"Shall I leave it for tonight?"

"Half an hour," Berger said. "When you go off watch. I think that should suffice."

"Very well, sir." Sturmm drained the last of his rum with reluctance. "If you'll excuse me, I'd better get back on the quarterdeck."

He turned and put his hand to the door—and from somewhere outside came the agonized cry of a woman.

It was hot below and very close. To Lotte, this voyage seemed interminable. From nowhere to nowhere. There was a gentle and continuous snoring from beneath her. Sister Angela had moved Sister Else into the cabin without any explanation.

Lotte lay on the top bunk, the roof no more than two feet above her face, hot and uncomfortable in spite of the fact that she was wearing only a linen night-dress. She was thinking of Helmut Richter, concentrating with an intensity that was almost frightening, trying to conjure him up from the darkness—the slow smile, the wild blond hair and beard.

Lotte was a quiet, self-contained girl. Most of her life had been totally enclosed—first by the demands of a rigidly orthodox Catholic family, and then by the self-discipline of nursing training. And afterward, the Order of the Sisters of Mercy. Nothing more demanding than God.

She had learned to live within herself. But Richter—Richter was something different, a totally new experience. When she thought of him, she smiled spontaneously.

Her body was damp with sweat. It was impossible for her to stay in that cabin another minute. She needed air—clean salt air. She dropped to the floor softly, reached for her cloak, and slipped outside.

Lightning flickered on the far horizon, moving nearer. There was an eerie phosphorescence to everything, so that the ship was a place of darkness and light, warm rain drifting across the deck in a silvery haze.

Kluth leaned on the wheel, his foot against the binnacle, thoroughly enjoying himself as the *Deutschland* stormed on through the night, every sail full. Weber leaned on the rail beside him, smoking a pipe. Neither saw Lotte emerge from the companionway.

But Ernst Walz, making himself coffee in the galley, saw her. The girl kept to the shadows by the port rail and paused at the mizzen shrouds, head lifted to feel the rain.

She moved away from the rail, and as she passed the galley entrance, Walz reached out and caught her around the waist.

Lotte was not certain what was happening. From surprise as much as fear she cried out—a sharp cry of terror that sounded clearly above the wind and rain.

Helmut Richter, asleep in one of the hammocks that had been rigged in the forecastle to take care of the extra crew, was awake in an instant, was up the ladder and out on deck before Berger and Sturmm had even emerged from the captain's cabin.

Lotte staggered across the deck, losing her balance as the ship heeled, and falling at Richter's feet. As he picked her up, the cloak fell back from her shoulders.

Sister Angela emerged from the companionway. "Lotte!" she called.

Richter put the girl to one side and took a pace forward to stand waiting as Walz came hesitantly from the galley.

"Walz!" Richter said softly.

He stood there, bare feet apart, dressed only in seaman's denims. Lightning flickered overhead as the storm moved in. St. Elmo's fire flared at each masthead, so that the entire ship seemed to glow as it plunged forward.

"Richter!" Berger cried.

The bosun ignored him and moved forward. Walz, terrified, sprang into the ratlines and started to climb the foremast. Richter went after him, picking his way with care as if he had all the time in the world.

Walz moved with remarkable speed. When he reached the lower topsail yard, he paused to look down, then drew the knife at his belt and slashed at the ratlines. Lotte cried out. There was a sudden groan from the assembled crew, followed by total silence as they held their breath.

The ratlines parted and Richter reached for the downhaul nearest to hand, swinging from it to a shroud line with the skill of a trapeze artist.

He hung there for a moment before starting upward again. Walz, holding on to the yard, waited for him, reaching down to slash at the bosun's hand with the knife. Richter twisted out of the way, but Walz kicked him in the side of the face.

Richter slipped several feet down the line, then came to a halt, spinning around. Lotte stared up, her knuckles tight against her teeth. Sturmm took a step forward.

Berger grabbed his arm. "Leave it!" he said in a low voice.

"In God's name, Herr Kapitän," Sister Angela said. "Do something."

"What would you suggest, Sister?" Berger asked, without taking his gaze away from the scene above for a moment.

It was an extraordinary sight, with sheet lightning exploding from one horizon to the other, the strange ball of light of the St. Elmo's fire pulsating at each masthead, the eerie phosphorescence of the electrical discharge flowing along every rope and stay, picking Richter and Walz out of the darkness with total clarity.

With an incredible effort, the bosun went up the line hand over hand, grabbed for the lower topsail yard, and a moment later was secure in the footropes.

Walz backed away and started upward again, climbing toward the upper topsail yard. Each flash of lightning had a dazzling white intensity to it that seemed to imprint the scene on the brain for those on deck, but in between was a brief interval of total darkness so that they might have been looking through the eyeholes of an old-fashioned moving picture machine, the action moving jerkily forward, scene by scene.

As Walz reached the yard, the bosun swung to one side on a lift, pulled himself up to a position on the extreme end of the yardarm, and began inching along the footropes. Walz backed away, out toward the other end of the yardarm.

Richter was very close now. He hung there no more than three feet away from Walz who struck out blindly. The point of the knife caught the bosun's right cheek. He came forward implacably and Walz gave a cry of despair.

He grabbed for the main upper topsail brace and slashed at it in a frenzy with the knife. The line parted and the yardarm, freed from restraint, swung viciously from one side to the other, the sail flapping as air spilled from it.

Richter should have been hurled into space, but he managed to scramble to the temporary safety of the lower topgallant yard.

Walz swung crazily backward and forward. A particularly wild roll of the *Deutschland* sent him half over the yard, and he only managed to save himself by hooking an arm in the footrope.

Richter worked his way across the back of the lower topgallant from one lift to another. He paused, suspended in space, watching carefully, judging his moment, as Walz, on the end of the yardarm, swung far out over the sea.

The ship heeled, Walz swung in very fast, hanging on with one arm, striking with the knife. Richter, a rope in each hand, gave him both feet in the face. Walz cried out and went back over the yard into space.

He hit the water some distance from the starboard rail. His arm swung up in mute appeal, but in spite of the wildly flailing sail, the *Deutschland* was still making ten knots, and he receded, became one with the night, taken by the sea.

"We're heaving to, Mister Sturmm. Douse jibs, if you please. Clew up forecourse, topsails, and t'gallants, then get to work and repair that damage. I want to be under way again in an hour," Berger ordered.

"Is that all you have to say?" Sister Angela's voice was low, intense. "A man is dead."

"It shall be so noted in the log," Berger said impassively.

Richter dropped to the deck and Lotte ran forward, arms outstretched. When she was a yard or two away from him she swayed, half fainting. Richter caught her quickly. He stood there for a moment looking down at her, blood oozing from his slashed cheek, then went toward the companionway.

The other nuns, gathered together at the bottom, got out of the way quickly. Sister Kathë said, "Is she all right, Mister Richter?"

Richter didn't reply. He walked across the saloon to Lotte's cabin, went in, and laid her on the lower bunk. He reached for a blanket to cover her and the girl's eyes fluttered.

For a second only she stared blankly into space, then recognized him. "Mister Richter?"

"It's all right," Richter said.

He made a movement as if to turn away and there was instant panic. "Don't leave me."

He took her hand and crouched beside the bunk, stroking her forehead as one might gentle a child. "Never," he said softly. "Never again. Sleep now."

She closed her eyes, the face growing calm. After a while, the breathing became slow and regular, the hand slackened in his.

He got to his feet and turned to find the nuns peering in at the doorway, a uniform look of astonishment on their faces in the dim light. Sister Angela stood at the foot of the bed, pale and composed, hands folded. He waited for her comment, drained of emotion, quite indifferent, and as always, she surprised him.

"And now, I think you'd better come with me, Mister Richter," she said calmly. "From the looks of things, I'd say you need another stitch or two."

In the gray light of dawn far to the northeast, U-235 surfaced at the rendezvous buoy a mile off Bergen. She presented an extraordinary sight, for in place of her prow there was only a jagged stump of twisted, rusting metal. In mid-Channel it had soon been discovered that eight meters of the forecastle were bent to one side. Friemel had managed to detach the damaged portion by alternating as rapidly as possible between full speed ahead and full speed back.

But the rest of the trip had been an unqualified nightmare. He had not closed his eyes in thirty-six hours, and when he followed Engel up the ladder to the bridge, it was very slowly indeed.

An escort of two armed trawlers raced out to meet them, signal lamps flashing. Engel examined them through his binoculars, then turned. His face was gray, the eyes dark, no life there at all. The bandage around his forehead didn't help the general appearance.

"We made it, Herr Admiral."

"So it would appear."

A seaman came up the ladder behind them quickly and passed a flimsy across. "Signal, sir."

He offered it to Friemel who shook his head. "You read," he said to Engel.

"WELL DONE, OTTO. DÖNITZ, HIGH COMMANDER OF THE KRIEGSMARINE AND BDU," Engel said in a low voice. "That's all it says, sir."

"Well done." Friemel laughed harshly. "Well done indeed."

There was a further flurry of activity as the minesweepers circled to take up position, men cheering from the rails as U-235 plowed forward slowly.

From somewhere below there was a cry, a muffled cheer, feet scrambling on the iron ladder, and Heini Roth erupted onto the bridge, another flimsy in his hand. His face was white with excitement. "What is it, for God's sake?" Friemel asked.

"Further signal from BdU, Herr Admiral. It simply says: INFORMATION FROM ABWEHR THAT GERICKE ARRIVED LONDON CAGE ON THE NINETEENTH."

He turned, leaned heavily on the rail, totally overcome. Friemel took a crumpled cigarette pack from his breast pocket. There was one cigarette left, which he carefully inserted into his holder. Heini gave him a light, hand shaking.

Friemel inhaled deeply, then sighed. "The last of those lousy French weeds, and yet I don't think a cigarette ever tasted better in my life."

Barkentine Deutschland, *20 September 1944. Lat. 46°55'N, long. 17°58'W. Another bad night. Wind force 7. Rain and heavy seas. At four bells of the morning watch outer jib parted at the clew and jib-boom ripped away when a huge sea came up to windward. Kluth and Schmidt who had jumped to the mizzen pipe-rail were hurled into the lee scuppers. I expected to see them swept away, but by some miracle they survived, Schmidt sustaining a fracture of the left forearm. As it was imperative to go about with such a sea running, I decided to wear ship to give Mister Sturmm a chance to repair damage. At two bells of the forenoon watch, Obersteuermann Richter reported eighteen inches of water in the bilges. I immediately ordered him to call the starboard watch from below and to commence pumping. It was two bells of the first dogwatch before Mister Sturmm was able to report all damage secure. Obersteuermann Richter's watch having pumped her dry again and the storm having abated a little, I was able to bring her around and resume our original course, having lost some forty miles as we drifted to leeward. I estimate we are now some seven hundred miles due west of the Bay of Biscay.*

Seven

*I*t was considered useful propaganda to let the public see German prisoners of war being led through Euston station. Sublieutenant Fisher was in charge of the escort, which consisted of Carver and two leading seamen, Wright and Hardisty. They all wore gaiters and webbing belts, carrying Webley .38 revolvers like any normal shore patrol, but they took Gericke through the crowd as unobtrusively as possible, just another naval prisoner, a blue raincoat draped over his shoulders.

Fisher identified himself to the guard, who led them into a luggage van. The rear section was walled off by a metal grille, behind which lay a jumble of red GPO bags.

The guard produced a key. "He can go in there if you like."

"Fine," Fisher said. "Can I keep the key?"

"Don't see why not," the guard said. "I've got a spare. I don't suppose you're likely to steal the mail."

He went out. Fisher unlocked the iron gate and Carver nodded to Gericke, scrupulously polite. "If you don't mind, sir."

Gericke moved inside, the sublieutenant locked the gate, and handed the key to Carver. "Right, Chief. You look after things here while I see if I can find Lieutenant Jago."

"You take your time, sir. We'll be fine in here," Carver told him. "A damn sight better off than they are further up the train."

123

Fisher went out and Carver passed a pound note across to Leading Seaman Hardisty. "You and your mate cut along to the station buffet and grab what you can in the way of sandwiches and fags."

"But we've brought a load of stuff with us from the canteen, Chief," Hardisty told him.

"I know, son, I know," Carver said. "Which is fine, till we roll into Leeds or somewhere like it at two in the bloody morning and find the cupboard's bare. Now do as I say "

Gericke leaned against the metal grille and examined a notice on the wall. It said: IF AN AIR RAID OCCURS WHILE YOU ARE ON THE TRAIN:

1. *Do not attempt to leave unless required by the guard to do so. You are safer where you are.*
2. *Pull the blinds down, both by day and night, as a protection against flying glass.*
3. *If room is available, lie down on the floor.*

Carver said, "Thanks to you buggers, that little lot."

"Tell me something, Chief Petty Officer," Gericke asked, "how long have you been in the service?"

"Thirty years. Joined up in 1914 when I was sixteen."

"Ah, a regular," Gericke nodded. "You surprise me. War, after all, is the name of the game for the professional. Yet you seem to object to the fact that there's one on. Perhaps the only reason you stayed on after the first lot was to wear a pretty uniform and have a girl in every port."

Carver was furiously angry. "You wait, you bastard."

They heard Fisher's voice approaching. The sublieutenant entered, followed by Captain Vaughan and Harry Jago, to find Carver passing a cigarette through the mesh to Gericke.

"Care for a smoke, Commander?" he was asking with perfect civility.

"That's very kind of you, Chief." Gericke accepted the cigarette and a light.

Vaughan said, "A little primitive, but it could be worse. Any complaints, Commander?"

Gericke raised his handcuffed wrists. "Could I possibly have these removed? After all, I *am* caged in."

"Sorry." Vaughan shook his head. "But if it makes you feel any better, we had an intelligence report in from our Norwegian friends in Bergen a couple of hours ago. It seems U-235, under the command of Rear Admiral Otto Friemel, arrived safely, minus seven or eight meters of her bows."

For a moment Gericke couldn't take it in, but in any case there was no time to say anything, for outside the guard's whistle blew, and there was the sound of running feet.

Vaughan said stiffly, in that careful, precise voice, "Well, Commander, I can only wish you a safe voyage, in spite of the exigencies of the North Atlantic."

Gericke smiled. "Ironic to find myself in the periscope sights of an old comrade."

Vaughan saluted, beckoned to Fisher, and limped out on the platform. Jago said to Gericke, "I'll look in from time to time. It can take twelve hours or more to make Glasgow."

"I'm in no particular hurry."

Jago went out and Carver moved across to the grille. "And neither am I, son," he said softly. "But just for starters, let's have those medals back."

On Fhada, rain blew in across the harbor and drummed against the windows of the old cottage. Reeve was seated at his desk, his diary open before him. His daily entry was an old habit, engaged in from his earliest days at sea. Not so much a record of events as an attempt to formulate his thoughts. He put a match to his pipe, picked up his pen, and started to write.

*This life of mine, if life I can call it, has be-
come a strange affair, a kind of metamor-
phosis in which everything has changed.
Oliver Wendell Holmes once said that it was
required of a man that he should share the
action and passion of his times at peril of
being judged not to have lived, and for most
of my life I have followed his precept with
uncommon faithfulness. But now I find myself caught in a web of days, time passing in
a kind of slow motion, and to what purpose?
What end?*

He put down his pen and stirred the wolfhound,
sprawled on the rug before the hearth, with his foot.
"Out of the way, you red devil."

Rory moved reluctantly and Reeve added a few
turfs to the peat fire, then glanced at his watch. "Almost time, Rory. Shall we see if they've anything for
us today, eh? Maybe someone out there will actually
remember that we still exist."

The radio was on a table by the window. He sat
down, adjusted the headphones, and started to transmit.
"This is Sugar One on Fhada calling Mallaig. Are you
receiving me?"

Rory crouched beside him and Reeve fondled the
dog's ears and tried again. There was an almost in-
stantaneous response. "Hello, Sugar One, this is Mallaig receiving you loud and clear. Stand by, please. I
have a message for you."

Reeve was aware of a sudden excitement.

"Admiral Reeve? Murray here, sir."

"What can I do for you?" Reeve demanded.

"Had a signal from London for you, sir. Just to let
you know that your niece is on her way to stay with
you for a few days."

Reeve said automatically, "That's wonderful.
When does she arrive?"

"Sometime tomorrow. I can't be more exact than that, I'm afraid. You know what the trains are like these days. What about transportation to Fhada, sir? I don't think I'll have anything official available."

"That's all right," Reeve said. "I'll see to that end of things." He braced himself. "Anything else for me, Murray?"

"I'm afraid not, sir," Murray said, and added, "I'm sorry, Admiral."

"Don't be," Reeve said bitterly. "I don't think anyone else is, so why should you be different? Over and out."

He switched off the set and sat staring into space, one hand idly playing with Rory's ears. It would be nice to see Janet again, to hear her news, but it wasn't enough. Not nearly enough.

The dog whined as his hands gripped too tightly, and he stood up quickly. "Sorry, boy. I'm not at my best today. Let's get a little fresh air."

He took down his reefer from behind the door and went out, Rory at his heels. The wind was in the wrong direction to use a sail so he hand-pumped his way on one of the trolleys for the entire length of the line to South Inlet. When he went down to the lifeboat station, the rear door of the boathouse was open. Murdoch was sitting on an old chair, sheltered from the rain, mending a net across his knee.

He looked up, the weather-beaten face showing no emotion, his hands still working. "A good day or a bad day, Carey Reeve?"

"Since when have I had a choice?"

"Like that, is it? Would you care for a dram?"

"Maybe later. My niece is arriving at Mallaig tomorrow on the London train."

"That will be nice for you." Murdoch spread his net. "Young Lachlan MacBrayne is coming home on leave off that same train. His mother told me yesterday."

"A paratrooper, isn't he?"

"That is so. If you've no objection, I've promised to run across in your *Katrina* and pick him up. You would like me to bring your niece back also?"

"That would be fine," Reeve said.

On the train, Gericke sprawled back on the mail sacks, eyes closed, apparently asleep. Carver and the two leading seamen were playing cards. Fisher was reading a book.

There was a knock on the door, and when Fisher unlocked it, Harry Jago stepped in. "Everything okay?"

"I think so," Fisher said. They walked across to the wire mesh screen. "He's been asleep for the past hour."

"Fine. If you've got time I'd like you to come up to the sleeping car and meet Dr. Munro. There's a bottle of Scotch in my bag we could do a little damage to."

"Sounds good to me," Fisher said as they went out.

Carver lit a cigarette and scratched himself. "They've got it made, these bloody Yanks."

"How's that, Chief?" Hardisty asked.

"This Dr. Munro. A nice bit of skirt, I can tell you, going all the way to Mallaig. Her uncle's an American admiral living on some island in the Outer Hebrides. She's got a private berth up there in the sleeping car. Jago's shacked up with her." He threw in his cards. "Another lousy bloody hand. Deal 'em again, Wright, only make sure you give me some good ones this time."

He got up and stared through the mesh at Gericke. "You awake, Commander?"

Gericke made no sign, breathing softly, eyes closed, and Hardisty said, "Leave him, Chief, for Christ's sake. He isn't going anywhere."

Carver turned away reluctantly, sat down, and

picked up his cards. Behind him, Gericke's eyes opened for a brief moment.

It was raining in Trondheim, heavy, drenching rain as Horst Necker went up the steps of the main entrance to the operations building with Rudi Hubner. They were still in flying gear, having just returned from an eight-hour operational flight that had taken them far out into the Barents Sea and back again.

Necker was tired and bad-tempered. "They'll have to do something about that port engine. It sounds more like a bloody tractor every time we go out."

"I know, Herr Hauptmann," Rudi said soothingly. "I spoke to Vogel myself. He said he was waiting for our next furlough."

"Christ Almighty, we could be dead by then."

He pushed open the door of the intelligence room, expecting to find Altrogge, the intelligence officer, but he pulled up short, for Colonel Meyer, the Gruppenkommandeur, was sitting on the edge of the desk, smoking a cigarette and leafing through some papers.

He glanced up. "You don't look too pleased with life, Horst. Did you have trouble?"

"You could say that." Necker dropped his parachute on a convenient chair and accepted a cigarette. "Eight hours of nothing but bloody sea and a port engine with asthma. Otherwise the flight was sheer delight."

Meyer grinned. "Never mind. I've brought your two-day furlough forward. That should please you."

"Why should it?" Necker demanded sourly. "You'll have a damn good reason, I'm sure."

"A change of routine. Our masters would like you to concentrate on the west coast of Scotland and the Hebrides again for the next couple of weeks." He smiled. "You wanted action, Horst. You've got it. Two new Spitfire squadrons moved up to the east coast this week. That should make it interesting for you."

"Thanks very much," Necker said, suddenly feeling surprisingly cheerful considering the circumstances. "What's it all about?"

"Convoys from Canada have been using the northern run lately, according to intelligence. Coming up a lot closer to Iceland. From now on your patrol must take you much further out into the Atlantic. At least five hundred miles west of the Outer Hebrides."

"We won't be able to stay there long."

Meyer pulled a chart across the desk and nodded. "We'll give you improved drop tanks. That should add another five hundred miles. And there's a modification to your GMI system that should make it possible for you to cross Scotland without dropping below thirty-five thousand. They claim forty, but I wouldn't count on it. In any case, it should keep you out of the way of those Spitfires."

The GMI system employed nitrous oxide, which was injected into the superchargers where, during high altitude flights, it supplied additional oxygen for combustion, increasing the engine power by twenty percent.

Necker examined the chart and nodded. "That's a long way to go."

Meyer smiled and slapped him on the arm. "It will seem shorter when you've had a couple of days' rest."

The wind dropped considerably toward evening and the *Deutschland,* under full sail, moved on into the gathering darkness, pushed by a light breeze from the southwest.

Richter had the first watch, alone on the quarter-deck except for a petty officer torpedo mechanic named Endrass, who was at the wheel. The bosun stood at the rail smoking one of his cigarillos, enjoying the night, the horned moon, and the stars scattered to the far horizon, their glow diffused by a damp, clinging sea mist.

At nine o'clock he went forward to speak with the lookout in the bows. On his way back he paused by the mizzen shrouds on the port side to check a lashing that had worked loose on the mainsail boom. There was a movement behind him, and Lotte stepped out of the shadows between the lifeboats.

"Helmut!"

Her hands reached out through the darkness, her face a pale blur. Richter took them instinctively. "Lotte —what are you doing here?"

"I've been watching you for the past half hour, pacing from one side to the other of that wretched quarterdeck. I was beginning to think you were never coming down."

"You must return below," he said. "At once."

"Why?"

"Because Sister Angela is concerned for your welfare. I've given my word to the Kapitän that I'll stay away from you for the rest of the voyage."

"And you?" she said. "Are you concerned for my welfare?"

"God help me." He tried to release his hands. "Let be, Lotte. I've given my word—don't you see?"

"I understand only one thing," she said. "That all my life I have been afraid. But when I am with you . . ." Her hands tightened on his. "Is this what love is always like, Helmut? Have you known love like this before?"

His arms went around her as his last defenses crumbled. "No, never like this, Lotte."

She tilted her chin to peer up at him. "As a novice, I can leave the order at will and with a minimum of fuss when we reach Kiel. And then . . ."

He kissed her gently. "What happens in Kiel is one thing. As for now, there can be no more such meetings."

"How much longer?" she asked.

"Two weeks if we're lucky, though we'll need to make better time than this."

"Shall I whistle up a wind for us?" she demanded. "A real wind?"

"No need." He looked up at the night sky. "I think this is only a temporary lull. Storm before morning."

There was a slight movement behind. They turned quickly and found Sister Angela standing by the mainmast.

"Mister Richter—Lotte," she said calmly. "A fine night."

It was Lotte who spoke first, reacting instinctively in Richter's defense. "This was my fault, Sister, believe me. None of Mister Richter's doing."

"I'm well aware of that, child. I've been here for the past five minutes. But now, I really do think you should go below."

Lotte hesitated, then started toward the companionway reluctantly. When she was halfway there, Sister Angela added, "I'm sure Mister Richter will be happy to talk to you again tomorrow, if his duties permit."

The girl caught her breath, paused, then turned and fled down the companionway.

Richter said, "Do I understand from this, Sister, that I actually have your permission to . . ."

"Come courting, Mister Richter?" She smiled faintly. "How old that makes me feel. So old."

She turned from him and walked to Berger's door. Richter watched helplessly as she knocked and entered.

Berger was at his desk, writing. Otto Prager lay on the bunk reading a book. The consul sat up, swinging his legs to the floor, and Berger laid down his pen.

"Sister?" he said politely.

Prager stood up. "You would like me to leave perhaps?"

He took a step toward the door, but she shook her head. "A moment of your time only, Kapitän. In the matter of Mister Richter and Lotte."

"Well?" Berger asked bleakly, ready for trouble.

"I would be obliged if you would release him from his promise not to speak to her again until we reach Kiel."

"A rather surprising change of attitude on your part, wouldn't you say?"

"A new viewpoint, perhaps. All I have ever wanted was what was right for Lotte. Her decision as to her future when we reach Kiel must be made of her own free choice with no voice to aid her but God's. I see that now. In the meantime, it would seem pointless to keep her and Mister Richter apart artificially. As I have discovered for myself, he seems a singularly honorable young man."

Berger couldn't think of a thing to say. She gave him a moment, then added, "And now, if you gentlemen will excuse me. I'm really very tired."

The door closed behind her. The consul turned, total astonishment on his face. Berger, without a word, opened the cupboard and took out the rum bottle and two glasses.

It was very dark as the train plowed on into the night, rain lashing against the windows. When Harry Jago knocked on the door of the sleeping compartment and went in, Janet was in the single bunk, a blanket pulled up to her chin.

"I'm freezing."

"Well, I could suggest a remedy for that condition," he told her cheerfully.

"Not tonight, darling. I've had it. I could sleep for a week. You'll have to make do with the floor and a blanket."

He shrugged his shoulders. "Okay," he said. "There are guys sleeping in the luggage racks back there." He took off his shoes, wrapped himself in one of the blankets, and lay on the floor, head pillowed on a canvas holdall; he was almost instantly asleep.

They reached Glasgow at six-thirty on a gray, sullen morning. Janet had slept badly and had awakened to find that Jago had gone. It took her a moment or so to pull herself together—to realize that they were standing still.

As she threw the blanket aside and sat up, there was a tap at the door and he looked in. "Alive and well," he commented. "That's nice."

He passed a thermos. "Coffee. We're in Glasgow, by the way. They seem to be disconnecting about half the coaches."

"Then what happens?"

"We pull out in about ten minutes. Bridge of Orchy, Rannoch, Fort William, and Mallaig. Another five hours if all goes well. I'm just saying good-bye to Fisher and our mutual friend Gericke. I'll be right back and we can have breakfast. It's all arranged."

He went out before she could reply. For a moment only she sat there, then got up, raised the blind, and pushed down the window. The platform was almost deserted. Jago was hurrying along to a small group consisting of Lieutenant Fisher and the escort, Gericke standing in the center, the blue raincoat over his shoulders again.

As she watched, Fisher and Jago moved to one side. She caught a brief glimpse of Gericke's sardonic face, and then Carver turned him around and gave him a push. They went through the door of the station waiting room, leaving Fisher and Jago talking on the platform. Quite suddenly Janet had had enough. She pushed up the window and pulled down the blind. When she turned back to the bunk, she was trembling.

"I'm tired," she said softly. "Too little sleep for too damned long. That's what it is." And she got back into the bunk.

"I was expecting your people to meet us," Fisher said. "I wonder what's keeping them?"

"God knows." Jago looked at his watch. "Say, I'd better get back on board. This thing pulls out again at any moment."

"I can't hand him over quickly enough, believe me," Fisher said. "There's something about him. The way he looks at you."

"I know exactly what you mean." Jago shook hands. "A good trip back, anyway."

He got into the train, and Fisher turned and walked toward the waiting room where a coal fire burned in a small grate. Hardisty and Wright warmed themselves in front of it, smoking cigarettes.

"Where's the prisoner?" Fisher demanded.

"He wanted to go to the lavatory, sir." Hardisty nodded toward a green door with the sign GENTLE-MEN painted on it. "The chief said he'd see to it."

Fisher turned, and at that moment the door opened violently and Carver staggered through, half doubled over. He seemed to find difficulty in speaking, his mouth opening and closing as he gasped for air.

Fisher grabbed him by the lapel. "What is it, man?" he demanded.

"He—he's got away, sir," Carver groaned, clutching at his groin. "The bastard's got away."

Gericke had asked to go to the lavatory for the most genuine of reasons. The idea of escape at this stage hardly seemed to be in the cards, especially when one considered those damned handcuffs. What had happened had been a spur-of-the-moment decision, the briefest of opportunities instantly seized.

"I'll see to this, lads." Carver had pushed him toward the door and kicked it open. "You two have a quick smoke while the going's good."

Inside, there was a row of stalls, a urinal, a broken washbasin, and rain drifting in through the open window above the basin. It was the sight of that window that stirred Gericke.

The chief petty officer leaned against the door. "All right, get on with it."

Gericke moved toward one of the stalls, turned, and held out his handcuffed wrists. "A little awkward with these things."

"Oh, a sit-down job, is it?" Carver laughed, eager to extract every last ounce of humiliation from the situation. "I think we might stretch a point there, Commander." He produced the key and unlocked one handcuff. "There, that will do you. And you'll have to leave the door open, of course. I'm sure you won't mind me watching, under the circumstances."

"Thank you, Chief," Gericke said calmly, and lifted his right knee into Carver's crotch.

Barkentine Deutschland, *21 September
1944. Lat. 49°52'N, long. 14°59'W. Wind
force 5–6. Intermittent squalls. Heavy rain.
It is now necessary to pump four hours out of
each twenty-four, which seems to suffice, and
thanks to the size of the crew is less of a bur-
den than it otherwise would have been. Our
position now approximately 220 miles southwest of Ireland.*

Eight

Fisher moved out of the parcels' office with Carver
hobbling at his heels and paused outside the waiting room. "Goddamn you, Carver, I'll have you for
this."

Hardisty and Wright came around the corner on
the run. "He hasn't gone through the barrier, that's
definite, sir," Hardisty said. "Two redcaps on duty
there. They're putting the word out now."

"Go through that damned luggage room again,"
Fisher ordered. "He's got to be here somewhere. Nowhere he could go, not in the time."

The two leading seamen went off. Carver said

bitterly, "When I get my hands on that German bastard I'll . . ."

"Oh, shut up, for God's sake, and let me think,"
Fisher said.

There was the shrill blast of a whistle; the guard's
flag fluttered. A sudden hiss of steam and the train
started to ease forward. One or two sailors leaned out
of carriage windows to see what the fuss was about,
but most of the passengers on board were still hardly
stirring.

"I mean, where in the hell could he have gone?"
Fisher demanded, and then, as realization dawned, he
almost choked. "The train, Chief!" he shouted. "He
must have got back on the train. It's the only possible
explanation."

It was already moving fast, but there was still
time, and he jumped for the open door of the guard's
van as it passed, turning to pull Carver up behind him.
Hardisty and Wright, running along the platform to
join them, were too late.

"Here, what's going?" the guard demanded.

Fisher ignored him, drew his revolver, and turned
to Carver. "All right, Chief, let's rout him out," he
said.

Janet Munro's travel voucher being marked TOP PRI-
ORITY, the sleeping car steward served her first that
morning, a good English breakfast of bacon, scrambled egg, marmalade, toast, and tea.

Jago could hardly believe his eyes. "Did I say
there was a war on?"

"Not for people with my influence, darling."

"I certainly joined the right ship this time."

He sat down on the other side of the small table
that the steward had pulled up from under the window.
Janet poured the tea.

"You know, I've actually managed to acquire a
taste for this stuff," Jago said.

There was a knock at the door. Janet, who was

nearest, reached to open it. Fisher moved in, revolver in his right hand, Carver behind him.

"What in the hell is going on?" Jago demanded.

"He gave Carver the slip back there in the station, sir," Fisher told him. "Asked to go to the lavatory . . ."

"Save it for your court-martial, Lieutenant," Jago said brutally. "Just tell me one thing." He turned to Carver. "Did you unlock his handcuffs?"

Carver licked his lips nervously. "Just one, sir. I mean, he wanted . . ."

"I can't believe it." Jago exploded. "One chance —any chance—that's all a guy like that needs." He turned away, white with anger. "So, he's on the train, is that what you're saying?"

"I think so, sir." Fisher hesitated and then added awkwardly, "I mean, there wasn't anywhere else for him to go. There wasn't time."

"You *think* so?" Jago said. "All right then, Lieutenant, where is he? German lieutenant commanders must be kind of thin on the ground, wouldn't you say, especially on the West Highland Line?"

Fisher glanced nervously at Carver, then back at the American. "I—I just don't know, sir. We started with the guard's van and worked our way forward."

"And there was no sign of him. Well, that figures. He'd hardly advertise. Is he armed?"

Carver hesitated, debating whether to lie or not, but one look from Jago was enough. "I'm afraid so, sir. I was carrying a spare, sir. A Mauser. Just in case."

"In case of what?" Jago demanded and then waved a hand. "Don't bother, Chief, we've got more important things to consider." He opened his holdall and took out a service-issue Colt automatic and slipped it into one pocket. "Put those pistols away for the moment. No need to set the entire train on its ear. If he is on board, which I doubt, any confusion can only assist him."

Fisher, delighted to hand over the reins, said eagerly, "What are we going to do, sir?"

"Carver stays up here at one end, you and I go back to the guard's van and work our way forward. Every compartment, every lavatory. We'll find him— if he's here at all. In my personal opinion, he's on a streetcar right now, heading for Glasgow and a Portuguese or Spanish boat if he can find one."

"In German uniform?" Janet said. "He wouldn't last five minutes."

"Last year a London journalist walked down Oxford Street to Piccadilly dressed as an SS colonel," Jago said grimly. "And no one took any kind of notice. There are so many uniforms around these days people are punch-drunk." He nodded to Fisher and Carver who moved outside. "You stay close to home. I'll be back soon."

It was a good hour later and the train was approaching the northern end of Loch Lomond when they reappeared, Fisher paler than ever, a picture of total dejection. Carver lurked in the corridor outside.

"No Gericke?" Janet said.

"What do you think?"

The guard, an old man long past his prime who had only stayed on because of the war, appeared behind Carver. "Any luck, sir?"

Jago shook his head. "Wherever he is, it isn't on board this train. We've checked every inch."

The guard said, "Not quite, sir. They coupled a flattop on at Glasgow behind my van with three jeeps on it for delivery to the Royal Navy at Mallaig. Mind you, there's no way he could have got out there as far as I can see."

"Is that so?" Jago said, and he reached up and pulled the communication cord.

Gericke had enjoyed a surprisingly comfortable trip in the back of one of the jeeps on the flattop. He was out of the rain and the views were spectacular—the kind of country he liked.

He had no set plan, allowing things to happen as the cards fell. The opportunity to put Carver down had been too good to miss—the decision to get back on the train so obvious that he hadn't really thought about it. He'd simply jumped for cover, head down.

And one thing was in his favor. The fact that, in regard to uniform, most naval officers looked the same the world over. All he had to do was remove the swastika and eagle from the *Kreigsmarine* badge on his uniform cap; and he was doing just that, the hand-cuffs swinging from his left wrist, when the train started to grind to a halt with such violence that he was thrown from the seat.

The game was up, so much seemed obvious, for the train was passing through a long narrow cut with sides that were almost perpendicular. Yet Gericke was reluctant to throw in the towel. He had nothing to lose. While the train was still sliding to a halt, he moved along the flattop to the rusting iron ladder at the rear of the guard's van.

There was a catwalk on the roof and he ran along it, jumping to the first coach, almost losing his balance as it swayed violently from side to side. He made it to the next roof and threw himself flat on his face as the train came to a halt.

There was silence, only the heavy rain, the hiss of steam, and then windows going down, doors opening —excited voices. Someone was running along the side of the track. He heard Fisher say, "Nowhere for him to go this time."

"Exactly," Jago called. "So play it cool. No need for gunplay. Much better to get him back in one piece."

They moved on. Gericke, daring all, went over the edge and slipped down the ladder to the bridge be-tween the coaches. He opened the door before him and moved inside.

The corridor was lined with people, mostly sailors on their way to the naval depot at Mallaig, leaning out of the windows, looking back along the track. There was a great deal of speculation going on as to what it was all about. Gericke moved along the corridor, thrusting his left hand and the dangling handcuffs into his pocket.

No one took the slightest notice of him until he reached the end, and then a young sailor, moving back from a window, pushed into him. He turned, took in the raincoat and uniform cap, and said quickly, "Sorry, sir."

"That's all right."

"What's going on back there, sir?"

"God knows," Gericke said. "I saw a couple of officers with guns in their hands. Maybe some prisoner or other has given them the slip." He stood at a window for a while, just one of the crowd watching, and saw Jago and the others climb back on board. The guard's whistle sounded, there was a hiss of steam, the wheels spun, and the train moved forward again.

People started to go back into their compartments and he carried on. He crossed to the sleeping car and immediately found himself in a calmer, more ordered world. The corridor was deserted, and as he started along it, a door at the far end opened and the steward came out of his tiny kitchen.

He paused, "Can I help you, sir?"

Gericke, improvising fast, remembered the conversation he had overheard earlier about Jago and the girl he was sharing a sleeping compartment with. What was her name again? Dr. Munro, an American admiral's niece. It had a certain black humor to it.

"I'm Lieutenant van Lott, Royal Netherlands Navy," he said smoothly, "I was looking for Dr. Munro."

"Compartment fourteen. This way, sir."

He turned, moved a little way along the corridor, and knocked at a door. Gericke followed.

The door opened and Janet peered out. "Gentleman here was looking for you, Doctor. Lieutenant van Lott of the Dutch navy."

Janet looked Gericke over calmly. "Thank you," she said and added to Gericke, "Won't you come in?"

The steward departed and Gericke moved past her into the compartment. When he turned, she was standing against the door, arms folded, watching him gravely. "You don't look too good to me, Lieutenant. What's the trouble?"

"I'm not sure. I wasn't feeling marvelous in Glasgow. Nearly got off the train there, but it's essential I get to Mallaig today. Someone told me there was a doctor on the train so I asked the steward."

"You'd better sit down."

He perched on the edge of the bunk. She put a hand on his forehead. "You could be running a fever."

"You think so?"

"But definitely."

She was close enough for him to smell her perfume; she sat down beside him and took his pulse, crossing one knee over the other.

"You've got excellent legs, Doctor."

"It's been said before," she said calmly and stood up. "A large Scotch, I think, is my prescription for you."

"You think so?"

"I'd say you're going to need it."

She found the bottle in Jago's holdall, took a glass from the small washbasin in the corner, and poured him a large one.

"Good health," Gericke said.

"Prosit," she replied and smiled. "How stupid of me. That's German, isn't it?"

Gericke sighed and took the whisky down in a single swallow. "That was really most kind of you," he said and reached out and shot the bolt on the door.

Jago made his way along the swaying train, Fisher and Carver behind him. "But what in the hell am I going to do, sir?" Fisher asked plaintively.

"Run for the hills. Blow your brains out. Why ask me?" Jago demanded. "It's your problem, Fisher. I wasn't even there. I was back on the train."

He had no intention of being dragged down by this young fool's incompetence. As he opened the door and entered the sleeping car, the steward was just emerging from the end compartment with a tray.

"We'll have some tea or coffee," Jago told him. "Anything you can rustle up."

"In Dr. Munro's compartment?" The steward hesitated. "Actually she has someone with her at the moment, sir. A Lieutenant van Lott. Dutch naval officer."

Jago looked at him. "A small guy with a pale face," he said carefully. "White cap, navy blue raincoat?"

"That's right, sir. I'm short of coffee, but I think I can manage tea for you gentlemen. I'll see to it directly."

He moved along to his kitchen. Jago took the Colt automatic from his pocket and turned to Fisher. "Well?" he said.

"I can't believe it." Fisher looked stunned. "It doesn't make sense."

"Just give me a minute, sir," Carver said eagerly, "and I'll have the sod out of there."

"Like hell you will. We've got Dr. Munro to consider, so we play this very carefully indeed till we know what's going on. Understand?"

He moved quietly along the corridor to Janet's compartment. He tried the door handle gently without success, took a deep breath, and knocked. "Janet, you in there?" His voice was muffled.

She took a step toward the door but Gericke pulled her back, the handcuffs dangling from his wrist, plain to see now. "I don't think so. Not at the moment."

Jago rapped on the door again, a little more insistently. "Hey, come on, Janet. Open up."

Gericke sat on the edge of the bed. "How did you know?"

"When I first saw you at the London cage there was an eagle and swastika above the badge of that rather sweet, white cap you're wearing."

He smiled good-humoredly. "How could I have missed you?"

"One of your bad days, I expect. Charm, like most things, has its limitations. Now would you mind very much if we bring this little farce to an end?"

She put a hand to the bolt and Gericke produced the Mauser from his pocket and cocked it. "I don't suppose you'd like to take my pulse again?"

"Not today, I'm fully booked."

"Ah, well, I shall always have the memory." He clicked his heels, gave a little bow, and handed the Mauser across, butt first. "Isn't that how Conrad Veidt does it in all those Hollywood movies?"

She stopped smiling. "You fool," she whispered. "And in the end, where has it got you?"

He shrugged. "The rules of the game, Doctor. You have to keep moving."

She pushed back the bolt, opened the door, and stood to one side. Jago and the others crowded in, Carver grabbing Gericke roughly and turning him around, jerking his arms behind his back.

"You all right?" Jago demanded.

She handed him the Mauser. "He behaved like a perfect gentleman."

"I'm sorry about that," Gericke said cheerfully over his shoulder.

She laughed harshly. "Get him out of here, for God's sake."

Carver shoved Gericke, whose wrists were by now handcuffed behind him, into the corridor. Jago handed him the Mauser. "Try not to lose it again. Or him."

"I won't, sir. You can count on that," Carver

said grimly, and he put a knee behind Gericke and sent him staggering.

The train stood in Fort William for twenty minutes while Fisher used the phone in the stationmaster's office. Finally he came out, climbed into the guard's van, and knocked on the door of the luggage compartment. As Carver opened it, the train started to move again.

"What's the form, sir?"

"We're taking him on to Mallaig. Back to Glasgow on the afternoon train. How is he?"

"Trussed up like a Christmas turkey."

Fisher walked over to the cage and looked inside. Gericke sprawled across the mailbags, wrists handcuffed behind him, ankles tied together with twine. The lieutenant sat down, suddenly very tired indeed, and lit a cigarette. Thank God the nightmare was over at last. No court-martial, no inquiry. Well, an inquiry perhaps, but then he might not come too badly out of that. After all, it had been Carver's fault in the first place, the whole wretched affair.

On the *Deutschland,* there were rumblings of discontent amounting almost to mutiny when Richter descended to the forecastle for his midday meal.

"Something's crawled in there and died, if you ask me," he heard Leading Seaman Roth observe.

The watch below were grouped around the narrow central table on which stood the cause of their dissension—two large pans that had just been brought down from the galley. The smell, when someone raised a lid, was really quite special, Richter had to admit that. Enough to take the edge off the strongest appetite.

"What's all this?" he demanded, pushing his way through.

"The food again," Endrass told him. "Not fit for pigs. Weber's gone too far this time."

"He's no cook," Richter admitted, peering into one of the pans with distaste.

"Which Walz was, whatever else he might have been."

There was an uncomfortable silence, for it was an undeniable fact of life that the cook's death had left a gap that had proved almost impossible to fill. Richter, by implication, did bear a certain responsibility for the present situation.

Riedel said, "I served my time in sail, Mister Richter, you know that. I was with the old *Kommodore Johnsen* out of Hamburg in the last grain race just before the war. One hundred and seven days, Australia to Queenstown. I know my rights and, according to regulations, each man is entitled to one and a quarter pounds of salt beef and three-quarters of a pound of pork per day." He dipped the ladle into the pan. "And what do we get? A mouthful each if we're lucky."

"Supplies are running low," Richter said. "That pork is half rotten when it comes out of the barrel. You can't blame Weber for that."

"Which is still no excuse to serve what little there is like something off the pavement," Endrass said. "I think we should see the Kapitän."

"All right." Richter nodded. "You and Riedel here, and you'd better bring one of those pans so he can see what we're talking about."

Not that there was any need, for when the bosun knocked at Berger's door and entered, he found the captain and Prager seated opposite each other, plates of stew before them.

"What's this?" Berger demanded.

"Deputation from the crew, Kapitän. Petty Officer Endrass and Leading Seaman Riedel ask leave to speak for the men."

Berger looked at Endrass coldly. "Well?"

"The food, Herr Kapitän," Endrass said. "It's getting so the men can't stomach it anymore, and the stink . . ."

He lifted the lid of the pan that Riedel was

holding. Berger grimaced at the first whiff. "You've made your point. Get it out of here." Riedel retreated. "All right, so it's not too good, but we're all in the same boat." He indicated his own plate and said to Richter, "Who's in the galley now? Weber, isn't it?"

"That's right, sir, and he had to be pressed into service. Nobody wanted the job so the men drew lots."

Berger nodded. "I don't really see that there's anything much I can do about this. It's an old problem on sailing ships, as you know. Once the food starts going off, especially the meat, it needs an experienced cook to handle it, and that's something we just don't have. I'm sure Weber is doing his best."

"I beg leave to doubt that." Sister Angela stood in the doorway, a pan in one hand, the other nuns behind her. She lifted the lid. "What would you say this is exactly?" she asked Berger.

He eyed the greasy scum on the surface with distaste. "Pea soup, I think, Sister."

"So dirty that it's almost black," she said. "A rare phenomenon, which is explained by the simple fact that the cook has omitted to wash the peas."

"All right." Berger held up a hand. "No need to go on. So what do you want me to do about it?"

She handed the pan to Sister Kathë. "We could start with an inspection of the galley. With your permission, of course."

Berger, for once allowing himself to go with the tide, reached for his cap. "For you, Sister, anything. If you'd follow me, please?"

So it was that the unfortunate Weber, sitting disconsolate in the tiny galley, surrounded by greasy pans and dirty plates, observed through the open doorway a sizable group bearing down on him, headed by the captain.

He got to his feet, wiping his hands hastily on his soiled apron, and Berger said, "Outside, Weber. On the double."

Weber did as he was told. Sister Angela paused

in the doorway. She surveyed the scene inside, briefly leaning down to sniff at the rotting pork in its barrel, then turned.

"Take off your apron," she said to Weber.

He glanced nervously at Berger, then did as he was told. She took it from him, holding it at arm's length for a moment, then tossed it over the side.

"I suggest you return this man to his normal duties. This is obviously not the place for him."

"And the cooking?" Berger asked.

"There, you will have to show a little faith, Kapitän. But first, I want every inch of this disgusting hovel scrubbed clean." She turned to the nuns. "Every pan sparkling. Then and only then will we be in a position to do something about the food. You agree, Kapitän?"

"We are, as you so frequently remind me, in the good Lord's hands," Berger told her.

But later, toward evening, when he went up on the quarterdeck with Prager, the aroma that drifted up from the galley on the damp air was so appetizing that for the first time in days he felt genuine hunger.

"What's that?" he demanded of Richter who had the watch.

"I think it's what's called the woman's touch, Herr Kapitän."

"And thank God for it," Prager added piously.

Janet stood at the window of her sleeping compartment, looking out morosely. Even the spectacular beauties of Ben Nevis didn't improve the way she felt. She sat down at the table and picked up a book.

An hour passed, an hour and a half, and Jago continued to sleep as they moved on, passing through some of the most spectacular mountain scenery in Scotland. Glenfinnan, Lochailort, and then the sea and the Sound of Arisaig, shrouded in mist and rain.

She had long since discarded her book. She sat smoking a cigarette, watching raindrops roll down the window, thinking of Gericke, mainly because the thought of him simply wouldn't go away. And that would never do. She picked up the book again and forced herself to read.

Lying face down on the mailbags Gericke couldn't see Carver, but he was conscious of his approach. The chief petty officer squatted beside him, a knife in his hand, and jerked Gericke's head around.

"Very foolish," Gericke said. "You'd never be able to explain it away."

Carver took the Knight's Cross from his pocket. "Did you do something special for this one then? Big hero, is that it?" The anger welled up in him like hot lava. He sliced through the cords that bound Gericke's ankles and grabbed his arm. "Come on—on your feet."

Gericke stood there swaying, almost crying out with pain as blood moved in his cramped legs. Carver pushed him out through the gate, then tripped him so that he fell to his knees, head resting on the floor. Carver booted him in the ribs.

"You feel better now, sir?"

Gericke pushed himself up on his knees. "Was this how you won those fights of yours, Chief? Using men with their hands tied behind their backs as punching bags?"

Carver produced the keys to the handcuffs and swung him around. "I'll show you if I can use myself or not."

Gericke, his wrists free, shrugged off his raincoat, a smile on his face. Carver rushed in and swung a wild punch, which the German sidestepped with ease, dropping into a fighting crouch, his right arm extended in front of him, fist clenched, his left guarding the body. And there was something terribly professional-looking about the way he moved.

The chief stamped in again, swinging a punch that Gericke once more evaded with ease, this time pivoting and delivering a left to Carver's kidneys. Carver cried out in agony and turned to face him.

"Yes, I'm afraid I haven't been really honest with you, Chief," Gericke said, sinking another left under Carver's ribs followed by a right that landed high on the cheek, splitting flesh. "As a young man, I served my apprenticeship in a clipper ship on the nitrate run to Chile. A hard school. Plenty of discipline enforced by belaying pin, knuckle-duster, and boot. I grew up fast."

He seemed to be moving in a kind of slow motion, one punch after another finding its target, and Carver's blows repeatedly landed on thin air.

The chief petty officer was in a bad way, face covered in blood, unable to speak, gasping for breath as the German drove him back across the van relentlessly.

"My friend, you are a disgrace to the uniform you wear and the country that nurtured you. Someone should have cut you down to size long ago," Gericke said, striking Carver three terrible blows on the face that sent him back against the wall of the cage.

He slid to the floor, head lolling to one side. Gericke stood there looking down at him, then dropped to one knee and went through his pockets, retrieving his decorations.

He found the Mauser, which he slipped into his own pocket, picked up his cap, and put on the raincoat. He pulled back the sliding door and rain flooded in.

Janet, standing at an open window in the corridor of the sleeping car, caught a brief glimpse of him landing in heather and rolling over and over down the slope. And then there was only the mist and the rain.

Barkentine Deutschland, *22 September 1944. Lat. 50°59'N, long. 15°35'W. At six bells of the midwatch, the iron collar of the mainsail boom fractured. In the ensuing tangle, the mainsail itself was split from top to bottom and we had to heave to for repairs, drifting under sea anchor until Mister Sturmm reported all clear and ready to proceed at noon. The weather deteriorated into heavy rain and mist soon after. Wind NW 5–6.*

Nine

*T*he *Mary Masters,* a nine-thousand-ton Liberty ship out of Halifax, Nova Scotia, with a cargo of pig iron destined for the steelworks of South Wales, had just gone through a very bad twenty-four hours. Most of the crew, including the captain, were snatching a couple of hours' sleep below.

Visibility was poor, owing to driving rain and mist, and the third officer, alone on the bridge, was tired. When he raised his binoculars for perhaps the twentieth time in half an hour and the *Deutschland* sprang into view, he received a considerable shock.

He went to the voice pipe to call up the captain. "Braithwaite, sir. Sorry to bother you, but I've sighted a sailing ship."

"What did you say?"

"A sailing ship, sir. A quarter of a mile away on the port quarter."

"I'll be right up."

Braithwaite turned to examine the *Deutschland* again, and a few moments later Captain Henderson hurried onto the bridge. He was a small, white-haired man who should have retired in 1940 but had stayed on for the duration.

He reached for the binoculars and focused them. "You old beauty," he said softly. "Alter course, Mr. Braithwaite. I think we'll take a closer look."

There were no more than half a dozen men visible on the decks of the *Deutschland* as Berger and Sturmm stood together on the poop, watching the other vessel move in toward them.

Sturmm lowered his glasses. "A Tommy, Herr Kapitän. The *Mary Masters,* registered Liverpool."

Richter came up the ladder holding the signaling lamp. "What happens now, sir?"

"That's a merchant ship out there, not the Royal Navy." Berger glanced up at the Swedish ensign. "We're still the *Gudrid Andersen* until someone proves different."

A signaling pennant was hoisted on the *Mary Masters,* and Sturmm examined it quickly through his glasses. "May I be of assistance?" was its message.

Berger frowned, one hand gripping the rail. She was very near, moving on a course that would take her astern, close enough for him to see the men on the bridge clearly.

"I think we'll try a real bluff this time. You speak the best English, Mister Sturmm, so you take the signaling lamp. Get ready to transmit on my orders. Plain language, if you please."

"Aye, aye, sir."

Sturmm made a preliminary signal. There was a pause and then an answering flash.

"Here we go then," Berger said softly. " 'Gudrid Andersen, twenty-eight days out of Belém for Göteborg. Thank you for your offer, but in no need of assistance.' "

The lamp flashed in reply from the bridge of the *Mary Masters,* even closer now. Sturmm waited until it had finished, then translated.

" 'Out of Halifax, Nova Scotia, for Swansea. Compelled to drop out of convoy yesterday owing to temporary engine fault.' " The lamp flashed again. " 'Do you wish me to report your position?' "

"Accept his offer. After all, we don't really have a choice. You agree, Helmut?"

Richter nodded, his face grim. "I'm afraid so, Herr Kapitän."

"With luck, it will take them a couple of days, perhaps three, to discover that the real *Gudrid Andersen* is still in Göteborg harbor, and we'll change course as soon as they're over the horizon."

The signal lamp clattered in Sturmm's hands; the *Mary Masters* acknowledged. Most of her crew seemed to be lining the port rail, waving, calling cheerfully through the rain.

"Ask him if they are still winning the war." Sturmm turned, mouth open in astonishment. "Get on with it, man!" Berger told him impatiently.

The reply was noticeably brief. " 'Definitely.' That's all he says, sir."

"Somehow I thought they might be," Berger said. " 'Thank you and good-bye,' Mister Sturmm."

The lamp clattered for the last time, and as the *Mary Masters* passed astern, they heard three long blasts on her steam whistle.

"Mister Richter, return the salute."

The bosun hurried down the ladder and ran

along the deck to dip the ensign. The hooter sounded again, a lonely echo drifting across the water.

"Right, Mister Sturmm, let's get the hell out of here," Berger said.

On the bridge of the *Mary Masters,* Henderson watched the *Deutschland* slip away, and she was already partly obscured by rain and mist when he lowered his binoculars.

"Everything I ever learned at sea, everything worth knowing, I learned by the age of eighteen on an old hooker just like her."

"Is that so, sir?" Braithwaite said.

The old captain nodded. "Watch her go, mister. Drink your fill. I don't think you'll get a second chance —not in your lifetime."

There was mist on the hills, but in Mallaig, it was relatively clear. Janet waited in the outer office of the naval commander's headquarters, staring out across the harbor. It was busier than when she was here before, fishing boats, several naval patrol craft, a submarine even, and a lighter unloading at the pier.

Her eyes were gritty from lack of sleep and she was impatient to be on her way. She had answered their questions, made an official statement and signed it, and still there were delays.

A young Wren was typing at a desk in the corner, but in spite of that the murmur of voices was clearly audible from the inner office. She turned from the window as the door opened. Fisher hurried out, his face flushed, and brushed past her without a word.

Jago appeared with Captain Murray, the base commander, a pleasant, gray-haired man of fifty or so. He smiled. "Sorry about the delay, Miss Munro, but we're all through now."

"I can go?"

"I don't see why not. You've told us all you know. As regards your passage to Fhada, Murdoch

Macleod hasn't arrived yet. The arrangement was that he would report here when he did. If I were you, I'd book in at the hotel for the moment. I've told them to expect you."

"And Gericke? What about him?"

Murray smiled. "My dear Miss Munro, I'm filled with admiration for the gentleman."

She was suddenly angry again. "Good God, he *is* on the other side. Or had you forgotten that?"

"Not at all, I assure you. Professional regard for a superb seaman, that's all. However—" Here he turned to a one-inch ordinance survey map of the western Highlands that was pinned to the wall. "—if he came straight over the mountain from where he left the train he would find his way blocked by Loch Morar. If he cut down to the coast road, it would only bring him to Mallaig—and he won't come here."

"So where will he go?"

"Not very far, I'm afraid, because there isn't anywhere for him to go. One road and the railway line coming in, as you can see. Only a question of time. He won't stay up on those hills for long, not in this weather."

Jago picked up her bag. "I'll walk you to the hotel."

Murray shook hands. "I'll send word the moment Murdoch arrives. Have a nice trip," and he turned and went back into his office.

They walked back toward the station, heads down against the rain. Janet said, "What about Lieutenant Fisher?"

"They'll probably post him to Cape Wrath."

"And Carver?"

"Patching him up now at the base hospital. That must have been something to see. I mean, Gericke really sorted him out. He's finished, of course. I'm not saying he'll end up in the brig, but he'll lose all rank."

As they came abreast of the station, a voice called, "Dr. Munro?"

A young paratrooper in red beret and camouflage jump jacket hurried across the road.

"Why, Lachlan," Janet said. "Were you on the train?" She turned to Jago. "This is Lachlan MacBrayne, Harry. He's from Fhada, too."

"Is that so?" Jago held out his hand.

Lachlan was eighteen, and his untidy red hair, freckles, and snub nose made him look even younger. "Fourteen days' leave. I've just finished jump training. Murdoch is supposed to pick me up, but when I checked down at the harbor he hadn't arrived."

"He's taking me, too," she said. "I'm going to wait at the hotel. They'll send word when he arrives. Why not join us?"

He glanced at Jago awkwardly. "Would it be all right, do you think?"

"Sure it would," Jago said. "You get your gear and follow us on."

The boy ran back across the road.

Janet and Jago paused outside the hotel as the rain increased in a sudden rush, and Janet looked up to the peaks on the other side of Loch Morar shrouded in mist.

"I shouldn't think it would be too comfortable up there on a day like this," Jago said.

"An understatement."

They went up the steps into the hotel.

Gericke was slightly northwest of Sitheon Mor. His intended destination was Mallaig. There was nowhere else to go; he remembered enough of the charts for the west coast of Scotland to realize that. All he had to do was keep going, straight over the top and down to Loch Morar, impossible to miss even in the worst of weather, then along the shore to the coast road. That he could last longer than a day seemed highly improbable, but at least there were boats at Mallaig. Some kind of a chance, however remote. And it was good to be free. Anything was worth that.

After jumping from the train he had started up

the hillside, coming across a mountain stream after ten minutes or so. He followed its course, moving fast, with mist pressing in on either hand giving him a safe, enclosed feeling, somehow remote from the world outside. There were birch trees at first, which grew sparser as he climbed higher, working his way through bracken that in places was waist high.

Occasionally, grouse or plover lifted out of the heather, disturbed by his passing. He kept on the move, stopping after an hour to catch his breath, sheltering from the rain under an overhang. Not that it mattered by now, for his raincoat was soaked through.

He set off again, climbing strongly. Three miles to the loch, perhaps four, and the mountains to pass over, but he was conscious of no feeling of fatigue, the first elation of freedom still carrying him on.

Half an hour later, the bourn petered out into a small loch, and he moved onto the flank of South Moror, climbing across a boulder-strewn hillside. The mist totally enveloped him and he was by now soaked to the skin, for the first time aware of the cold.

He climbed on doggedly, and two hours after leaving the train he scrambled over the edge of a great uptilted slab of granite and found himself on a plateau. There was a special kind of cold here, a wind on his face that told him he was on top. Then a sudden current of air snatched away the gray curtain.

The view was incredible. Loch Morar below him, Mallaig on the far point four or five miles beyond and, out to sea, the islands, crouching in the rain: Eigg, Rum, and Skye, across the Sound of Sleat. There was a cairn of stones ten or fifteen yards away, a track snaking down toward the loch. The curtain of mist dropped back into place but he had seen enough. With renewed energy, he started down the mountainside.

The *Deutschland* was making good time, plunging into the waves, carrying every stitch of canvas she possessed.

From the quarterdeck, Berger addressed the crew and passengers.

"The final run," he said. "Our meeting with the *Mary Masters* was unfortunate, but we've had a lot of luck on our side. I altered course as soon as I could, just in case anyone should come looking, but I don't think it likely. However, one thing is essential. Now, more than ever, we must watch those lights at night. There have been occasions when carelessness in this regard has been much in evidence."

There was a moment of silence, every face turned up to him, expecting more, and there was so little to give. He clutched the rail tightly and tried to put confidence into his voice. "Look, it's going to be all right. Another seven or eight days, that's all, and those of you with families to think of will be greeting them again, I promise you. We've come too far to fail now." He nodded to Sturmm. "Dismiss the crew, please, Mister Sturmm."

There was a general movement as the starboard watch returned to their duties and the others went below. Berger checked the course, then descended the ladder and went into his cabin. He was pouring himself a glass of rum when there was a knock on the door and Prager entered.

"Join me?" Berger held up his glass.

"No, thanks," Prager said. "But I'll have one of your cheroots if you have any left."

"Help yourself."

Berger sat down at his desk and pulled a chart of the western approaches forward. Prager said, "You sounded good out there, Eric."

"Did I?" Berger said wearily. "That's something anyway."

"Where are we? Is it permitted to ask?"

"Here." Berger tapped on the chart with his forefinger. "Now all we have to do is work our way up west of Ireland, the Outer Hebrides, Shetland, across to Norway. We should be safe enough then. Follow the coastline down through the Kattegat to Kiel."

"It seemed like a dream when we started," Prager said. "An impossible dream."

"Yes, it did, didn't it?"

And something touched him, a wave of grayness running through his entire body, like a cold wind brushing the face on deck at night, first warning of a storm to come.

In the galley, Sisters Angela and Lotte, sleeves rolled up to the elbows, worked together preparing the evening meal. The door was pushed open and Richter entered, an enamel washbasin in his hands.

He dropped it on the table. "Salt beef. The last of the crop, and it doesn't smell too good."

Sister Angela prodded it with a knife.

"Half of it rotten, the rest teeming with life."

"Not to worry, Sister. I'm sure you'll manage to do something with it."

He exchanged glances with Lotte, who smiled as she kneaded dough, flour to her elbows. She wasn't wearing her coif, and the slender neck and cropped hair made her look strangely defenseless. Richter would have liked nothing better than an opportunity to take her in his arms.

He pulled himself together hurriedly. "Anything else I can do?"

"Yes," Sister Angela told him. "There are still a few potatoes left. You can peel them. Outside."

He took the bowl she indicated, went out, and squatted by the port rail. He took out his gutting knife, sprang the blade, and started on the potatoes. They were mainly rotten, sprouting roots, but he did the best he could, whistling between his teeth as he worked.

After a while, Lotte appeared, a bucket of garbage in one hand. He got up quickly, took the bucket from her, and emptied it over the side. When he returned it, their hands touched briefly and she smiled. As a token, he had given her his signet ring. Impossible to wear it, of course, and for the moment she kept it hidden in her bunk under a corner of the mattress.

"It will be all right, Helmut?" she said. "We will get through?"

"Of course we will. Why do you ask?"

"Kapitän Berger. It was something in his voice. Something I can't explain."

"Nonsense, he's tired, that's all. We all are. It's been a hell of a trip." He reached up and held one of her hands. "You've nothing to worry about."

She smiled. "And when we get to Kiel?"

"You'll never be alone again, I promise you. From now on nothing parts us. Not ever. I swear it."

She smiled warmly. "Then that's all that matters," she said and returned to the galley.

Janet peered out across the harbor from the bridge of the *Dead End*. "I always forget when I'm away just how much it rains up here."

"Five days out of seven," Jago said.

Jansen entered, a cup of coffee in each hand. "Just had our orders, sir. Stornoway, by dawn's early light."

Noting Janet's expression, Jago explained. "He always speaks that way. In quotation."

"A well-known disease," Jansen told her. "It's called education."

A seagoing launch rounded the pier and moved into harbor. Janet leaned forward. "I believe that's the *Katrina* now. Yes, I'm sure of it."

Jansen said, "I'll go and tell him you're here."

He went out. She turned to Jago. "Well, Harry— the end of something."

"Or the beginning."

"That's what I like about you, darling. The last of the great romantics, and that's a quality hard to come by these days."

There was a surprising amount of light on the pier in spite of the blackout. A crane was working powered by a diesel engine that thumped hollowly through the night as a party of sailors unloaded oil drums from a lighter into two large trucks.

At least it gave Gericke, standing in the shadows, a view of the general state of things. There was an old gunboat that looked prewar, with a couple of ratings on the deck. Americans, to judge from their headgear.

Beyond the gunboat was a coaster, a single-stacker of eight or nine hundred tons, and then a gaggle of fishing boats. And perhaps twenty yards farther on as the light faded, the dim shape of a seagoing launch.

He glanced at his watch. It was just coming up to nine. Those sailors couldn't work all night. At least he hoped so, for to attempt to reach that boat as conditions were presently on the pier was obviously impossible.

He needed somewhere to lie up for three or four hours, preferably with a roof over his head, for the rain showed no sign of abating. There were half a dozen naval trucks parked at one side in a rather confined space, crammed together nose to tail.

He made a cautious reconnaissance, but there seemed to be no guard, probably because they were empty. He climbed over the tailgate of one, made himself as comfortable as possible on the floor, and waited.

Janet and Harry Jago were sitting in a corner of the bar of the Station Hotel when Murdoch came in. He wore seaboots and his reefer coat, a yellow oilskin over one arm, a splendidly archaic figure that made heads turn as he moved past.

"Can I get you a Scotch, Mr. Macleod?" Jago asked, standing up.

"Murdoch, lad, Murdoch to my friends," the old man said. "And yes, a wee dram would go down just fine, you being the one with the influence to get it."

Jago moved over to the bar and Murdoch took out his pipe. "Do you mind, girl?"

"Not at all," she said. "Now tell me about the island. How's my uncle?"

Murdoch filled the pipe methodically from his oilskin pouch. Instead of answering her question, he said, "Where would young Lachlan be?"

"In my room. I thought the bed might as well get some use, and he looked as if he needed the sleep."

Jago returned with Murdoch's Scotch. The old man raised the glass and examined the contents in the light with a connoisseur's appreciation. "How in the devil do you manage it, Lieutenant?"

"Oh, I let them have a couple of bottles now and then, so they always keep one under the bar for me."

"How is Uncle Carey? You still haven't told me," Janet demanded.

He said carefully, "Have they work for him yet? Have you news?"

"Yes, I think you could say that."

He nodded. "His only problem."

"Mind you, it's not what he's hoping for. No more boarding parties, sword in hand, if you know what I mean."

"I was afraid of that." Murdoch sighed. "He has —how can I explain it to you—a hunger for action. It is, I think, meat and drink to him. A great pity he cannot bide still for a while, and a good woman to hold his hand."

"Jean?"

"That is the impression I get."

"And the best thing for him." Janet was pleased. "I'll have to see what I can do."

"Look to your own affairs, girl," he told her gently. "Some things grow better on their own."

Jago was vastly amused to see her slapped down. She kicked him under the table. "When do you plan to leave?"

"Oh, about two o'clock in the morning if that will

suit. The tide will be flowing well by then. I'll leave you now if you don't mind. I'm promised to supper with my sister." He produced an old tin watch from some inner pocket and consulted it gravely. "I should have been there ten minutes ago. She'll have the skin off me. Terrible sharp since her husband died last year."

"Is it far?" Jago stood up. "I could get the jeep."

"The top end of the main street. A step only. I'll see you here at one-thirty."

He moved away through the crowded bar, and Jago sat down. "There goes one hell of an old man. Pity you had to be so openhanded with young Lachlan. There's a perfectly good bed going to waste up there."

"Good deeds is my second name."

He leaned across, offering her a cigarette. "As it happens, being a young man of some resource, I have a special arrangement with the landlord."

"Somehow I thought you might."

"You know how it is. Home is the sailor and all that. Somewhere to lay his weary head. There *is* only one difficulty. It's a single bed."

"And two into one won't go?"

"I was always lousy at mathematics."

"Me too."

They got up and moved out of the bar into the hall. Rain rattled against the door in a sudden flurry of wind and she paused, one hand on the banister. "A hell of a night to be out."

"Not fit for man, beast, or an old stray tomcat," he told her cheerfully. "As my old granny used to say."

"I was thinking of Gericke," she said and started upstairs.

Gericke actually dropped off to sleep, waking in something of a panic to find that a good two hours had passed. Not that it mattered, for it was one o'clock before the sailors on the pier finished unloading. The lights were extinguished, the trucks driven away.

It was very quiet now. A dog barked hollowly somewhere in the distance. He waited for another quarter of an hour just to make sure that no one was coming back, then moved out from the shelter of the trucks and went cautiously down to the pier.

He kept to the shadows, pausing to remove his seaboots and stuff his white cap inside his raincoat. There was a murmur of voices as the two men on watch in the gunboat chatted, the glow of a cigarette inside the wheelhouse. He moved on, soundless in stockinged feet, past the coaster and the fishing boats.

The launch was tied up at the bottom of a flight of stone steps. He stepped over the rail, put his seaboots down gently, and descended the companionway, the Mauser in one hand.

There was a decently sized saloon, a cabin aft with two bunks, both unoccupied, and a small toilet. The galley was forward. Nothing could have been more satisfactory. He found a towel, dried his feet, then went back up the companionway and pulled on his seaboots.

Next, he made a cautious exploration of the wheelhouse. This was no fisherman's boat, so much was certain. A rich man's craft. Penta petrol engine, twin screws, depth sounder, automatic steering. Such boats commonly had a range of seven or eight hundred miles, perhaps more. It all depended on what was in the tanks.

He found the correct dial that seemed to indicate that they were full or nearly so. What he needed now was an oar so that he might sweep her out of the harbor before switching on the engine. He moved out on deck cautiously and pulled back into the wheelhouse at the sound of voices, footsteps approaching along the pier.

He stayed in the shadows, waiting for them to stop, perhaps at one of the fishing boats, already aware with a strange kind of fatalism that they would keep right on coming.

Someone laughed clear on the damp air, harsh, distinctive, and familiar. Gericke smiled incredulously as Janet Munro said, "Don't you ever take anything seriously, Harry?"

"Not if I can help it," Jago told her. "You know, I've had a great idea, Murdoch. Why don't you choose the deepest spot you can find between here and Fhada and put her over the side with about eighty pounds of old chain around her ankles? I'd say the world would be a whole lot more comfortable for all of us."

"Bastard," she replied.

"Mind your manners, girl," Murdoch said in reproof, "for if you do not act in a more seemly fashion, I might take the lieutenant here up on his suggestion."

Gericke, smiling again, was already out of sight and halfway down the companionway.

Barkentine Deutschland, *23 September 1944.*
Lat. 53°59′N, long. 16°39′W. Wind NW
6–7. Rain and intermittent squalls. During
the midwatch, Mister Sturmm requested per-
mission to shorten sail as we were taking so
much water inboard that life was becoming
very uncomfortable for the passengers. I re-
fused his request, anxious to make as much
time as possible now.

Ten

Jago switched on the light in the saloon. The blackout curtains were neatly drawn, and he turned as
Janet followed him down. "This is nice. Where do
you want these, by the way?"

"The aft cabin," she said.

He kicked open the door and dropped the suit-
cases and medical bag on one of the bunks. As he
went back into the saloon, Lachlan came down the
companionway, his rifle slung over one shoulder, a kit
bag under his arm.

The boy made a face. "So help me, Doctor, but
I feel sick already."

He dropped his kit bag on the floor and Janet took

the rifle from him and pushed it out of sight under one of the divan seats. "I hate those things. Never mind, Lachlan, I've got some pills in my bag. I'll give you a couple and you can get your head down and sleep all the way across."

The boy went into the galley and she turned to Jago. "He's always been like that, ever since he was a kid. Believe it or not, but his father was captain of a local fishing boat out of Fhada."

"Was?"

"Apparently he was killed in action recently serving as a petty officer under Murdoch's son."

"I know," Jago said. "About what happened, I mean. Not about Lachlan's father, though. They were torpedoed in the North Sea. I had the unpleasant task of bringing the bad news. As I told you before, I'm just a bloody postman."

She was suddenly angry, irritated at the recurrence of the same old theme. "For God's sake, grow up, Harry. Stop feeling sorry for yourself." She grabbed hold of his sweater. "You try turning up at Fhada in that mood and I'll throw you straight back into the sea."

"Yes, ma'am."

He tried to kiss her, but she slipped from his arms and made for the companionway. "I want to get out of here."

They found Murdoch in the wheelhouse with Jansen. "I've been trying to suggest to Mr. Macleod," the chief petty officer said, "that maybe it would be a good idea to wait for a little more light."

"And what was his reaction?"

"As I have been sailing these waters, man and boy, for at least seventy years now, I told him to mind his own business and go to hell," Murdoch said. "A terrible sentiment for a man of my persuasion, but there it is."

"Admirably put," Jago observed.

Murdoch took out his pipe. "A couple of plates of

good Scots porridge in you and you'll be ready for that dawn start to Stornoway."

"Porridge?" Jansen asked. " 'A grain which in England is generally given to the horses, but in Scotland supports the people.' It was Dr. Samuel Johnson who said that first, by the way. Not me. As a matter of interest, he actually traveled in these parts."

"Lieutenant Jago," Murdoch said grimly, "will you get him off now or do I pitch him head first over the side?"

"No offense, sir." Jansen backed out hurriedly and stepped over the rail.

"I'm sorry," Jago said. "He isn't really responsible. Something gave him when he was very young."

"On your way, Harry." Janet gave him a push.

Jago joined Jansen at the bottom of the steps and they cast off the lines. Janet hauled them in, then stood watching them, hands on hips. Jago blew her a kiss. She waved and went into the wheelhouse.

She stood at Murdoch's elbow peering out into the darkness. "What's the forecast?"

"Three to four winds with rain squalls. A light fog generally in the Sea of the Hebrides just before dawn."

"How disappointing."

"Oh, so it's excitement you're seeking? You must wait a day or two."

"Why do you say that?"

"Heavy weather coming."

"Something really bad, you mean?" Janet frowned, for she knew that it was not uncommon for Fhada to be cut off from the mainland for weeks at a time. But that was usually in the winter. "How do you know?"

"It is to be found in the wind's breath, the touch of the rain. The smell of things." He smiled. "Or in the sum total of a lifetime at sea, perhaps."

She stuffed her arm through his. "I know—you're just an old Highland mystic. Can I take the wheel?"

"Later. Go you and see to the boy. You know how this trip distresses him."

She left him and went downstairs. Lachlan was seated at the table and already looked ghastly. She went into the aft cabin, opened it, and found the pills she'd promised.

"Take these with a glass of water, then get on one of the bunks. I'll bring you a cup of tea."

She went out to the galley. Lachlan stood there by the bunk for a moment then, stomach heaving, reached for the handle of the toilet door. When he pushed it open, Gericke was sitting there, the Mauser in his right hand.

Janet leaned against the bulkhead in the galley and smoked a cigarette, arms folded, as she waited for the kettle to boil. She was aware of the creak as the door swung open, turned casually, and saw Lachlan standing there, hands clasped behind his neck.

Gericke peered over the boy's shoulder, smiling. "Ah, there you are, Doctor."

Her heart pounded, and so great was the shock that she had difficulty in speaking at all.

"You," she whispered.

"I'm afraid so." He stepped back, motioning with the Mauser. "Now you will please be so good as to come out here and tie this young gentleman's hands behind him."

He threw her a coil of thin rope that he had found behind the cabin door. Janet folded her arms quite deliberately and it landed at her feet.

"You won't shoot me. You couldn't on the train —you won't now."

He smiled calmly. "You're quite right. But the boy here—now he is something different. A paratrooper as well, so it may be argued that I am helping the war effort. The left kneecap first, I think."

She picked up the coil of rope hurriedly. Lachlan looked sicker than ever. "Sorry, Doctor, but he was in the lavatory when I opened the door, sitting there bold as brass. Would he be the U-boat captain they were on about in Mallaig?"

"At your service," Gericke said. "Now lie down like a good boy and all will be well."

Lachlan lay on one of the divans and Janet lashed his wrists, Gericke observing her closely.

"Satisfied?" she demanded.

"Not bad. Now the ankles."

She did as she was told, and when she was finished he said, "And now we will go to see your friend upstairs, Mr. Murdoch Macleod. Have I got the name right?"

She had recovered enough from her initial astonishment to be able to assess the situation more coolly and became aware, with a kind of clinical detachment, that she was not afraid of Gericke in the slightest. Which was interesting. On the other hand he was very obviously a man who would kill, if he had to, without a second's hesitation.

He smiled down at her. "Of what are you thinking?"

The feeling of intimacy was really quite disturbing, but she forced herself to stay calm. "Murdoch's an old man. One of the finest men I know. I don't want him hurt."

It was delivered almost as a command. Gericke inclined his head. "Very well, Doctor, let's see if we can deal with this in a civilized manner, then."

She led the way up the companionway and opened the wheelhouse door. Murdoch stood there, his head disembodied in the light of the binnacle.

Gericke leaned in the doorway and thumbed the hammer on the Mauser very deliberately. "You will please do exactly as you are told, Mr. Macleod."

Murdoch looked him over calmly. "And who might you be, laddie?"

"He's Gericke, the U-boat commander who escaped from the train," Janet informed him.

"I see," Murdoch said. "It's the boat you're after, is that it? And where exactly do you intend to take her?"

"Norway, by way of the Orkneys."

"A possibility. But only just. You'd need to know what you were doing. A lot different from those sardine cans you're used to."

"I have a master's certificate in sail," Gericke told him. "Is that good enough?"

Murdoch nodded gravely. "Like that gun of yours —difficult to argue with. And what about us?"

"I'll drop you off on the way. Somewhere nice and remote on the coast of one of the larger islands. Lewis, perhaps. And now, as I am perfectly capable of reading a chart, you will oblige me by putting her on automatic pilot and coming below."

"You feel you are familiar enough with these waters?"

"I do."

"Then who am I to argue?"

He locked the automatic steering device in position and moved out, Janet leading the way. They descended to the saloon where he lay on the opposite divan from Lachlan and allowed her to lash his wrists and feet.

When she was finished, she said, "Now it's my turn I suppose."

"Good heavens, no. I shouldn't dream of such a thing," Gericke said. "You, my dear Doctor, are far too useful. First, you will make a flask of hot tea and some sandwiches, then we will continue in the wheelhouse."

"Continue what?" she demanded suspiciously.

"Why, where we left off in the train if you like." He smiled. "The galley, by the way, is right behind you."

It was very peaceful in the wheelhouse. Janet swung from side to side in the chart-table chair and watched Gericke at the wheel.

"You like that, don't you?" she said.

"A deck under the feet, a wheel kicking in the hands?" He smiled. "The finest feeling in the world. Well, almost."

"Aren't you ever serious?"

"Not possible. I realized rather early in life what a bloody unpleasant business it all was. No man of intelligence could possibly take it seriously. We had a hard time when I was a boy, you see. My father was killed on the western front."

"Was he a soldier?"

"No, a fighter pilot. One of the first. He lasted three years. A long time, but not long enough."

"And your mother?"

"Died in the influenza epidemic of 1918. I went to live with her brother, my uncle Lothar, in Hamburg. Poor as a church mouse, but one of the kindest men I've ever known. He was a teacher of mathematics. Had a house at Blankanese on the Elbe from which you could see every ship that entered or left Hamburg. I used to sit in my room at night for hours with the window open watching the lights on cargo boats slipping out to sea. Going somewhere romantic—always that. And I wanted to sail with them."

"The beginning of a love affair?"

He carried on, "And if it was too foggy to see them there were always the foghorns growling out there somewhere at the edge of things."

He took one of her cigarettes from the packet on the chart table. Janet said, "When I was a girl I used to spend summers at my uncle's place on Cape Cod. Lots of fog there. Sometimes at night you could hear the fishing boats calling to each other far out to sea."

Gericke nodded. "A lonely sound for a lonely place."

She swung around on the swivel seat to face him. "You know it?"

"I sank eleven ships off that coast between mid-March and late April of '42." There was a slight ironic smile on his mouth. "The Happy Time all over again. For five consecutive minutes the thought actually crossed my mind that we might win the war."

"American ships?"

"All except one. A Spanish tanker that got in the way of the action, so to speak."

"I see," she said. "So even a neutral wasn't safe from your attentions?"

He smiled sardonically. "Sea wolves. Isn't that what they call us?"

"And you're proud of that?" She reached for the thermos, mainly to give her hands something to do, and poured tea into the plastic cup. "Now let me tell you something. Lieutenant Jago let me read the report on you back there on the train."

"Strictly against regulations that, I should imagine."

"That Spanish boat was an oil tanker, the *San Cristobál* out of Bilbao. There was a big fuss in the newspapers at the time because she was a neutral, then it turned out that she'd been chartered by the American War Department. You knew that when you sank her."

"Naturally." He peered down at the compass and altered course a point to starboard.

"Then why try to make me think something different?"

He smiled good-humoredly. "But I thought that was what you wanted to believe. The brutal Hun about his evil work. Machine-gunning the lifeboats, after making sure there weren't any women available among the survivors, of course."

"Damn you, Gericke!"

"Taken care of long since."

She lit another cigarette and sat leaning her elbows on the chart table, frowning and staring into the dark glass. "You love ships, yet you destroy them."

"I'm perverse by nature. You should try me some time."

"No, thanks—and still not good enough."

"What would you prefer—some neat psychological explanation on the lines that each man kills the thing he loves? Come now, Doctor. Even the great Freud once said that sometimes a cigar is only a cigar."

"They certainly didn't teach us *that* in medical school."

"Just put it down to the bloody war, then."

There was a savage tone in his voice that had not been present before. For a moment she stood on the edge of something, peered into a dark and private place and drew back.

He checked the course again and stared grimly in the dark, his face set, that slight, perpetual smile missing for the first time.

"Your English," she said lamely, "is really very good."

"We lived in Hull for a while. That's a port on the east coast of England."

"I know."

"My uncle taught mathematics there for two years." He smiled. "People tell me I have a Yorkshire accent. When we returned home, I tried a year at university. Philosophy and mathematics because Uncle Lothar wanted it. It didn't work out so he allowed me to enroll in the school for naval petty officers at Finkenwärder in Hamburg. After that I went to sea as an apprentice on a square-rigger."

"A hard school."

"As friend Carver discovered earlier today. I sailed in clippers for a while. The Chilean nitrate trade, grain from Australia by way of the Horn. Then I served as third officer on a cargo boat to complete my navigational training. I was all of twenty-two when I took my master's tickets in both sail and steam."

"And then?"

"Nobody wanted me. I tramped the streets of Hamburg. Visited every shipowner there was, but nothing doing. Times were hard; the Depression was at its height. We all used to meet at a bar in the David-strasse called the Star of David. The man who ran it had served as a bosun under sail and gave credit. I finally shipped as first mate on a clipper doing the big circle. Chile, the States, then across to Australia, and home again. When I got back, everything was changed."

"When was that?"

"It was 1933 and the *Kriegsmarine* was offering equivalent rank to officers of the merchant service. I couldn't get to Stralsund fast enough to sign on."

"To learn how to sink ships?"

"It's a living."

There was silence between them for a while. The wind had shifted and the sea was rising, the *Katrina* rocking in the turbulence. Janet said carefully, "And women? A family? No mention of them. Haven't they ever had a place in your scheme of things?"

"Not really. Women, yes, in the most basic way. But shore leave, as I have always found, seldom lasts long enough for more permanent arrangements to grow."

"Strictly ships that pass in the night?"

"An apt analogy." He shrugged. "And then the important things in life have one hell of a way of happening at exactly the wrong time. At least as regards being able to do anything about it. Don't you find that?"

He turned to face her. She was aware of a cold excitement, a need to breathe deeply—then a sudden violent squall struck *Katrina,* swinging the boat to port. Janet fell from her seat.

Gericke wrestled with the wheel and brought her head around. "Are you all right?"

She scrambled to her feet, white and shaken. "Yes, but I'd better get below and check on the others." She hesitated, peering out into the dark. "You think it will get worse?"

"I should imagine so. I'll put on the automatic steering device and come down myself."

"Is it safe to have only that thing in control in this kind of weather?"

"A whole lot safer than allowing you to go below on your own."

She slipped through the door and was gone. He cursed, locking the steering, and went after her, already too late, for when he entered the saloon, she had Lachlan's Lee Enfield in her hands. She thumbed off the safety catch, worked the bolt, ramming a cartridge into the breech, and backed off.

"Loaded, I presume?" he inquired.

"You can take my word for it," Lachlan said, struggling to sit up.

Gericke produced his Mauser and cocked it. "Stalemate, I think."

"Don't make me shoot you, darling," she said harshly. "I will if I have to and I could hardly miss at this range."

There was determination on her face, but a kind of panic also, as if she knew that whatever happened, he would not pull the trigger. Suddenly, there was a desperate appeal in her eyes.

Gericke smiled very gently and placed the Mauser on the table. "Ah, well," he said. "It was fun while it lasted," and he clasped both hands behind his neck.

Richter, flat on his face because of the confined space, was examining the bilges with the aid of a storm lantern. The pumps had been working constantly for two hours, but it was still a foot deep in there. Every so often, as the *Deutschland* plunged over a particularly large wave, filthy, rancid water washed over his head.

He finished his inspection and came up through the hatch in the aft hold, passing his lantern to Sturmm. "God, but you stink," the young lieutenant observed.

"I know," Richter said in disgust. "It's like crawling along a very old sewer down there."

"How does it look?"

"It could be worse."

"Good." Sturmm was relieved. "Better let the old man know straight away."

When they went out on deck, there was a terrific beam sea running and Berger, in oilskin coat and sou'wester, leaned on the quarterdeck rail.

"Just in time, Mister Sturmm," he called. "Clew up the topsails and fore lower t'gallant and make them fast, quick as you like."

"Aye, aye, sir."

"And get the foresail off her."

Berger went down to his cabin and the crew tumbled into action as Sturmm relayed the orders, Richter springing into the ratlines and leading the way aloft, no place for the faint-hearted in such weather. But on deck, conditions were just as hazardous. The men at the clew lines were up to their necks in water, hanging on for dear life every time another sea washed over them.

Richter, on his way down to the deck again, saw Lotte emerge from the galley. She carried a bucket in each hand and was wearing an old oilskin coat and sou'wester. At the same moment, he noticed a huge sea coming aboard.

He cried a warning, jumped for the nearest line, and slid down to the deck very fast. There was a tremendous crash as the sea poured aft. Richter caught a brief glimpse of Lotte washing along with it, then he dropped into the welter of foam and went after her.

The *Deutschland* pointed into the slate-gray sky, riding high over the next wave. Richter hauled the girl to her feet and discovered that she was still clutching the two buckets, both quite empty now. And she was laughing.

"Little fool," he cried. "How often do I have to tell you?"

"I don't think I'll ever be dry again," she answered.

He put a hand under her elbow and helped her along the deck to the galley. When he opened the door, there were a couple of feet of water inside, pots and pans swilling around, and Sister Angela on her hands and knees.

From the look on her face, that inexhaustible patience had finally run out. Richter retreated, leaving Lotte to handle the situation.

Berger toweled his head dry, then sat down at his desk, selected a cheroot, and lit it. The last box and only a dozen left. He inhaled the fragrance of Brazil with conscious pleasure, reached for his pen, and started the daily entry in his private journal.

> *We are, by my estimation, perhaps a hundred miles due west of Galway Bay in Ireland and making excellent time, mainly because I have maintained a policy of carrying as much canvas as possible in rough weather. An unfortunate consequence of this is the fact that we take water inboard in large quantities, and this makes things difficult for both crew and passengers. The fanlight has smashed again, water cascading into the saloon without pause, making life wet and uncomfortable for the nuns who pray constantly during such weather, although whether their plea is for the Good Lord to take them up to heaven or save them for it, I have never been able to determine. . . .*

There was a knock at the door and Richter entered. Berger put down his pen. "How was it down there, Helmut?"

"Smelly, but sound, Herr Kapitän. We worked the pumps for two hours before I went in and there were still twelve inches, but when you consider this weather and how much water we've been shipping that seems to me not too bad."

"Good," Berger said. "Very good. I've a feeling

we may hit rough weather all the way now and it's a comfort to know things are still no worse than they were below the waterline."

He reached for his pen and had already started to write in his journal again as Richter went out.

It was just after eight-thirty as the *Katrina* moved in toward Fhada. Geriche, seated in the swivel chair at the chart table, hands tied behind his back, looked out with interest at the gray-green hump crouching there in the rain, cliffs splashed with lime, seabirds wheeling in great clouds, cormorants, razorbills, gulls of every description.

"So this is Fhada?"

Murdoch, at the wheel, nodded. "They say the name is derived from an old Gaelic word *Fuideidh,* meaning an island that lies apart from other islands."

"Interesting." Gericke filled his lungs. "I like islands. They have a special quality. In April 1941 I did a patrol in the Aegean and came down with some kind of fever. I convalesced on the island of Corfu. A marvelous place. It was April. The most beautiful wildflowers I've ever seen in my life and the butterflies . . ."

"Whatever else it is, Fhada isn't like that, darling." Janet came in through the door carrying a mug of tea. "I thought you might like to have yours below," she said to Murdoch. "Put her on automatic pilot and I'll keep my eye on things while I feed the pride of the *Kriegsmarine.*"

Murdoch hesitated, then locked the steering device in position. "Ten minutes, that's all you get," he said and went out.

"It would seem he assumed you wanted to be alone with me," Gericke observed. "How romantic."

"Nothing could be further from the truth," she said. "I just wanted him to sit down for ten minutes and have a hot drink. He's an old man, or hadn't you noticed?"

"The doctor in you coming out. Does this happen often?"

"Not on Fhada, believe me. They're a healthy lot here."

She unlocked the automatic pilot and took the wheel herself. "You love the place, I think," he said.

"It has a strange attraction for me. It's as if the outside world has ceased to exist, which it very frequently does. On Fhada, they boast winds four-to-seven for two-thirds of the time as early as April. From September on, anything goes. They tell a story of a constable sent from the mainland to escort a local man to serve a six-week sentence at Stirling prison."

"What happened?"

"The weather was so bad that by the time it was fit for the boat to leave, the sentence was finished."

"So—I may be in for a long stay?"

"They also boast the worst hazard to shipping on the entire west coast. The Washington Reef. That's why they stationed the first lifeboat here back in 1882. Murdoch's the present coxswain."

"Isn't he a little old for such work?"

"He handed over to his son in '38. Came back into harness when Donald was called up by the navy. Uncle Carey says he's a genius. One of the greatest coxswains in the history of the Lifeboat Institution."

"I see. And how do people live here?"

"A little crofting. Sheep. A few cattle. Fishing. The population's very small now. A place of women, children, and old men. All the others are away, mostly serving in merchant ships."

As they drew nearer to the island they met the only four fishing boats still working from Fhada, moving out to sea.

Janet waved. Gericke said, "Old men."

"And boys," she said. "All that will be left soon if this damned war lasts much longer."

They moved into harbor and Gericke noticed a small dark man with a black eye patch in old seaboots and reefer coat standing at the edge of the upper jetty.

Janet placed her hands lightly on his shoulders. "And that," she said, "believe it or not, is my uncle, Rear Admiral Carey Reeve, United States Navy, not quite retired."

Barkentine Deutschland, *23 September 1944.*
Further entry. Sister Angela and Herr Prager
visited me formally to raise the question of
low morale among the crew and passengers
because of the lack of hot food and drink,
owing to the impossibility of keeping a fire
going in the galley under the present weather
conditions. Sister Angela made the point,
which I had to accept, that my own cabin
was the driest in the ship owing to its posi-
tion, and prevailed upon me to allow her to
use it for cooking purposes with the aid of
a portable oil stove. A run of 225 miles this
day.

Eleven

*I*t was very quiet in the small study where Gericke
sat, hands still tied behind his back. Murdoch
leaned in the window seat, filling his pipe.

"This house," Gericke said. "Quite impressive.
Who does it belong to?"

"Mrs. Sinclair. She owns the island. What we call
the laird in these parts. Also bailie—that's magistrate.
And coroner and harbor master."

"Quite a lady, from the sound of it."

"You'll see soon enough. She is responsible for you in a sense. The only law we have here. Her husband was in the same trade as yourself. He went down with the *Prince of Wales* in the Pacific. That would be in 1941."

"I see," Gericke said. "I shouldn't imagine I'll be too popular in that quarter."

"We are not savages, Commander. Put that from your head. During the past fortnight we have buried eight of your comrades, washed up from a U-boat that was sunk in this area on the ninth of the month. I took the services myself and almost every soul on this island attended."

There was a moment's silence. Gericke, for once at something of a loss, said, "I thank you. On their behalf, I thank you, sir."

The door opened and Reeve came in. He was still wearing his reefer coat and there was rain on his face. "I've been in touch with Captain Murray at Mallaig. He insists that under no circumstances should any attempt be made to take you back to the mainland in anything other than an official vessel. Lieutenant Jago is apparently en route for Stornoway now. He'll receive instructions by radio to call in here for you sometime tomorrow."

"Another day's grace before the door closes finally."

Reeve said, "And now Mrs. Sinclair would like to see you."

He nodded to Murdoch who moved out, and Gericke followed, the admiral bringing up the rear. They went along a corridor, passed through a large stone-flagged hall, and paused at a green baize door. Reeve opened it and motioned Gericke through.

It was a pleasant room, two of the walls lined with books from floor to ceiling, French windows giving a view of the garden outside. Janet and Jean stood in front of the log fire.

They turned at once. Gericke came to a halt and inclined his head formally. "Ladies."

"Lieutenant Commander Paul Gericke," Reeve said. "Mrs. Sinclair."

A handsome woman, she was wearing a Shetland sweater, brogues, and a kilt, which he presumed to be in her clan's tartan, and her hair was tied back with a blue velvet bow.

She looked him over calmly and her voice was formal. "I don't know if Admiral Reeve has explained, Commander, but I am bailie here and responsible for you at law."

"That has been made clear to me."

"There is no policeman stationed on the island, but the police station is still here from the old days and I do have to make use of its cells on occasion."

"I understand."

"You will be locked up there until Lieutenant Jago arrives to take you into custody tomorrow. And you will be guarded, naturally."

There was really nothing to say. Janet had moved to the window and was looking outside. Reeve touched Gericke's arm. "Let's go. Murdoch and I will take you down."

Gericke hesitated, glancing toward Janet. She did not turn around. He inclined his head again, turned without saying anything, and went out, followed by Reeve and Murdoch.

The door closed. "Damn you, Paul Gericke," Janet whispered, still staring out into the rain. "I wish I'd never set eyes on you."

The three men went down the cobbled main street, Gericke in the center. The heavy rain kept most people indoors, but here and there a woman stood on a step watching curiously, and two small boys trailed behind until Murdoch chased them away.

The old police station was at the bottom of the street and faced out over the harbor, solidly built of granite like every other dwelling in Mary's Town, with only the bars at the windows to distinguish it.

Reeve tried to open the oaken door that was bound with iron, but it refused to budge. Murdoch hammered with the toe of his boot. "Lachlan, are you asleep in there?"

There was the sound of heavy bolts being withdrawn, and Lachlan MacBrayne peered out. He wasn't wearing his jump jacket, but was otherwise in uniform, the battle-dress blouse open at the neck.

"Time to lock up when we've got him inside," Murdoch said.

There was an old desk in one corner, a chair, and not much else, and a peat fire smoldered in a tiny grate.

Lachlan picked up his rifle, slung it from his shoulder, then took a large bunch of keys down from a nail on the wall. "Will we be putting him straight in, Admiral?"

"The sooner the better," Reeve said.

They went down a flight of steps to a narrow corridor. There were three cells on either side, each closed by a gate of iron bars. Reeve untied Gericke's wrists and pushed him inside. There was an iron bed, three or four army blankets, and a bucket. Lachlan closed the gate and locked it.

"That's it, then." Reeve slipped a packet of cigarettes, a box of matches, and a newspaper through the bars. "Something to read. Three days old, but you'll see you're still losing the war."

Murdoch took a small bottle from his pocket. "It will be cold in there after a while, I'm thinking."

"A surfeit of riches indeed." Gericke clicked his heels. "Gentlemen—my thanks."

Reeve smiled in spite of himself, and they went back to the office and left Gericke alone. He crossed to the barred window, peered out across the harbor, then sat on the edge of the bed, unscrewed the neck of the bottle Murdoch had given him, and sampled the contents. It burned all the way down, exploding in the pit of his stomach.

He gasped for breath. "God Almighty!" he said, and stiffened as he heard steps in the corridor.

Lachlan was on the other side of the gate, the rifle still hanging from his left shoulder. He unslung it awkwardly and stood staring at Gericke, gripping the rifle lightly in his two hands. Gericke got up slowly, muscles tightening. As casually as possible, he took out the cigarettes Reeve had given him and put one in his mouth.

"Do you smoke?" He moved to the bars, holding out the packet.

The boy shook his head, and when he spoke, his voice was hoarse. "You had a round up the spout of that Mauser. I unloaded it myself. I saw it."

"That's right."

"You could have shot her. Why didn't you?"

"Could I?" Gericke said gently. "You think that?"

The boy sighed, relaxing suddenly, and rested the butt of the rifle on the floor. "No, I don't suppose you could." He moved away, then paused. "I'll be making a cup of tea in a little while. Do you want one?"

"I don't think I'd like anything better."

Lachlan said very slowly, "I thought I could shoot you. I had it all worked out, because of my father, but when it came to it, I couldn't do it."

"I know," Gericke said.

The footsteps died away along the corridor. He sat down on the edge of the bed again very carefully and when he struck a match to light his cigarette, his hand was shaking.

The *Dead End* was five miles southwest of Idriggil Point on the Isle of Skye and making heavy weather of it. Peterson had the helm and Jago sat at the chart table checking their course. When the door swung open behind him he turned, expecting coffee, and found instead Jansen, a signal flimsy in one hand and a peculiar glint in his eye.

"I think the lieutenant might find this one particularly interesting."

"A signal?" Jago said. "From Mallaig. Christ, we only left the damned place an hour ago. Read it to me."

"As the lieutenant pleases," Jansen was enjoying himself. "LIEUTENANT COMMANDER GERICKE APPREHENDED AS STOWAWAY ON KATRINA. NOW ON FHADA. REQUEST YOU CALL THERE ON YOUR WAY BACK FROM STORNOWAY TOMORROW AND TAKE INTO CUSTODY."

Jago looked at him incredulously, then snatched the flimsy and read it for himself. "It's not possible."

"I'm afraid it has to be, sir. The good word came direct from Captain Murray himself."

"All right—if you can find a brief moment in that crowded schedule of yours, signal Mallaig 'Message received and understood. Will leave Stornoway at dawn tomorrow, weather permitting, and should arrive Fhada around noon.' Now kindly get the hell out of here."

Jansen withdrew, grinning hugely, and Jago picked up a pencil from the chart table and snapped it between his fingers.

Janet put another log on the fire, pushing it into place with a long brass poker, then sat back and waited. Her uncle stood at the window reading the letter she had brought him.

"He says here that he's spoken to you personally."

"That's right," she said. "In the back of his staff car at Guy's." There was no immediate response, and she was seized with a sudden impatience. "He's offered you a job, Uncle Carey. The supreme commander himself. A chance to get back in the thick of things. Isn't that what you wanted?"

"Deputy director, supply and personnel coordination," he said bitterly, and crumpled the letter in his hand.

"For God's sake, what do you want—blood?"

The door opened and Jean came in with tea things on a silver tray. "Family argument?" she asked cheerfully. "Or can anyone join in?"

"Show her," Janet ordered. "Go on—show her. She's as much right to know as anyone."

Jean put the tray down on a small brass table by the fire. She crossed to Reeve, prised the letter from his grasp, smoothed it out, and read it.

"But that's wonderful, Carey." She kissed him on the cheek. "I'm so pleased for you."

"Good God, woman, you're as bad as she is. A desk job, don't you understand? A glorified clerk, signing papers all day."

Jean pulled him toward the fire and Janet shook her head, "You and Harry Jago. You just can't wait to get back into the glorious fight. Death before dishonor."

Jean said, "You two should be celebrating, not fighting. I've got a marvelous dinner laid on for tonight. Game pie, jugged hare, and there are still four bottles of that special champagne Colin laid down in the cellar."

"I'm sorry, Jean," Janet told her, "and thank you. That sounds wonderful. I'd love to come."

Reeve stood in front of the fire, filling his pipe. "You know, Gericke interests me. It's not often one gets a chance to meet a legend face to face."

"Is he really that special?" Jean asked.

"In naval circles certainly. Probably the most successful submarine commander on either side in the war. That information's not exactly on release for public consumption, mind you. But he's a remarkable man, no doubt about it."

"Whose side are you on, for God's sake?" Janet demanded.

"Oh, don't misunderstand me. Respect of one professional for another, that's all. Mind you, that attack on Falmouth was quite something. I'd love to know just how he pulled it off."

"Then ask him to dinner, why don't you? Make up the four—isn't that the civilized thing to do? You can talk war to your heart's content."

The sarcasm was heavy in her voice, together with a certain anger.

Reeve frowned, a slight fixed smile on his mouth. "That's not a bad idea."

"You've got to be joking."

"But why not?" He turned to Jean. "Would you mind?"

She hesitated. "I'm not sure, Carey. If you'd asked me that yesterday I'd have thought you were mad, but now . . ." She frowned. "The enemy—everything I should hate—and yet I liked him. He's a human being."

"Does he come or doesn't he?" Reeve demanded impatiently. "Your decision. You are the civil power here, after all."

"Are you suggesting he gives his parole for the evening?"

"Nothing so old-fashioned. Young Lachlan in attendance with that rifle of his, of course."

"Why?" Janet asked. "Why are you doing this?"

"Why not? At least I'll hear how the war's going at first hand for a change." There was a glint in his eye, a hint of that wild and unpredictable Carey Reeve she knew and mistrusted. "And anyway—I would have thought it might make for a rather entertaining evening."

Gericke, lying on the bed, was surprised to hear that distinctive laugh from the office. He got to his feet as her step sounded in the corridor.

She stood on the other side of the gate. "I've seen them do this scene so often in the movies that I have the dialogue by heart. Are they treating you all right?"

"No complaints. To what do I owe the pleasure of this visit?"

"An invitation to dinner from Jean Sinclair."

Lachlan appeared behind her looking slightly bewildered. "A joke perhaps?" Gericke suggested.

"Half-seven for eight. As you don't have a black tie, uniform will do. Lachlan will bring you up to the house—and please don't try to do anything silly like starting to run in the wrong direction. He'll shoot you if he has to."

He bowed slightly. "How could I refuse such a charming invitation?"

"I know," she said. "The honor of the *Kriegsmarine* is at stake."

She walked away briskly and the boy stared at Gericke, mouth open. Gericke smiled. "Don't fight it, Lachlan; just go with the tide like me."

He lay down on the bed and pillowed his head on his hands.

Berger's cabin was a scene of confusion. The oil stove stood on the cabinet in a corner and his desk had been cleared to take a selection of pans. Sisters Kathë, Else, and Brigitte were serving food to some of the crew, and not without considerable difficulty. Outside, the wind howled in full gale and the floor tilted beneath their feet as the *Deutschland* rolled through heavy seas.

The captain stood in a corner out of the way, a glass of rum in one hand, the bottle in the other. He was just in from the quarterdeck, chilled to the bone, his oilskin streaming.

Sister Kathë looked across at him. "Something to eat, Herr Kapitän?"

Berger shook his head. "No time, Sister, I've things to do. Any problems?"

"The men come in when they can. Three or four at a time. At least we're managing to keep a stove going in here."

"Meaning hot food?" Berger said. "All the difference in weather like this. I'm very grateful to you ladies. We all are, believe me." He drained his glass. "I'd better get back to it."

He opened the door and went out, struggling to close it again in the high wind. The *Deutschland* fought her way through heavy seas under full sail, water pouring over the bulwarks as she rolled. There were two men on the wheel, and her hatches were buried under a maelstrom that on occasions was waist deep as he made his way to the companionway. He entered with a flood of water, got the doors closed again, and went down.

Water a foot deep swirled about the floor of the saloon. The fanlight had been boarded over and two storm lanterns swung from hooks in the ceiling.

Four of the crew waited their turn for attention at Sister Angela's afternoon clinic. A young electrician's mate named Sporer lay on the table, his left sleeve rolled up, exposing a ring of very bad sea boils on his wrist.

Sister Angela stood on one side of him, the hem of her skirt tucked into her belt. Lotte faced her, holding a tray containing instruments and a small basin. Richter stood at the head of the table.

"What's all this?" Berger demanded.

"The infection is now so bad that his arm is almost paralyzed." Sister Angela reached for a scalpel. "Hang on, Karl, like a brave boy. I'll be as quick as I can."

Sporer, only eighteen, was frightened to death, his face damp with sweat. She nodded to Richter, who placed his hands on the boy's shoulders. The *Deutschland* staggered in a sudden squall, a minor wave flowing from one side of the cabin to the other.

One of the crew lost his balance and ended on his hands and knees in the water, but Sister Angela, bracing herself against the table, leaned down and went to work.

The scalpel lanced into the boils one after another, and there was an immediate stench of corruption as pus spurted. The boy cried out, bucking, in spite of Richter's weight on him—and then he fainted.

She worked on at an incredible speed, no need to be gentle now, Lotte handing her one instrument after another without a word. As she started to bandage the suppurating sores, Berger said, "Are many of the crew suffering with those things now?"

"About half," she said.

Berger turned and found Richter watching him. "A long voyage, Herr Kapitän."

Berger nodded wearily. "So it would appear."

It was just before seven-thirty and dusk when Gericke and Lachlan turned in through the wide gate of Fhada House and moved along the gravel drive. They went up the steps and the German tugged at the chain of the old-fashioned bell-pull.

Steps approached, and the door was opened by a pleasant-looking woman of sixty or so, gray hair pinned back in a bun. She was wearing a black bombazine dress and a starched white apron.

She smiled, showing no surprise at all. "Won't you come in, sir?"

"Thank you." Gericke stepped into the hall, Lachlan behind, the Lee Enfield ready in both hands.

"Let me take your coat, sir." She vanished into a small cloakroom and was back in a moment. "The others are in the drawing room. If you'll come this way." She paused, a hand on the door. "Who is it again, sir?"

Gericke, convinced more than ever that he was engaged in some privileged nightmare, said, "Lieutenant Commander Paul Gericke. I'm expected," he added gravely.

"Oh, yes, sir." She opened the door and led the way in. "Lieutenant Commander Gericke, madame."

"Thank you, Mary."

Jean Sinclair, Reeve, and Janet were by the fire

drinking sherry, Rory sprawled across the carpet. Jean held out her hand. "I'm so glad you could come, Commander." She turned to Reeve. "Do get Commander Gericke a drink, Carey."

Lachlan took up position beside the door. She said, "Good evening, Lachlan. How is your mother?"

"She is well, Mrs. Sinclair."

"You will tell her I was asking after her."

Gericke found himself a moment later in front of the fire, slightly bewildered, a glass of excellent sherry in one hand, a cigarette in the other.

"I hope they've made you as comfortable as possible down there," Jean said.

But it was a remark not to be taken seriously, for there was a glint in her eye, laughter hardly contained.

"I should describe the facilities at your police station as adequate rather than comfortable," he replied smoothly.

Reeve burst out laughing. "I like that." He took Gericke by the arm. "Let's leave these two to cackle on and come over here and tell me about Falmouth."

He and Gericke moved over to the window and stood, heads together. Jean said, "He's a handsome man, isn't he?"

"Which one?" Janet said.

The older woman smiled. "Point taken, but you know what I mean."

Janet nodded. "He's like no other man I've ever known. There is a quality to him I can't define. I've always been too busy for men, Jean. For any deep relationships, I mean. Medical school, then the war. Work and sleep mostly, with the occasional affair when I felt the need."

"And Gericke?"

"I'm just a little bit afraid of him."

"I know what you mean."

"It's there in the eyes mostly," Janet said.

"Or not there, haven't you noticed that? Nothing shows, for he gives nothing away. He seems a man remote from life, that constant wry smile of his a sign perhaps that he thinks it all a rather black little joke. A brilliant officer, a seaman of genius—his record, those decorations prove that. And like all such men, totally unpredictable. No rule that was ever made was made for him."

A gong sounded outside and Mary appeared in the doorway. "Dinner is served, madame."

Jean stood up. "Shall we go in, gentlemen?"

She moved out with Reeve. Janet and Gericke followed, Lachlan bringing up the rear.

The meal, served in a dining room of baronial proportions, was everything Jean had promised. There was a minstrel gallery at one end, the most enormous fireplace Gericke had ever seen, three great logs burning brightly on the open hearth. Above it hung two tattered battle flags.

There were mounted animal heads on the stone walls. Everything from leopard to Thompson's gazelle, taking in most things in between. A magnificent suit of medieval armor, halberds, targes, and crossed claymores, muskets of every description.

"Extraordinary," he said. "You have a very remarkable place here, Mrs. Sinclair."

"We know," Janet said. "Stage six at MGM. All we need is Errol Flynn in a kilt, swinging down from that gallery, claymore in hand."

Jean Sinclair laughed. "Actually she's not too far from the truth, Commander. This place is really the most awful fraud. Victorian Gothic. An ancestor of mine, one Fergus Sinclair, was responsible."

"The trophies, are they from his time also?" Gericke asked.

"No, those were my grandfather's. Hunted all over the world. He was one of those men who would rather shoot anything than nothing. He used to insist on taking me deer stalking in season when I was quite young. Something of an experience."

"I just bet it was," Janet commented.

"Oh, yes, I learned many things. That you must never hurry. That you must never talk and stay downwind, even at a thousand yards, and always to shoot low if the target is downhill."

"Interesting," Gericke said. "I must remember."

"To weave from side to side when making a run for it?" Reeve said.

He was already opening a third bottle of champagne, fumbling with the cork, supporting his bad arm on the edge of the table. There was a touch of aggression in his voice that had not been there earlier. Janet stopped smiling.

Jean went around the table and reached for the bottle. "Let me, Carey. They can be difficult, those corks."

"I can manage." He tried to jerk the bottle away from her, one-handed, lost his grip, and it smashed on the floor. "Would you look at that," he said bitterly.

"It's all right, Carey." She picked up a napkin and wiped down his uniform where it had been splashed.

"That was a good year," Reeve said slowly. He passed a hand over his eyes for a moment, then turned to Janet and Gericke. "I must apologize. I haven't been quite myself lately."

Jean patted him on the shoulder. "Coffee in the drawing room, I think."

She nodded to Janet, who glanced at Gericke, then pushed back her chair. They returned to the drawing room and Lachlan followed without a word.

"He's not well?" Gericke asked.

Janet took a cigarette from a box and he gave her a light. "You noticed his arm, and there's the eye. He got that little lot on D day going into action when he shouldn't. The story of his life. He's been trying to get back into the fight ever since."

"I know the type well. His last words in this life will probably be: 'Follow me, men.'"

She shook her head. "The only job he's been offered, and that took all the influence in the world, is behind a desk. That's what I've come up to see him about."

"And he didn't like it?"

"He has nothing," she said. "In *his* eyes, he has nothing."

"A beautiful woman is nothing?"

"To some men."

"But not all, I think."

She put a hand to her throat, at a loss for words, then turned quickly, sat down at the grand piano, and lifted the lid.

"But then, how seriously can one take that kind of thing? The war can do strange things to people, make them act in a way they otherwise would not."

"Or with complete honesty for once. A Bechstein, I see? Only the best. I didn't know you could play."

"One of the more useful by-products of an expensive education, but if it's Beethoven you're after, I'm afraid I'm not your woman."

She started to play "A Nightingale Sang in Berkeley Square" and Gericke leaned on the piano, watching her. "You're good."

The wolfhound came over from his place in front of the fire and flopped down beside her. "I'm afraid so. Isn't it a bore? Even Rory agrees."

He burst out laughing, and Reeve and Jean Sinclair came in. The admiral looked considerably more cheerful and crossed to the piano. "That really takes me back. What about 'Moonlight in Vermont'?"

She moved smoothly into the new melody, and Reeve went and sat by the fire with Jean, who was pouring coffee. They had their heads together and were talking softly.

"Doesn't that make you feel the world's a better place?" Janet asked.

"Envious," Gericke whispered. "It makes me feel envious."

She started to play "Lili Marlene." "Is that any better?"

"Not really. Reminds me too much of the way the war is going, the British having taken that over, too. Do you know 'A Foggy Day in London Town'? It was extremely popular with the *Luftwaffe* for a while."

She hesitated, remembering that night of the Embankment with Harry Jago. "No, I'm afraid I never did get around to that one."

Reeve had taken Jean Sinclair's hand. They were totally engrossed in each other. Janet closed the lid and stood up. "I think I'd like a little air. Could I have my wrap, please?"

It was hanging over the back of a chair. Gericke got it at once and draped it around her shoulders. "We're going on the terrace for a while to look at the evening," she called and smiled up at Gericke. "An old Scottish custom. Coming, Lachlan?"

Reeve glanced across. "Oh, sure—fine." He turned back to Jean and took her other hand.

"You see?" Gericke said. "How a good woman can work wonders?"

"In this case, a miracle," Janet said. "Believe me."

She opened the French windows and moved out on the terrace. The sky was very dark and streaked with orange flame on the horizon, so that to the north the islands stood up starkly and the sea was perfectly calm.

They stood on the edge of the terrace, shoulders touching, and Lachlan paused beside the French windows. "It's as if everything is waiting for something," she said.

Gericke nodded. "Once in the West Indies, we surfaced off Martinique at night to charge the batteries. It was just like this. Incredibly quiet."

"That's what I like about it here," she said. "The stillness. At least in the brief interludes when the wind isn't blowing."

"The following day it blew the worst hurricane they'd known in those islands in living memory. We had to go down and stay down. Nature took care of the convoy we were after. Eleven ships out of twenty-six were sunk."

"Did you claim a medal for that, too?"

"Now why didn't I think of that?" he said lightly.

In the pale evening light her face was barely visible. "I'm sorry."

Reeve appeared behind Lachlan. "Hey, you two, the coffee's getting cold."

"We're coming," Janet replied.

Her wrap slipped from her shoulders, falling to the ground. Gericke picked it up and handed it to her. The last flicker of orange on the horizon seemed to flare suddenly—and was extinguished as total darkness fell.

At Trondheim, Necker walked across to the operations building. He was in a thoroughly bad temper. His eyes were sore as if from lack of sleep, though he'd been sitting around for three days now with absolutely nothing to do.

When he went into the intelligence room Colonel Meyer was sitting behind Altrogge's desk. The major leaned over beside him and they were examining a chart of the western approaches together.

Meyer glanced up. "There you are, Horst. A little action for you at last."

"It would be nice to think so," Necker said with a certain amount of sarcasm in his voice. "But as the Herr Oberst is well aware, I've been called out on three separate occasions during the past thirty-six hours, only to have the operation canceled at the last moment."

"Not this time," Meyer said. "It's too important. To put it briefly, you take off at 0200. Your flight plan will take you over Scotland, then south of the Outer Hebrides and west of Ireland to this map reference."

He indicated the spot with a pencil. "According to the *Abwehr*, there should be a large convoy inward bound from Halifax, Nova Scotia, in that area about now. It's essential they have the information regarding its position in Kiel before noon tomorrow."

"Or we'll lose the war, I suppose."

"Very funny," Meyer said coldly and got to his feet. "You're a good pilot, Horst, but there are times when you behave with the intelligence of a fourteen-year-old. One of these days, you will make that kind of remark just once too often."

"I'm sorry, Herr Oberst."

"No, you're not," Meyer smiled and clapped him on the shoulder. "Altrogge will fill you in on the wearisome details and I'll expect a personal report the moment you get back."

He went out and Necker examined the chart. "I'd say it's a nine-hundred-mile flight to that map reference."

"And nine hundred back, which leaves you with six to play with when you get there. Say two hours' flying time in the target area, just to give you a margin for error."

"I don't make them," Necker said. "That's why I'm still here. What about those Spitfire squadrons?"

"Up here near Inverness, but they'll give you no trouble if you stay at thirty-five to thirty-eight thousand, which you can do in comfort with the improvements we've been installing. The outward journey will be in darkness anyway. A milk run."

"If you say so," Necker said acidly and sat down. "All right, let's go into it in detail."

Reeve opened the police station door and he and Gericke walked in, followed by Lachlan. The boy got his keys and led the way down the steps to the passageway. Gericke moved into his cell and Lachlan double-locked it.

"Herr Rear Admiral." Gericke saluted. "My thanks for your part in a delightful evening."

Reeve hesitated. For a moment it seemed that he might speak. Instead, he returned the salute punctiliously and moved away along the passageway to the office, Lachlan following.

The door closed. Gericke stood there for a moment, listening, hands on the bars, then moved to the window. The stonework of the sill was cracked, the cement where the bars fitted into it old and crumbling. He lifted his mattress, removed one of the coil springs from the iron bed, and went to work on that cement with the hooked end.

There were steps in the corridor. He sat down quickly, and Lachlan appeared on the other side of the gate, rifle over his shoulder, a sleeping bag under one arm.

"What's all this?" Gericke demanded.

The boy placed a thermos flask on the floor, unrolled the sleeping bag, stepped into it, and zipped it up around his body. Then he sat down, back against the opposite wall, rifle across his knees.

"Just keeping an eye out for you, Commander. Admiral Reeve thought you might sleep better knowing I was close by."

Gericke smiled. "You know something, Lachlan? I think he may very well have a point there."

He lay down on the bed, pulled the blankets up to his chin, and was asleep almost instantly.

Barkentine Deutschland, *24 September 1944. Lat. 56°N, long. 9°51'W. 110 miles southwest of the Outer Hebrides. Starts calm and strangely still as I cannot remember it in these waters within my experience. Just after midnight a ship crossed our bow, for we heard her engines and saw a light plainly, presumably carelessness on the part of her crew. In the midwatch it began to rain again and the wind freshened considerably. At four bells in the morning watch, it being Sunday, Sister Angela held her usual early-morning service on deck in spite of the inclement weather.*

Twelve

The *Deutschland*, with every stitch of canvas set, was making twelve knots. The sea was beginning to lift into whitecaps under a sky of uniform slate gray.

Rain was driving in from the southwest, yet Sister Angela stood at the rail in front of him and addressed the other nuns on the deck below with the dozen or so crew members who had felt religious enough to turn out.

202

Although a few of the men were Roman Catholic, the rest, when they were anything at all, were Lutherans, and she had opted for a service of such a nature that it would offend no one.

She was just coming to the end of general confession, her voice clear on the damp air.

". . . and grant, O most merciful Father, for His sake; that we may hereafter live a godly, righteous, and sober life, to the glory of thy holy name."

There was a moment of silence as she prayed, eyes closed, hands clasped. She crossed herself and said, "We will now sing a hymn, especially for those at sea and well known to you all. 'Eternal Father, strong to save, whose arm hath bound the restless wave.' "

Lotte and the other nuns took up the words bravely and Richter, standing behind her, joined in, taking the other crew members along with him in a ragged chorus. Sister Angela turned once to glance at Berger and Sturmm, and the captain found himself joining in helplessly.

"O hear us when we cry to Thee for those in peril on the sea."

And then, as the chorus started to peter out, there was a roaring in the heavens and Berger swung around in alarm to see a black plane coming in over the sea from the southeast at no more than 150 feet.

God in heaven, this is it! At last this is it, he thought, and in the same moment grabbed Sister Angela and pulled her down. There was total confusion on the deck below as the crew scattered and Sister Kathë screamed piercingly.

Sturmm, crouching on one knee beside Berger, cried excitedly, "Herr Kapitän—look! It's one of ours!"

Berger caught a glimpse of the Junkers as it passed over, saw the crosses on the wings clearly, the swastika tail plane, and then it banked to port and started to climb.

On the deck below men were running to the rail,

two or three actually climbing the rigging, everyone cheering, and Richter and Lotte stood together, the bosun's arm around the girl's waist as they stared up into the sky.

"Now what, Herr Kapitän?" Sturmm demanded.

Berger, recovering his scattered wits, got to his feet. He leaned over the rail and bawled, "Richter, run that Swedish flag down. You'll find a *Kriegsmarine* ensign in the main locker in my cabin." He turned to Sturmm. "Get on the radio, quick. Let's see if we can make contact."

"Swedish?" Necker demanded. "Are you certain?"

"Definitely, Herr Hauptmann," Rudi assured him. "I saw the flag plainly."

Kranz, the rear gunner, cut in on them. "I can confirm that, Herr Hauptmann."

"A sailing ship," Necker said. "If I hadn't seen it for myself I'd never have believed it. Let's take another look."

He throttled right back, making his pass at no more than 150 this time, aware himself as they approached that the Swedish flag was fluttering down.

"What on earth are they striking their colors for, Herr Hauptmann?" Rudi Hubner asked in bewilderment.

"Search me," Necker said, and then grunted in astonishment as another flag was run up.

As they flashed past, the flag stretched in the wind and Kranz called excitedly, "A *Kriegsmarine* ensign, Herr Hauptmann! I swear it!"

"Don't worry," Necker called. "I saw it, too. But it doesn't make any sense. I'm going around again."

Schmidt, the wireless operator, touched his shoulder. "I'm getting something now, Herr Hauptmann. It must be them. I'll switch over."

A moment later, to his total astonishment, and with a clarity only to be expected at such short range, he heard Johann Sturmm's voice clearly in his headphones saying, "This is the *Deutschland* calling Big Black Eagle. Are you receiving me?"

"Big Black Eagle?" Schmidt said in bewilderment. "What's he talking about?"

"He doesn't want to identify us, you fool, in case anyone else is picking the message up," Necker said. "Here, let me speak to him."

Jean Sinclair was having a last cup of tea before leaving for church when Reeve and Janet arrived.

"This is a pleasant surprise," she said. "I don't usually have much success when I try to persuade him to turn out on a Sunday morning."

"Business, I'm afraid," Janet said. "But I persuaded him to put his uniform on anyway, so grab him if you can."

Jean looked puzzled. Reeve said, "I've had word from Mallaig that Lieutenant Jago's got engine trouble. His deadline for fixing it is the middle of the afternoon, otherwise they'll send someone else to pick up Gericke. Whoever it is, they obviously can't make it before late evening. Possibly even tomorrow morning."

"I see." She glanced at her watch. "The service, I might remind you, starts in fifteen minutes, and unless you want one of Murdoch's public rebukes as we creep in at the back of the congregation, we'd better hurry."

"All right," he said heavily. "I'll come, only I'll have to catch up. I want a word with Mary about butter and eggs. I'm fresh out."

The door closed behind him and Jean turned to Janet. "What about you?"

"I don't think so—not this morning."

"What are you going to do?"

"I'll think of something."

Jean smiled. "I'm sure you will."

Gericke had breakfasted well on porridge and fried bacon and tomatoes supplied, surprisingly enough, by Lachlan's mother. After she had gone, Lachlan resumed his place against the wall.

Gericke said, "Sleep, Lachlan. When do you expect to get some sleep?"

"Och, I need terrible little of that. An awful problem I was to my mother as a wee boy." Lachlan glanced at his watch. "No sweat, Commander. Murdoch takes over from me at eleven o'clock after morning service."

"Ah, yes," Gericke said. "He is some kind of pastor, is he not?"

"That's right—and coxswain of the *Morag Sinclair*."

"The *Morag Sinclair*?"

"The great love of Murdoch's life. She's a forty-one-foot Watson-type motor lifeboat. The station's at South Inlet at the other end of the island, and Murdoch lives there."

Gericke said, "I don't understand. Why not here?"

"Because in really rough weather, the sea builds up so bad across the harbor bar it's impossible to get out. Much easier from South Inlet."

"And this is always so?"

"No—once or twice a year, it's impossible to launch from the inlet."

"And what happens then if there is a call?"

"There's another lifeboat stationed at Barra."

"And you, Lachlan, were you a member of the lifeboat crew before joining the army?"

"Not with my belly," Lachlan said. "But my father was."

He stopped smiling and Gericke, at a loss for words, stood there gripping the bars. The outer door banged and Janet called, "Anyone home?"

She was wearing a sheepskin coat, tweed skirt, knee-length boots, and tam-o'-shanter. "Has he been behaving himself, Lachlan?"

"No choice," Gericke said. "Lachlan sat against the wall looking in on me all night with that rifle across his knees."

She passed a packet of cigarettes and a couple of magazines between the bars. "To help you pass the time."

"Not long now," he said. "Lieutenant Jago will be here at noon to take me away. Is it not so?"

"Engine trouble at Stornoway. Tonight at the earliest—maybe even tomorrow."

He stood there looking at her through the bars as if waiting for something. Suddenly, she felt awkward, half-angry with herself for being there at all.

"I'll have to go now. I've got things to do."

"My thanks," Gericke said gravely, and held up the magazines. "For these—among other things."

She turned and walked out quickly.

In the intelligence room at Trondheim, Necker paced up and down moodily, smoking a cigarette. He still wore flying clothes, his face streaked with dirt and sweat, the marks of his goggles plain.

Altrogge, at his desk, glanced up from the report he was writing. "That won't help, Horst. Why don't you sit down? Have some coffee."

He reached for the pot on the tray at his right hand and Necker shook his head. "No, thanks." And then he exploded. "Why all the delay? I mean, what in the hell goes on?"

"The Gruppenkommandeur is handling it personally, you know that, but with a thing like this, there are bound to be delays in channel. You'll have to be patient." He leaned back and added carefully, "I suspect, my friend, that you may also have to prepare yourself for a rather large rocket."

Necker stopped his pacing. "What are you talking about?"

"You didn't do as you were told, Horst. You didn't follow orders."

Necker gaped at him in astonishment. "Didn't follow orders? For God's sake, Hans, what did you expect me to do?"

The door opened and Meyer entered. He carried several signal flimsies and his face was grave. "I've been on to the *Kriegsmarine* in Kiel and the news has gone right up to Dönitz himself. I've had a signal acknowledging and thanking us for the information."

"Is that all?"

"No, they also sent another signal expressing their extreme displeasure at the lack of information concerning the whereabouts of the Halifax convoy."

"Never mind that," Necker said. "What about the *Deutschland*?"

Meyer sat on the edge of the desk and selected a cigarette carefully. "They know all about her from intelligence sources in the Argentine. Left Brazil some weeks ago with a crew of assorted *Kriegsmarine* types under a Fregattenkapitän Berger. They also have some civilian passengers on board—nuns, I believe."

"How fantastic," Necker said. "To sail a thing like that from one end of the Atlantic to the other right under the noses of the British and American navies. It'll set the country on fire."

"No, it won't, my friend, for the good and sufficient reason that the news will not be released. For such an intelligent man, Horst, you can on occasion be exasperatingly stupid. You kept your radio contact with *Deutschland* to a minimum, didn't you? Improvised a crude code, for example. Why did you do that?"

"In case anyone picked up the transmission and was able to get a fix."

"Exactly. The British navy, Horst, can have had no more than a passing interest in the activities of a broken-down old sailing ship attempting to reach Kiel from Brazil, mainly because no one would have given a snap of the finger for her chances of getting even halfway."

"So?"

"But now the situation changes. Our friends on the other side of the North Sea are as alive to the value of propaganda of the right sort as we are. Let them even suspect that the *Deutschland* is in that area and so close to home and they'll do anything, deploy every ship they have in those waters, to stop her getting through."

There was silence for a moment and it was Altrogge who said, and with considerable sympathy in his voice, "So you see, Horst, no one must know. Any public announcement at this stage would be fatal."

Necker nodded slowly, suddenly very tired, and slumped into a chair. "The *Deutschland,* Horst, must be left to her own devices," Meyer said. "You understand this? We can pray for her, but no more than that."

"Yes, Herr Oberst."

"And you were wrong, Horst. You had no right to break off from your search pattern. You could have stayed in the area another hour and a half at least. You may very well have sighted the Halifax convoy."

Necker nodded wearily and Meyer put a hand on his shoulder. "We all make mistakes, but of this kind you are permitted only one. You understand?"

"Yes, Herr Oberst."

"Good. Now go and get something to eat, then sleep, Horst. Lots of sleep. Sometime during the next twenty-four hours you'll be going out again."

Necker stood up. "The same area?"

"The same." Meyer nodded. "But the Halifax convoy this time, Horst."

Necker went out slowly, boots drubbing. The door swung behind him. There was silence for a moment, then Meyer sighed heavily. "A funny thing, Hans," he said to Altrogge. "And I'll always deny having said it, of course."

"What's that, Herr Oberst?"

"Oh, just that in his place I've a nasty suspicion I'd have done exactly what he did."

In Stornoway, the mist had been swept away by the rising wind, and rain drove in from the sea as Jago went down the ladder from the bridge and moved aft. He dropped to one knee by the open hatch and peered into the cramped engine room.

"How's it going in there?"

Jansen squatted beside Astor and Chaney. "Another hour, sir."

"And are you certain it will work?"

It was Astor who looked up, slightly aggrieved. "Me and Chaney and that Limey warrant officer up at the RAF workshop, we made the new parts ourselves. Solid brass. She'll be as good as new, Lieutenant."

Jansen came up the ladder. "He's right, sir, they've done an excellent job."

"Good," Jago said, hauling himself up on the bridge. "Signal Mallaig we expect to be able to leave in one hour." He glanced at his watch. "Which means we'll only have overstepped Murray's deadline by ten or fifteen minutes. I'll confirm actual departure, naturally."

He pushed open the door, went in, and sat at the chart table. Jansen hesitated and said, "The glass has fallen quite substantially within the past hour, Lieutenant."

"So?"

"And the general forecast, not to put too fine a point on it, sir, stinks."

Jago laughed. "Aren't you the guy who once crossed the Atlantic single-handed?"

"The sea, Lieutenant, has fulfilled a need in me for most of my life," Jansen said gravely. "We enjoy a very special relationship. She has shaken me up a time or two, but I have always come back for more. A game we play."

Jago felt unaccountably chilled. "What in the hell are you talking about?"

"God knows." Jansen seemed embarrassed. "Perhaps I'm getting old." He peered out through the doorway. "These islands are different from anything I've ever known. The sea's different."

"Oh, I get it," Jago said mockingly. "You mean it's been waiting for you up here all your life?"

"Or I've been waiting for it," Jansen said. "Which is something else again. Anyway, I'd better get that signal off, sir."

He went out. Rain dashed against the bridge windows and outside the wind moaned through the steel rigging. Jago, still caught by what Jansen had said, sat there, head slightly turned as if listening for something.

There was a weather report on the desk and he picked it up. Sea areas Rockall, Bailey, Malin, the Hebrides—the picture was uniformly black. A deep depression moving in fast from the Atlantic. Heavy rain, winds four-to-five, increasing to full gale by evening.

He crumpled the flimsy and tossed it into a corner. "Ah, well," he said softly. "I guess it just isn't my day."

On the *Deutschland,* Berger sat at the charts in his cabin, plotting the course for the next few days. He was aware of the pump clanking monotonously outside, and of the rising wind. Otto Prager lay on the bunk reading a book. He sat up and removed his spectacles.

"That damn thing seems to be going on forever."

"You think so?"

There was a knock at the door and Sturmm entered. "You wanted me, Herr Kapitän?"

"How goes it?"

"Two hours yesterday—two and a half today."

"And still not dry?"

"Almost." Sturmm hesitated. "We ship water constantly, Kapitän, which doesn't help. It seems to me, sir, that if we took in sail . . ."

"Not a stitch, Mister Sturmm." Berger slammed a hand on the table. "Not one rag do you touch without my permission. You understand?"

"As you say, sir."

"Now return to your duties and send Richter in here."

Sturmm withdrew and Prager got up and crossed to the desk. "He's changed, that boy. A month ago he would have jumped to attention and clicked his heels if you'd spoken to him like that, but now—"

"He is a man," Berger cut in. "He has the *Deutschland* to thank for that. Nothing will ever be the same again."

"He is right then?"

"Only in part. That we are shipping a great deal of water is true, which doesn't help an already indifferent situation below the waterline. That the main reason for this is my insistence on hanging out all my canvas in rough weather is also true. But bad weather is the best friend we have, for it makes us difficult to find. We can use it, Otto, to make time, which at this stage in the game is what we need to do at all costs." He smoothed the chart with both hands. "I mustn't fail. Not now. Not having come so far."

Prager put a hand on his shoulder. "We owe you a great deal, Eric. All of us."

There was a knock at the door and Richter came in. He wore an oilskin jacket and his hands were covered in Stockholm tar. "Herr Kapitän?"

"Ah, Richter. You've been aloft, I see."

The bosun glanced at his hands. "A block came loose on the top foremast."

"Have you attended to the saloon skylight?"

"We've boarded it up permanently, Herr Kapitän. Dark for the ladies down there now, but better than water flooding through at all hours."

"Good," Berger said. "Now, I'd like your opinion on our general situation."

Richter appeared to hesitate. "You are the master, sir, not I."

"I know, man," Berger said impatiently. "But except for myself, you've had more time at sea under sail than anyone else. You, at least, know what I'm talking about."

Richter shrugged. "As the Herr Kapitän pleases."

Berger half-turned the western approaches chart and tapped it with his finger. "Most blockade runners in the past have attempted the Denmark Strait between Greenland and Iceland, then across to Norway. You agree?"

"One doesn't exactly expect to find traffic up there, Herr Kapitän."

"But not for us, eh? Why?"

"A possibility of spare ice floating around in the Greenland section, and we'd have to spend too much time north of the Arctic Circle."

"I agree. And once past the Hebrides, where should our present route take us? The Orkneys passage?"

"No, sir," Richter said. "In my opinion we'd do better to make our turn somewhere north of the Shetlands, then cut straight across for Bergen."

"Good, Helmut. Very good. It's nice to have one's judgment confirmed." Berger rolled up the chart. "There is just one other thing. Mister Sturmm thinks we're carrying too much canvas. Do you agree with him?"

"Not if the Herr Kapitän wishes to make time," Richter said. "However, I would point out that the glass is falling. In my opinion, we're in for a bad night."

Berger, who had started to smile, frowned in irritation. "All right, I wasn't born yesterday. You think I don't know the glass is falling?"

The bosun went out. Berger unrolled the chart and looked down at it, scowling.

Gericke moved his bed toward the gate to avoid the rain, which was driving in through the broken window every so often when the wind gusted. When he had things arranged to his satisfaction, he went back and peered through the bars.

It was just after seven, night falling fast, and as wild a scene as he had ever seen, ragged waves stretching to the horizon, driving rain, a sky of lead verging to black, yet here and there slashed with orange and gold.

Suddenly, far out to sea beyond the end of the pier, he saw the *Dead End* rise high over a wave, then plunge down again, her prow biting deep.

There was a step in the passageway and he turned to see Janet on the other side. She wore a sou'wester and an oilskin coat that glistened with rain, and she carried a covered basket. She dropped to one knee and pushed the basket through the small flap at the bottom of the gate.

"That should keep you going. What the Scots call a good ham tea."

Gericke picked the basket up and put it on his bunk. "Your friend, Lieutenant Jago. He's making his run into harbor now, and from the looks of that sea, I'd say he must be damn glad to get in."

"Harry?" she said, her face lighting up. "Here?"

She turned and ran out, and Gericke reached for a cigarette as Lachlan came along from the office, a mug of tea in his hand, which he passed through.

"Have you a match, Lachlan?"

"I have, Commander." Lachlan gave him a box between the bars. "You can keep them."

Gericke lit his cigarette and moved to the window. The gunboat was bouncing against the pier now, her crew hanging on to her lines.

He saw Jago come out on the bridge, then Janet,

her yellow oilskins clear against the evening light, running along the pier. Jago waved, came down the ladder, and stepped over the rail. A moment later she was in his arms.

"So that's the way of it?" Gericke whispered. And as the wind gusted, driving rain in through the bars, he turned away.

At Fhada House, the wind howled down the chimney, sending the logs roaring. Jago reached out his hands to the blaze. "That's marvelous, Mrs. Sinclair. I was beginning to think I'd never get warm again. One hell of a trip."

"Another coffee?"

"No, thanks. I've really done very well."

He glanced across at Janet, who played the piano softly. Jean said, "I'm sorry the admiral couldn't come."

"Well, as he said, he prefers to stick close to the radio on a night like this."

"I know," she said. "There could be a call for the lifeboat. I wish they'd get that submarine cable connected. It makes things very difficult for everyone. Carey, you know, is our only link with civilization."

The clock chimed eleven and Jago smiled. "I really think I should be getting back now. Early start in the morning." He turned. "I'm ready when you are, Janet."

"I'm staying the night, darling," Janet said, still continuing to play.

"Oh, I see. Well, I'd better get going then."

She showed no inclination to move. Jean Sinclair took him out into the hall. As she helped him into his reefer, she said, "You did say an early start in the morning, didn't you, Lieutenant?"

"That's right, ma'am."

She shook her head. "I don't think so. Not tomorrow, probably not for two or three days now." She smiled. "I know what I'm talking about. When the wind starts blowing over Fhada like this, anything can happen."

Jago grinned, suddenly much more cheerful. "Can you positively guarantee that?"

"I think so."

As she opened the door, struggling to hold it still against the wind, he kissed her on the right check. "Anyone ever tell you you're an angel?" he said and plunged out into the gale.

When Jean returned to the drawing room, Janet was standing by the fire pulling on her sheepskin. "Has he gone?"

"Obviously."

"Good." Janet moved past her into the hall and Jean followed.

"What are you playing at?"

"To be perfectly honest, I don't know," Janet said, and added, "I've just had a great idea. To hell with men."

"It's a thought." Jean opened the door. "I'd sleep on it if I were you."

"Exactly," Janet said, and she moved out into the driving rain.

"Personally, I think the search for the Halifax convoy to be a waste of time," Hans Altrogge said. "But they still insist you have a look."

It was just before midnight, and the intelligence room was a place of shadows. Necker leaned over the chart and nodded. "I agree. A waste of fuel, the whole exercise."

"Not entirely, Horst." Altrogge opened a briefing file. "There's something building up out there in the Atlantic, something pretty unusual according to our weather station at Cape Bismarck in Greenland."

"How unusual?"

"Deep depression coming in very fast and exceptionally severe storms forecast. Nothing to worry you, of course, not at thirty-five thousand."

"And what if I have to go down?"

"We must hope you won't have to. One thing is

certain: the trip should be worthwhile for the weather statistics you can bring back, if nothing else."

"All right," Necker said. "When do we leave?"

"O-five-hundred." Altrogge glanced at his watch. "Time to get some sleep in. You could manage three or four hours."

"I'll think about it," Necker said and went out.

Barkentine Deutschland, 25 September 1944.
Lat. 56°20'N, long. 9°39'W. A bad night.
Wind force 6–8 increasing. Heavy rain and a
pounding sea. At two bells in the midwatch
I gave orders to furl the fore upper t'gallant
and fore upper topsail. This was accomplished with considerable difficulty. Richter,
Winzer, and Kluth have the wheel at this moment, which I snatch to enter the log. The
barometer continues to fall. I greatly fear
things will get worse before they get better.

Thirteen

On Fhada it was Reeve who first became aware, for certain, that something completely out of the ordinary in the way of weather was building up. High winds always had made him nervous and restless. Unable to sleep, he got out of bed around two in the morning, made a pot of coffee, and sat at the radio for a while to see what he could pick up.

The air seemed alive with voices, crackling through the static. Some were faint and far away, others close at hand, but all had one thing in common: fear. Those who could were already running for shelter.

At one point, a Royal Navy supply ship, south of Iceland, came in urgently to report a wind speed of seventy-five knots increasing, with heavy seas and rain. She was trying to make Reykjavík.

It was almost three o'clock when he tuned in to the first really vital transmission from RAF Coastal Command at Stornoway.

"Suspect polar air depression imminent in sea areas Malin and Hebrides. Be prepared for winds of hurricane force within the next few hours. Expected direction northeast."

Reeve sat thinking about it for a moment, then padded into the kitchen, closing the door quietly behind him. He had often joked that the telephone in the wall was so old that Alexander Graham Bell himself must have installed it, but just now it was a lifeline. He turned the handle vigorously for some considerable time, knowing there would be no one on duty at the post office on the quay. It would be necessary to raise Mrs. MacBrayne from her bed.

There was no response at first. He tried again, and as he did so, the kitchen door opened and Janet entered, her dressing gown over her shoulders. "What's going on?"

He waved her to silence as Mrs. MacBrayne's sleepy voice said, "Hello?"

"Katrina? Reeve here. Can you put me through to Murdoch at South Landing? Sorry to bother you, but it's urgent."

She was instantly alert. "Is the boat called out, Admiral?"

"Not yet, but it could be before too long, the way things are building up."

"Hold on now. I'll put you through directly."

He turned to Janet, "Put the kettle on, sweetheart; we'll have some coffee. We could be in for a long night."

She was still slightly bemused, but went obediently to the stove, opened it, and fed wood into the still-glowing ashes.

Reeve waited impatiently. After a while, Katrina MacBrayne came back on. "I can't get through, Admiral."

"You mean there's no reply?"

"Och, no. The line's dead. Down in this wind, I'm thinking. Is there anything I can do?"

"No, I'll see to it. But I think the crew should be alerted."

"But there is no crew, Admiral. The fishing boats were working the grounds South Uist way this afternoon. They'll run for shelter to Lochboisdale to wait for it to blow over. If they call the boat out tonight, there'll be no one fit to handle her except old men and boys."

"Right, Katrina," Reeve said briskly. "Leave it to me. I'll be in touch."

He replaced the receiver and turned to Janet. "I've got a job for you." He took her by the hand, led her into the living room, and sat her down at the radio. He adjusted the dial quickly and locked it in. "That's the band that most of the local stuff comes through on. You can get dressed if you want, make your coffee, only keep listening. Any messages for me or for Fhada direct, write them down."

"But what about you?" she demanded. "Where are you going?"

"To see Murdoch," he said simply; then he went into his bedroom and started to dress quickly.

Reeve carried a storm lantern, but it only seemed to accentuate the darkness. Rain fell relentlessly, and the wind gusted with such force that it was out of the question to raise the sail on the trolley.

He pumped his way across the spine of the island one-handed, rain cascading from his oilskins. The wind snatched away the storm lantern when he was halfway there and he completed the journey in darkness.

He negotiated the track down to the lifeboat station with the aid of the electric torch he'd slipped into his pocket before leaving in case of emergencies. He could hear Rory barking, and then the cottage door was opened, light flooding out, and Murdoch appeared. The wolfhound bounded through the rain to greet Reeve. His hand fastened in its ruff and they went down to the cottage together.

Murdoch drew him inside. "A bad night to be out, Admiral."

"Worse at sea." Reeve took off his sou'wester and oilskin and crouched at the fire. "I've been trying to get you on the telephone. The line must be down."

"Is the boat called out then?"

"No, not that you could do much if it was. You haven't got a crew, Murdoch. The fishing boats didn't get back in this evening."

"I wouldn't say that," Murdoch told him calmly. "There is Hamish Macdonald, Francis Patterson, James and Dougal Sinclair."

Reeve stared at him. "Hamish Macdonald is seventy if he's a day. The Sinclair brothers must be the oldest twins in the business. I don't know about Patterson. . . ."

"We were born in the same year, Admiral."

"Come off it, Murdoch," Reeve said angrily. "There's a world of difference between you and those old guys and you know it."

"The *Morag* is a fine boat. If she capsizes, she rights herself again. Even if her engine compartments flood, her engines will still keep turning. You know the *Morag,* Admiral. It is not like the old days when young muscle was needed for the oars. Hamish and the others have fished these waters all their lives. They know their business. It is enough."

"Well, I hope to God they don't have to be put to the test."

Murdoch produced a bottle from a cupboard by

the fire and found a couple of glasses. "Here, now, this will put marrow in your bones again."

Reeve gulped, tears springing to his eyes as the *Uisgebeatha* exploded in the pit of his stomach. "Damn you, Murdoch, that not only hits the spot—it takes it right out. Anyway, you need eight to man the boat, so you're still three short. What would you do about that?"

"There is always Lachlan."

"Who spews his guts at the first ripple on the water. You must be joking." A sudden gust of wind slammed solidly against the roof of the house and the building shook. He shivered. "I don't like the sound of that. I caught a storm warning from Coastal Command on the radio before leaving. Winds of hurricane force within the next few hours from the southwest."

Murdoch frowned. "Let us hope they are wrong. If that is the way of it, the devil's own job we'd have in launching."

"You think so?"

"I know it, Admiral."

Reeve reached for his oilskin. "I'd better be getting back. At first light we'll see if we can find where your line's down."

"And if I'm needed before then?" Murdoch took his own yellow oilskin down from behind the door. "Better I come with you now and see what is happening out there in the wide world."

It was a quarter to five when they reached Reeve's cottage, and when they went into the living room, Jean was sitting with Janet at the radio.

"Hello, Carey," she said. "I couldn't sleep in this wind so I thought I'd come along and see how you were making out. I'll get some tea."

She went into the kitchen. Janet said, "Things have been warming up. The Stornoway boat was called out an hour ago to assist a fleet tanker in difficulties off Cape Wrath. Barra, twenty minutes later."

"Where to?"

"Somewhere up in the North Minch."

"Our turn soon, I'm thinking," Murdoch said as Jean returned with cups of tea on a tray. "No, not now, Mrs. Sinclair. I have one or two people to see. I'll be back later."

He went out and Janet said, "Where's he off to?"

"Oh, rousting out Hamish Macdonald, the Sinclair twins, and a few other members of the pensioners' club, just in case they're needed," Reeve told her.

"You must be joking. They're old men."

"You try telling Murdoch that." There were various other notes on the table and he picked one up. "What's this, another weather report?"

"That's right. From the meteorological office."

It was substantially the same as before. SEA AREAS HEBRIDES, BAILEY, MALIN, AN INTENSE DEPRESSION GIVING RISE TO HURRICANE-FORCE WINDS WITH HEAVY RAIN AND SLEET.

A moment later a voice crackled over the radio: "Mallaig calling Sugar One on Fhada. Mallaig calling Sugar One on Fhada."

The reception was poor, crackling with static, other voices crowding in. Reeve took the mike, "Reeve here. Receiving you strength five, Mallaig."

"I have Captain Murray for you, Admiral."

There was only the static for a moment, and then Murray's voice broke in. "Hull, sir, how are things with you?"

"Terrible. What about your side of the pond?"

"Total chaos. Two lighters sunk right here in the damned harbor and a nine-hundred-ton coaster loaded with fuel drums broken loose from her moorings. We've been trying to contact Jago during the past hour: routine check on all naval vessels. No success, I'm afraid. Any suggestions?"

"Last I saw of him he was safely tied up at the pier. I'll take a look and call back."

"Be obliged if you would, Admiral. By the way,

you're in for at least another really bad day. We've reports of winds gusting up to a hundred knots. The weather boys tell me we can expect an almost vertical fall in barometric pressure."

"For those few kind words, I thank you," Reeve told him. "Over and out."

It was bitterly cold in the cell. Gericke had slept little during the night, and at five-thirty he got up and went to the window, pulling a blanket around his shoulders.

It was still dark outside, but occasionally the horizon exploded with electricity, giving a split-second instant picture of the scene in the harbor. There were several small boats adrift down there as far as he could see, two of them upturned.

The noise of the wind was higher now, a grating moan that was a constant irritation. He looked out again, and in another flash of sheet lightning saw a figure in an oilskin, lantern in hand, plowing along the pier toward the gunboat. There was a step in the passageway, and Lachlan peered through the bars, an oil lamp in one hand.

"You must be cold in there, Commander."

"Yes, I think you could say that."

"I've a good fire up there in the office. If you'd give me your hand on it, I'd let you sit by it for a while." The boy grinned. "Not that there's anywhere for you to go—not in this lot."

"Why, thank you, Lachlan," Gericke said without hesitation. "My hand and my word. You are very kind."

The boy unlocked the gate and Gericke followed him up to the office. The peat fire glowed white-hot in the draft. Lachlan handed him a mug of tea as a great gust of wind struck the roof, loosening tiles.

"God help me, but it frightens me, that wind, Commander. Frightens me to death. The same since I was a wee boy. Isn't that a terrible thing to have to confess?"

"That one is afraid?" Gericke smiled and offered him a cigarette. "Have one of these, Lachlan, and join the club."

Mary's Town had never been a good anchorage, and though sheltered from the wind when it was from the southwest, a considerable sea was apt to build up inside the harbor.

The *Dead End* had had a bad night. Twice she had dragged her lines, on the first occasion being hurled back against the pier by a severe gust with considerable force, and she was under regular attack from loose boats in the harbor.

Jago and his crew had been at action stations for much of the night, engaged in a constant battle to save the old gunboat from dashing her brains out against the pier. By five-thirty, he was exhausted.

He was aware of the storm lantern on the pier, but didn't realize it was Reeve coming aboard until the admiral mounted the ladder to the bridge.

"How goes it?"

"We're hanging on, sir, that's about all. I think I'd rather be taking my chances in the open."

"Don't kid yourself. You think this is bad? Wait till it gets worse. Murray's been in touch. He can't raise you."

"I know. Our radio's taken a pounding. I'll be surprised if they can ever put it together again."

"Okay, I'll notify Murray you're still in one piece. If you can spare an hour when it gets lighter, come on up to my cottage. I've an idea I might need you."

"Will do, sir."

Reeve judged his moment to step over the rail and hurried back along the pier.

Berger kicked upon the door of his cabin and lurched inside, followed by a tremendous gust of wind and rain. The oil lamp above his desk was swinging in its gimbals, light and dark chasing each other back and forth in the corners.

Otto Prager, who had been lying on the bunk, sat up in alarm. "What is it, Eric?"

Berger was soaked to the skin in spite of his oilskins. His face was wild. "I lost another man."

He leaned heavily on the desk for a moment, then made his way around to the other side with all the care of a drunken man as the floor heaved. He sagged into his chair.

"I'm sorry," Prager said.

"Aren't we all?"

Berger opened the top drawer, took out the ship's log, and picked up his pen.

> *Five bells in the morning watch and conditions as bad as I have ever known. We have reduced sail to main lower topsail and storm staysail with great difficulty. Conditions aloft were atrocious. At four bells, two enormous waves swept down upon the ship. She rode the first, but while in the trough on the other side, the second wave struck, reaching halfway up the foremast. There were eight men in the rigging at that time by my orders, among them Leading Electricians' Mate Hans Bergman, who was swept away.*

"So far," Berger said bitterly. "Poor lad. All this bloody way—and for what?"

"You need sleep, Eric."

"You're right," Berger said. "Wake me in half an hour."

He laid his head on his hands and closed his eyes. Prager sat watching him, the light from the wildly swinging oil lamp flickering backward and forward across the room, and outside the several thousand voices of the wind seemed to rise to a crescendo.

"It's the sea, Otto," Berger said softly without

opening his eyes. "I think maybe it's decided to come for us."

In the saloon, the nuns grouped around the table, heads bowed, hands clasped. Water dripped in through the skylight, but the boards, for the present, seemed to be holding. And here, as in the rest of the ship, there was not a dry inch to be found, water pouring down the companionway, swilling in and out of the cabins.

Sister Angela prayed aloud in a firm, steady voice. "Thou, O Lord, that stillest the raging of the sea, hear, hear us and save us, that we perish not . . ."

The doors at the top of the companionway opened, and Richter clattered down the steps, carrying a large billycan, which he set on the table. His cap was soaked, his tangled beard and oilskin streaming with water. He stood there waiting, chest heaving. Sister Angela faltered, then continued her prayer to the end and crossed herself.

"Kapitän's compliments, Sister. Hot coffee. Just made on the oil stove in his cabin."

"My thanks to Kapitän Berger. How are things?"

"Bad," Richter said. "We lost another man. Young Bergman. Swept from the rigging."

"We will pray for him."

"Yes, you might well do that, Sister."

He turned and went back up the companionway. "Let us pray, sisters, for the soul of Hans Bergman, that he may find peace."

But Lotte, at the other end of the table, turned suddenly, mounted the companionway before a word could be said, and went out on deck.

It was a sight to take her breath away. Although it was well past dawn there was no day: the sky was black, mountainous, swirling clouds, touched with violet and red as if somewhere beyond in the gloom great fires burned. Lightning flickered constantly, and the wind howled like a mad dog, slashing at her face.

Everyone on deck had his hands full and no one noticed her. Sturmm had the wheel, while Winzer and Kluth and four men manned the pump, each one tethered to the mainmast by a line.

The sea swept in over the ship in a solid mass, taking all before it. Lotte hung on to the ladder. The *Deutschland* seemed to lie right over, then righted herself.

Without their lifelines the men on the pump would have been washed away. They floundered on the deck like stranded fish, and Richter, who had jumped into the ratlines, dropped down to go to their aid.

There was a sudden violent report, almost like an explosion, high above. He looked up. The lifts had parted on the fore lower topgallant. As he watched, the yard swung violently and the sail broke free.

It fluttered wildly in the gale, the entire mast vibrating. Richter knew that it could only be a question of time before it snapped the fore topmast itself like a rotten stick. He ran to the galley, snatched one of the fire axes from its mounting, and sprang into the ratlines.

He paused to jam the ax into his belt, turned, and saw Berger on the quarterdeck waving wildly. Impossible to hear what he was calling, but it was plain enough from his gestures that he wanted Richter down out of there.

But if that sail was left and brought the mast down . . . Richter kept on climbing, gritting his teeth. His oilskin was worse than useless, more a hindrance than a help, for it offered little protection against such heavy and continuous rain. The rigging was swollen, every rope stiff, and each time he raised an arm to pull himself up, a cold stream of water slopped in between clothes and skin. The wind was pulling and tearing at his clothes like a living thing.

He paused on the foretop for a moment to catch

his breath. The sea boiled white foam as far as the eye could see, rain and hail driving in, lightning glimmering balefully in the blackness of the sky.

He paused beneath the sail. It thundered free with a terrible roar. Facing death now, judging his moment, he moved close to the mast, got inside the flailing sail, hung on tight with one hand, and swung the fire ax, attacking the ring that held the yard to the mast.

The sail enveloped him, almost tearing him away. Then the line from one corner tightened, pulling it straight for a moment. He glanced down and found Berger standing on the foretop just below him, hanging on to the line.

Berger nodded, and Richter swung the ax again, aware of the entire topmast vibrating. Once, twice, the ax cut clean through metal, the yard swung, the ring parted. Berger released the line—only just in time, as the yard, the lower topgallant sail still fluttering wildly from it, whirled away on the wind.

Berger clapped Richter on the shoulder. Slowly, painfully, they descended, taking their time. Richter dropped to the deck, and as he moved forward, he saw Lotte by the quarterdeck ladder. She was gazing at him, a kind of awe on her face. As if by instinct, he held out his arms and she ran into their shelter.

Jago and his men moved the gunboat into the inner harbor at first light, where the groundswell was less of a problem. As soon as the *Dead End* was secure, he left Jansen in charge and went up to the cottage. Jean Sinclair let him in the front door, and when he went into the living room, Reeve and Murdoch were at the radio.

"How goes it?"

"Terrible," the admiral said. "A bloody shambles."

In Mallaig, another coaster had been driven

ashore and two more lighters sunk. Three trawlers
had foundered off Stornoway so quickly that nothing
could be done, overwhelmed in that terrible sea. South
of Iceland, the Royal Canadian Navy corvette *Mac-
michael* had disappeared, never to be seen again, along
with the eighty-five officers and men who comprised
her crew. And the Halifax convoy, striking for the
North Channel into the Irish Sea, was hopelessly
scattered.

But still, there had not been a specific call for the
Fhada lifeboat. Murdoch sat patiently smoking his
pipe, listening to the jumbled messages over the radio.
Jago went into the kitchen, where he found Janet with
Jean making sandwiches.

"Hey," he said. "You're a woman after all."

"Watch it, darling." She pointed the knife under
his chin.

He helped himself to tea. "I see the boat hasn't
been called out."

"It will be. That's what Murdoch's waiting for.
The crew are all ready down at the lifeboat station."
She shook her head. "Honest to God, Harry, you've
never seen anything like it. There isn't one of them
who isn't a grandfather. It's pathetic."

"Pathetic? A bunch of guys are willing to put
themselves on the line in the worst sea I've ever seen
in my life and that's all you can find to say?"

"They wouldn't last five minutes out there. What
would be the point?"

He went back into the living room and took a
chair next to Reeve. It was just after seven-thirty. At
ten to eight there was another weather forecast from
Stornoway.

"U.S. destroyer *Carbisdale* a hundred and ten
miles northwest of butt of Lewis reports winds of hurricane force, gusting to one hundred and twenty
knots."

"A hundred and twenty," Jago said in awe.

"A bad blow indeed," Murdoch said gravely. "As bad as I have known."

Janet brought in tea and sandwiches on a tray, put them down, and went back to Jean in the kitchen without a word. Jago helped himself to a sandwich and leaned forward to pat Rory on the head. The clock on the mantelpiece struck eight times.

As the last stroke died away, a voice sounded over the radio in broken English. "Three-masted bar-kentine *Deutschland* adrift and helpless. I estimate my present position some twenty miles southwest of Fhada in Outer Hebrides. For God's sake, help us. I have women on board."

The message faded, drowned in a sea of static. Reeve turned to stare at Jago. "Did he say *Deutsch-land*?"

"That's what it sounded like to me, Admiral."

"A three-masted barkentine," Murdoch said. "I did not think I would live to see the day."

Janet and Jean had come from the kitchen and stood listening. Reeve said, "It just can't be, for Christ's sake."

Berger's voice swelled through the static again. "This is barkentine *Deutschland* in urgent need of assistance, twenty miles southwest of Fhada. I have women on board."

"There he is again, Admiral," Jago said. "That guy *has* to be for real."

Reeve reached for the microphone, and then, as Berger started to repeat his message again, another voice broke in on the channel. *"Deutschland, hier ist Grosse Schwarze Adler."*

What followed was wholly in German. Reeve sat back helplessly. "What in the hell goes on here? One minute we have some guy screaming for assistance— the next, a lot of Kraut I don't understand a word of."

There was a moment's silence before Janet said carefully, "Gericke would, Uncle Carey."

On the *Deutschland* things had gone from bad to worse. By seven-fifteen it became obvious that she could no longer support the main lower topsail, and Berger gave Sturmm the necessary orders.

To clew up that sail proved to be incredibly difficult. Although the men had to work at no great height above the deck, they still had the appalling wind to contend with. Every rope was foul, swollen to twice its normal size, the blocks jammed at a touch, and all the time the wind tore at them, keen as a surgeon's lancet, splitting flesh with its driven spray.

Finally it was done and the men descended wearily to the deck. The wind now dominated everything, striking the ship one blow after another as it gusted. Ragged clouds passed by overhead, seeming low enough to touch the mastheads, sheet lightning flickered, and the rain fell relentlessly.

Another four men worked frantically at the pump. Berger, as he watched them at the quarterdeck rail, felt strangely impotent. Such puny insignificance in the midst of all this vastness. What could it hope to achieve?

He turned to check on Sturmm and the two men who had the wheel with him, and his mouth opened in a soundless cry as a tremendous following sea rolled in across the stern.

The *Deutschland* shuddered, Berger found himself on his back, clutching at the rail for life itself, as hundreds of tons of water swept on toward the prow. There was no sign of Winzer or Kluth, but Sturmm was still there, hanging on to the wheel.

Berger staggered across the quarterdeck to join him. The *Deutschland* put her lee rail under the water. They fought like demons, Berger cursing in a frenzy, and slowly, so slowly, she started to answer the helm. But the blow had been mortal. The mizzen topmast and much of the rigging had gone. The lifeboats had been swept away. The galley shack had totally disappeared.

Richter came up the ladder. Berger shouted in his ear, "Two more men on this wheel, Richter, then a damage report, quick as you can."

The bosun disappeared. A few moments later Holzer and Endrass came up to take over the wheel. "You're in charge here, Mister Sturmm. I'll see what the situation is below."

As Berger reached his cabin door, Richter came up the companionway. "Are the sisters safe?"

Richter nodded. "Shaken up and badly scared. But we've other problems now, Herr Kapitän. Twenty inches of water in the bilges and rising."

Berger turned to look at the *Deutschland*. Rigging lines danced on the wind, the fore lower topsail had torn free, and half of it still fluttered from the yard-arm like a ragged gray flag. Here and there planking protruded from the deck and the pipe rails were smashed. The entire ship shuddered as she wearily climbed another great wave and a squall hit her.

Richter knew what he was thinking, could smell defeat. "It's no good, is it, Helmut?" the captain said. "We're finished."

"I'm afraid so, Herr Kapitän."

Berger nodded. "Take over from Mister Sturmm and tell him to bring the radio to my cabin right away."

Necker had left Trondheim at five, and the flight over Scotland at thirty-five thousand feet, far above the weather, had been completely without incident. He had arrived in the target area, however, to find a very different situation.

Clouds boiled below him, dark and menacing, tinged with orange and fire, twisting and curling like black smoke. Schmidt said, "They're having a hell of a time down there today. My English is only fair, but I know SOS when I hear it. I'll cut you in, sir."

There was another message coming through now. "Sea areas Malin and Hebrides. Wind gusting to one hundred and thirty. Barometer reading nine-seven-o and still falling."

It was Schmidt who said, "I know one thing, Herr Hauptmann. The Halifax convoy won't be a convoy any longer. She'll have been smashed to pieces."

But Necker, gazing down into that black smoke below, was thinking of the *Deutschland*. He said to Rudi, "You've got the position where we saw the *Deutschland* yesterday. Average, let's say, ten knots on a northeast-by-north course. See what your dead reckoning can do with that for her present whereabouts."

"But Herr Hauptmann," Rudi protested. "Our orders—"

Necker said coldly, "Do as you're told, and shut up."

It only took the boy a couple of minutes to produce the desired information, and he passed it across. Necker altered course immediately, switching on his intercom at the same time.

"Listen to me, you lot. They told us this was the finest all-weather plane in the world. Claimed it would even operate under hurricane conditions. Let's see if they're right. I'm going down to find out what's happening to the *Deutschland*. My decision."

He pushed the column forward, taking the Junkers into a shallow dive, and started to descend. Within a few minutes they were enveloped in cloud and heavy rain, lightning flickering at the wing tips.

They continued to descend at speed, buffeted from side to side in the heavy wind. Necker had to hang on to the column with all his strength. At one point, they slewed to port, the wind striking a series of blows on the fuselage that stripped pieces from the wings, but he regained control and maintained his dive.

They were at ten thousand and still descending, still enveloped in dark, swirling clouds. Rudi had unclipped his oxygen mask and stared out through the windscreen, his face very white.

And it was all a waste of time, Necker told himself. In such weather it was highly unlikely that the *Deutschland* would have been able to maintain her original course, and her speed, after all, was only an estimation.

At three thousand, the Junkers burst out of the clouds into a great bowl of luminous light and torrential rain, a sea of foam stretching to the horizon. And there she was—quite incredibly, about half a mile away to the southwest.

"Rudi," Necker said. "I owe you a bottle of champagne," and he banked steeply to port.

Rudi had the binoculars out. "She looks in bad shape, Herr Hauptmann."

Schmidt broke in, "Something's wrong, sir. They're transmitting a distress call. In English. Berger is asking for help."

"Hook me in," said Necker grimly. "And I'll talk to him myself."

Barkentine Deutschland, *25 September 1944.*
Winds of hurricane strength and the Deutschland, *in my opinion, being in imminent dan-*
ger of foundering, I started to transmit
distress calls at the end of the morning watch.
Our signal, I fear, is very weak owing to
the effect of salt water on the batteries.
However, shortly afterward our friend from
the Luftwaffe *reappeared. To our mutual*
astonishment, a third party joined in from
the neighboring island of Fhada.

Fourteen

"*D*eutschland calling. Are you still with us, Necker? We lost you in low cloud."

"I still have you in sight," Necker replied. "Don't
worry. I'll stay close."

The exchange crackled through static, remote and
somehow far away. Gericke, at the radio, said slowly,
"*Deutschland?*"

"Well, speak to him," Reeve said. "Find out
what's going on."

"Very well." Gericke reached for the microphone

and started to transmit in German. *"Deutschland,* this is Fhada calling. Come in, please."

There was silence, and then Berger's voice crackled faintly. "Necker, who was that, for God's sake?"

"I don't know."

"Deutschland. Fhada calling. Will you please come in with fullest details on your present position? We may be able to assist."

There was a further silence and then Necker's voice: ". . . haven't any idea . . . suggest you answer . . . see what happens."

Once more there was silence, other fainter messages crowding in as if from far away. Jago said, "What's going on out there, Commander?"

"We're only picking up one side of the conversation now. Necker, whoever he is. As for the *Deutschland,* she's either foundered or lost radio contact."

"There's only one sure way to find out," Reeve said. "Speak to Necker this time."

"All right." Gericke tried again. "Fhada calling Necker. Come in, please. Fhada calling Necker. Come in, please. I cannot raise the *Deutschland.* Urgent I speak with you."

Only the silence. Jean Sinclair said softly, "He doesn't trust you, Commander."

Gericke tried again. "Necker, this is Korvetten-kapitän Paul Gericke of the *Kriegsmarine* calling from Fhada. I beg you to reply to me."

There was more static, then Necker's voice strongly, "Paul Gericke—the U-boat ace?"

"That's right."

"But how can this be?"

"I am a prisoner of war. Those in charge here have asked me to monitor your calls because they cannot understand German. Who are you?"

"Hauptmann Horst Necker, serving with K.G. Forty out of Trondheim. Shipping and weather reconnaissance. I'm circling the *Deutschland* at the moment in a JU Eighty-Eight S."

"I can't get any kind of reply from them," Gericke said. "What's wrong?"

"Their signal has weakened. Seawater in the batteries."

"Can you still monitor them?"

"Yes, if I stay close."

The admiral said impatiently, "Come on, Gericke, what's going on out there?"

Gericke told him. Reeve turned to Murdoch. "Think you can reach them?"

"We can try," Murdoch said. "It would help if that aircraft stayed overhead to give us a mark. Visibility at sea level will be very bad."

"That's asking one hell of a lot," Jago said. "Of Necker, I mean. Can you imagine what it's like trying to keep that plane in the air in this weather?"

Gericke reached for the microphone again. "Gericke calling Necker. We have a lifeboat here ready to leave at once. It would greatly assist if you could stay in the area as marker."

Necker replied, "That's asking a lot. The worst conditions I've ever known. But she's handling all right so far. We'll do what we can. Present position is as follows." He gave the essential facts slowly and clearly. "How long before this lifeboat reaches us?"

Gericke passed the details to Murdoch. The old man nodded. "About an hour. I'm leaving now."

"I'm coming with you." Reeve reached for his oilskin. But Murdoch shook his head. "You are welcome to watch, Admiral—nothing more. I have my crew."

"Now look here—" Reeve started to say hotly.

"I am coxswain of the Fhada lifeboat, Carey Reeve," the old man said. "Life or death this day, by my decision only. You can see us off with pleasure, but no more."

Reeve turned to Gericke. "Stay on that radio.

I'll be back as soon as I've seen the boat launched."

"Very well," Gericke said.

Murdoch plunged out into the gale with Reeve and Jago at his heels.

High up on the spine of the island the wind was ferocious, a living thing that seemed to be doing its utmost to force the trolley back. It took the combined efforts of Murdoch and Jago pumping together to make any kind of progress.

When they came to the end of track above the lifeboat station, the sea was enough to take the breath away. A ragged broken carpet of white water, one enormous wave after another flowing in a kind of slow motion. Now and then in the trough, the jagged black teeth of the reef gaped beyond the mouth of the inlet.

"Think you can make it?" Reeve bawled into Murdoch's ear.

"Perhaps," the old man replied.

There were people clustered around the lifeboat house. Mainly women and a few children. As the three men hurried down the track there was the sound of running behind and Lachlan overtook them.

"I came as soon as I heard," he said, slightly breathless. "And half Mary's Town behind me. Will you be needing me, Murdoch?"

"There are six of us, Lachlan. We can manage fine."

Murdoch moved on through the small crowd and entered the boathouse. His crew already waited in the boat wearing yellow oilskins and life jackets.

The doors at the end of the slipway were open. He pulled on an oilskin and moved a yard or two down the slope from where he could see into the mouth of the inlet. He looked up at his crew.

"There is a chance it can be done. One in ten only, but worth a try. There is a ship out there in a bad way and women on board. And if we don't go now, we don't go at all, not the way the sea builds up out here. If any one of you thinks better of it, speak up and get out of the boat."

This last remark was delivered in the same calm, matter-of-fact tone as the rest. White-bearded Francis Patterson replied with a touch of impatience, "Can we be off now, Murdoch, or are we going to hang about and jaw all day?"

"So be it," Murdoch said and went up the ladder.

The women in the small crowd moved down to the Strand, talking anxiously among themselves in low voices.

The *Morag Sinclair* emerged from the mouth of the boathouse a moment later, sliding down the slipway at considerable speed, and entered the water, her prow biting deep, spray fanning high into the air.

She moved on through the heavy swell, lifting as a great wave smashed in through the narrow mouth of the inlet. For a moment the reef gaped again through broken water. There was silence from the crowd, only the wind howling.

"It's no good," Reeve said. "They'll never make it. It's madness. Those waves must be thirty feet high. If they hit at the wrong moment, they'll be chewed to pieces out there."

But the *Morag* kept going, out through the entrance in a burst of speed. "He's trying to catch the next big swell for clearance over the reef," Jago cried.

Perhaps it might have worked, Murdoch's one chance in ten. But at that moment, the wind gusted with such violence that a woman screamed somewhere in the crowd. The *Morag Sinclair* staggered, then veered sharply to port and seemed to poise high on the swell above the black rocks suddenly revealed.

"She's going to strike!" Reeve cried.

An enormous wave bored in, rising thirty or forty feet into the mouth of the inlet, carrying the lifeboat broadside on, helpless before it. She struck close inshore, water boiling over her in fury, washing two of the crew straight over the side.

Harry Jago was running now, down into the surf, reaching out for a yellow oilskin. He was aware of Francis Patterson's face surfacing beside him, eyes closed, teeth bared.

And then there were others beside him, waist deep in the freezing water. Admiral Reeve, with his one good arm, floundering, the black patch lifting to reveal the ugly puckered scar, the eyeless socket. Jago turned the yellow oilskin over to find James Sinclair, and heaved him backward through the surf to where willing hands stretched out to help.

The next few minutes were a total confusion of shouts and screams, the *Morag Sinclair* grinding in through the surf on each succeeding wave. A line was thrown, another, and people running from the boathouse brought more.

Jago found himself heaving, bending his back in the surf, Lachlan and Reeve beside him. Once, falling flat on his face, he took a moment to collect himself and was astonished to see a dozen women on the next rope, skirts swirling up about their hips.

The wind blew sand straight into his face. He closed his eyes and kept on hauling, the rope burning his shoulder. Then he was on his hands and knees. This time, when he opened his eyes painfully and looked about him, everyone seemed to be roughly in the same position. And the *Morag Sinclair,* tilted to one side, was safe on the beach.

Jago and Reeve got to their feet and went forward. Murdoch appeared at the rail above them. His face was very pale and twisted with pain.

"Are you all right?" Reeve called.

"I took a knock when we broached. It's nothing."

Jago circled the boat. "Only superficial damage and the screws are intact."

"That's something," Reeve said. "At least there's been no loss of life. A miracle."

Murdoch hooked a ladder over and came down it awkwardly as the crowd surged forward. His left arm swung loosely at his side in a way that Jago thought was distinctly unhealthy.

The old man swayed and Jago tried to steady him. "Are you all right?"

Murdoch pushed him away. "Never mind me." He turned to Reeve. "There is a boat out there helpless, and women on board, and nothing to be done about it."

Jago heard someone say, "There's always the *Dead End*." Only afterward did he realize it was he himself who had spoken.

Jago sat at the chart table, Jansen at his side, and the crew crowded in around the door. "That's it," he said. "Now you know the score. It's going to be rough out there. Volunteers only this trip. Any man who wants to can collect his duffle and step over that rail to the pier and I won't think any the worse of him. Not to put too fine a point on it, I'd say that should particularly commend itself to those of you who are married."

It was Petersen who spoke for all of them. "We've been together a long time, Lieutenant. We've been in the water together more than once, and this is the first time I ever heard you talk crap. Begging your pardon, sir."

"I think what he's trying to ask in his own delectable way, Lieutenant, is when do we leave?" Jansen said.

Jago glanced at his watch. "The admiral's due at any moment with the *Deutschland*'s present position. I'd say we'll be moving out of here within the next ten or fifteen minutes." He looked up. "So what are you all hanging about for?"

Janet left Murdoch lying on the bed, closed the door softly, and went into the living room. Gericke was at the radio, Reeve and Jean beside him.

The admiral turned. "How is he?"

"The arm's broken. I've put it in a splint for the time being and given him a pain-killing injection. He should sleep for a while. How are things going?"

"Not so good. We've not been able to raise Necker again. Probably an electrical storm."

Gericke was still trying in the background, speaking urgently into the mike in German. "Come in, Necker. Come in, please."

Necker's voice sounded faint, but clear enough for them all to sense the urgency. "Necker here, Gericke. I've been calling for the past half hour. What's happening?"

"We've not been connecting, that's all," Gericke told him. "Too much disturbance. There's been a delay. The lifeboat couldn't get away, but there's a gunboat leaving now from Mary's Town. Please confirm present position." Necker did so and Gericke went on, "What about the *Deutschland*? Are you still in touch?"

"Only with difficulty. The signal is very weak. Another hour to wait, then?"

"I'm afraid so."

Gericke had written the details of the *Deutschland*'s position on a scrap of paper, which he pushed across at Reeve. The admiral slipped it into his pocket. "I'll get this down to Jago."

As he turned to the door, Jean caught his sleeve. "Carey, you wouldn't do anything silly, like try to go along for the ride, would you?"

"At my age?" He grinned and kissed her lightly. "Sweetheart, you've got to be joking."

He went out quickly. Jean turned, her face troubled. "He's going to go, Janet. I know it."

Janet said bitterly, "What did you expect?"

She went into the kitchen and slammed the door. Gericke reached for Jean's hand and held it tight for a moment. Necker's voice cut in on them.

"Have they left yet?"

"On their way."

"I have a problem. An hour and fifteen minutes, then we must head for home. A question of fuel."

"I understand," Gericke said. "You must leave when you think fit. Your decision."

He switched off and turned to Jean with a smile. "And now, if you dare venture in there, I think we could all do with one of your nice hot cups of tea."

The *Dead End* was ready and waiting, her engines turning, when Reeve went onto the bridge. Jago was bending over the chart, and the admiral passed Gericke's message across.

Jago quickly worked out the target position and nodded. "That's it, sir. We can get moving now."

"I'd like to come with you."

Petersen, at the wheel, glanced sideways. Jansen looked stolidly ahead. Jago said, "Well, now, Admiral, I'm not so sure that's a good idea."

"I could order you to take me."

"And I could point out, with the utmost respect, that as commander of this old bucket, I'm the only one whose words count around here."

Reeve came right down. "All right, Lieutenant, I'm asking, not ordering. I'll even say please if that helps."

"My command, sir. You understand that?"

"Perfectly."

Jago nodded and turned to Jansen. "Okay, Chief, let's move it."

Necker's voice exploded from the radio, full of excitement. "Come in, Gericke! Come in!"

"Receiving you loud and clear," Gericke replied. "What is it?"

"I can see it. I can see the gunboat, half a mile to starboard, in heavy seas, but making progress."

"He can see the *Dead End*," Gericke said.

"My God," Janet breathed, and her hand fastened tightly on his shoulder.

"I'll stay on the air," Gericke said. "Please keep close contact from now on."

The bedroom door clicked open and Murdoch appeared, his left arm in a sling. His face was drawn and full of pain, a slightly dazed expression in the eyes. "What is it?" he demanded.

Janet went to his side and drew him toward a chair. "You shouldn't be up. You should have stayed in bed."

The old man sat down heavily and it was to Gericke he spoke now. "What is happening, Commander?"

"Lieutenant Jago has gone out there in the gunboat."

"And the admiral?"

"We think he has gone with them."

"They should have taken me. I know how this game is played. They do not." There was only resignation in Murdoch's voice now. "God help all of them."

The *Deutschland* wallowed in gigantic seas, plunging drunkenly down the slope of each successive wave, climbing with extreme difficulty to the crest of the next. There were two or three feet of water in the saloon and it was rising. The nuns, in Prager's charge, were secure for the moment in Berger's cabin.

On the quarterdeck, Richter and two of the men had the wheel. Berger stood at the rail, hanging on tightly as one sea after another washed in. Below, four of the crew, tethered to the mainmast, pumped frantically, a losing battle.

He looked up to the Junkers, circling overhead, his brain numbed by the incessant cold, faintly surprised to find that she was still there. Sturmm stumbled out of the cabin below and hauled himself up the ladder.

The wind tore away his voice even when he put his mouth close to Berger's ear. The captain shook his head. Sturmm grabbed his arm and pointed to starboard. As Berger turned, the *Dead End* came over the crest of a wave two hundred yards away, poised dramatically, then plunged down out of sight.

Every window on the bridge of the gunboat was smashed, the door ripped from its hinges, and Petersen and Chaney struggled to hold the wheel between them. Reeve had jammed himself into a corner and Jago and Jansen crouched at the chart table, observing the *Deutschland*.

Jago had long since passed the point of feeling the intense cold, indeed, of feeling anything. His body had ceased to exist, only the brain turned still, sharp and keen. The trip had been a nightmare. He knew that to have gotten this far was some kind of miracle. But that didn't matter. They were here.

"Now what?" Jansen cried into his ear.

The *Deutschland* leaned over, her lee rail under water, then swung to port again.

"I don't know," Jago said. "Perhaps if we go in there under the lee. If they're quick."

This was unknown territory, a situation so extreme that it was not covered by any manual of seamanship. He was hesitating. And that was fatal. Two men at the quarterdeck rail were waving frantically. One of them, he presumed, was Berger, beckoning him to come in.

Reeve broke the spell, crying hoarsely, "Let's go, for God's sake! Let's go!"

Jago turned to Petersen. "Okay, straight in to her lee rail. This is crunch time."

He went out on the bridge, followed by Reeve. Jansen went down to the deck, calling the other five crew members to him, and they moved to the rail to get ready.

The *Dead End* went in fast, and Chaney turned the wheel frantically at the last moment as a wave caught them. Her prow smashed into the barkentine's rail. As the wave receded, the *Deutschland* rolled to port and the *Dead End* dropped sickeningly fifteen feet below her. In the same moment a great sea rolled in across the *Deutschland*'s port rail, rising forty feet up her masts, sweeping everything before it.

Jago, on his knees in a world of green water, hanging on to the rail, felt the gunboat sag beneath him. Another wave washed in as he grabbed for Reeve, throwing both of them bodily forward. When it receded, he found himself face down beside the admiral on the deck of the *Deutschland*.

Berger reached them a moment before the next wave struck and hauled Jago to his feet. The lieutenant grabbed at the mainmast ratlines to steady himself, turned, and saw, to his horror, the *Dead End* in the process of going down close to the rail, the *Deutschland*'s mizzenmast torn from its mountings by that first enormous sea, lying across her in a tangle of wreckage.

The surviving members of his crew were already on the move, jumping for their lives to the deck of the *Deutschland*. Petersen, blood on his face, but not Chaney. Crawford, Lloyd—but no sign of Jansen.

Another wave swept in and Jago held tight, aware that the *Deutschland* was foundering beneath his feet, already up to his waist in water as the combined weight of the mizzenmast and the gunboat pulled her over.

Richter came down the quarterdeck ladder, an ax in one hand, and started to attack the tangled web of lines that still held them tied to the mast. In a daze Jago turned to watch him. And then Reeve was tugging at his arm and pointing.

Jansen was out there, head and shoulders above the tangle where the mast had struck. He was bareheaded, one arm free. Jago stumbled toward Richter and pulled him away.

The German had him by the oilskin with one hand holding him off and Reeve was screaming into his ear. "It's got to be done, Jago. Otherwise we all go."

Jago turned to look out at Jansen as if in a dream, could have sworn he smiled, and then quite distinctly heard the chief call, "Get it done, Lieutenant."

Suddenly, unable to breathe, he tore the ax from Richter's grasp. "Damn you," he cried. "Damn you all to hell!"

There were tears in his eyes. The ax rose, descended, cutting deep, rose again and again in a frenzy.

The *Deutschland* lifted as the mast tore away from the gunboat, and Jago was hurled on his back. He got to his feet in time to see the mast and what was left of the *Dead End* drifting rapidly away. He caught a final glimpse of Jansen, his arm moving in slow motion, as if in a kind of benediction. Then another wave rolled in and there was nothing.

Jago hurled the ax into the sea, turned, and stumbled away.

At almost the same moment Necker's voice sounded on the radio again. "She's foundering. The gunboat has foundered."

Gericke turned and said gravely, "I'm afraid the *Dead End* has gone down."

Jean Sinclair slumped into a chair, stunned. Janet said frantically, "It can't be."

"Come in, Necker. Come in. Please confirm your last message."

There was silence, the crackle of static. Janet said in a dull voice, "All gone. All of them. Uncle Carey, Harry . . ."

Necker's voice cut in on her. "Have been in communication with the *Deutschland*. The gunboat foundered under her lee rail when the mizzenmast fell on her. There were six survivors from her crew, all of whom are now safe on board the *Deutschland*."

"Six survivors," Gericke translated rapidly.

Jean grabbed his arm. "Who? I must know who!"

"Admiral Reeve, Lieutenant Jago, and four others," Necker continued.

Gericke turned to Jean. "He's safe, Mrs. Sinclair, for the moment at any rate, on board the *Deutschland*." He glanced at Janet. "And so is your lieutenant."

Necker's voice broke in again. "What happens now? What shall I say to the *Deutschland*?"

Gericke sat there for a long moment. Then he told him.

When he had finished, Necker said, "Are you sure? You will see to it personally?"

"My word on it."

"I'll tell them what you say. The trouble is, I'm already ten minutes past the critical point as regards my fuel for the return trip."

"There is nothing more you can do here, my friend. Speak to the *Deutschland* and go home."

There was a brief pause. Janet said, "What's going on? What have you been saying?"

Gericke motioned her to silence. Necker's voice sounded again. "I've spoken to Berger. Told him what you intend."

"Has he told the admiral?"

"Yes, he's sent a rather peculiar message for you."

"What is it?"

"He says isn't it about time you realize you'd lost the war? Does that make any sense?"

"Of a sort. And now, my friend, you must be leaving."

Necker said, "Good-bye sir. It's been an honor to know you."

"And you, Herr Hauptmann."

And then there was only that damned static again. Gericke switched off the set and reached for a cigarette. "So," he said.

"What's going on?" Janet began, but Murdoch waved her down.

"Be still, girl." He leaned close to Gericke. "Well, Commander?"

"Necker's had to leave. He's already dangerously

short of fuel, but before he went, I asked him to send a last message to the *Deutschland*."

"And what would that be?"

"I told them to hang on because we'd be coming for them in the lifeboat."

"But that's impossible," Jean said. "She's on the beach at South Inlet."

"And even if we could launch her again," Murdoch said, "she will never make it over that reef and out to sea, not as the wind is. I told you that."

"I'm not suggesting that you launch her from South Inlet, but from here in the harbor."

Murdoch shook his head. "Madness. It can't be done and if it could—if you dragged that boat from one end of the island to the other—who could take her out there?" He looked down at his broken arm. "One hand is not enough—not in weather like this."

"I told them I would come myself," Gericke said simply. "I told them exactly what I intended." He turned to the two women. "The admiral knows and so does Jago. They must also know that it is their only chance of life now."

The door burst open and Lachlan ran in to collapse against the table, chest heaving as if he had run for some considerable distance.

"What is it, lad?" Murdoch demanded sternly. "Pull yourself together now."

"I've been up on *Feith na Falla*," Lachlan said, struggling for breath. "Along with half the town. The *Deutschland* has just come into view."

As Janet and Gericke went over the crest and stood on top of the hill, the wind almost knocked them back again. She held on to his arm tightly and Murdoch and Lachlan, Jean Sinclair between, followed after them.

There were dozens of women there, many of them wearing the oilskins of absent husbands, most with shawls bound tightly around their heads against the wind.

The sea raged in fury, a boiling cauldron. Visibility, because of blown spindrift and sleet, was poor, and yet they were able to see her a couple of miles out, lifting on the crest of a wave, only two masts now and the rag of a staysail still intact.

Murdoch raised his binoculars. "Aye, she is in a bad way sure enough," he said, and then swung the binoculars slightly to the northwest.

Lachlan said, "She is going straight on to the Washington."

"I fear so."

Someone in the crowd cried out, and then another voice was raised—another. Women were moving forward, arms outstretched—calling out, as if by the simple power of their voices they could haul her back. Prevent what was happening.

Gericke said nothing, but simply reached for Murdoch's binoculars and focused them on that place where the sea boiled in fury, spray lifting a hundred feet into the air over jagged rocks. The *Deutschland* was no more than three hundred yards away from the reef, drifting in fast to a rising chorus from the women on the hill.

"She'll strike," Murdoch said, taking back the binoculars. "Can't avoid it now."

He stood there, legs apart, watching intently through the binoculars, and when he finally turned, his face was surprisingly calm. "The old Washington will hold her tight for a while. Time enough if we move fast." He waved his arm at the crowd. "Follow me—all of you!"

He went straight down the hill. Gericke and Janet, Jean Sinclair, and Lachlan followed. As the word spread others went after them until, in a few moments, the top of the hill was deserted.

The track emerged at the side of the church. When they reached that point, the old man went through the lych-gate, hurried up the path, and entered the porch. A moment later, the bell started to toll.

Horst Necker burst out of cloud at eight thousand feet over the Moray Firth, in serious trouble and still descending. Things hadn't been right since leaving the *Deutschland,* but it was only within the past five minutes that the source of the trouble had become apparent—a fracture in one of the fuel pipes connecting the GMI system.

"I'll have to go down to floor level," he said over the intercom. "No choice. Anyone who wants to pray, start now."

There was a chance that in this weather the Tommies would be too preoccupied to bother about one stray intruder on their radar screen. In fact, although Necker wasn't aware of it, Spitfires had already scrambled at Huntly airfield near Inverness and were seeking him out.

"I have a kurier! I have a kurier!" The voice of Kranz, the rear gunner, sounded in his ears.

Necker went into a corkscrew instantly, the reflex of several years of combat flying coming to his aid. He was aware of the chatter of the machine guns, glanced up to see a Spitfire zoom overhead and turn away to port, and then the entire aircraft seemed to stagger. Miraculously, he was still in control.

"Everyone still in one piece?" he said over the intercom.

There was no reply. Rudi, blood on his face where a splinter had sliced his cheek, scrambled to the rear. Necker kept on going down, jinking from side to side, aware of the shock waves as cannon shell punched holes in the fuselage.

Rudi got back into his seat. "Kranz is dead. Schmidt is unconscious. Some sort of head wound. I've put a field dressing on him."

"Good boy. Now hang on while I show these bastards how to fly."

He took the Junkers right down to sea level—a hazardous undertaking; with forty-foot swells, it was possible to find on occasion that the seas ahead were above the plane.

And the Spitfires didn't like it, although two of them still hung on grimly for a while, even at that suicidal level.

Once, Necker looked down and observed strange waterspouts all around and wondered for a moment what they were—until the Junkers shuddered again under the impact of cannon shell.

Twenty minutes at three hundred miles an hour. Not so good with that fractured pipe. The engines would be overheating, but not long now, unless he had hopelessly miscalculated.

The aircraft staggered under a well-aimed burst of machine gun fire. The windscreen shattered. Necker felt as if he had been kicked in the left shoulder, turned, and found the port engine smoking. He feathered it at once and switched to the extinguishers. The Junkers slowed, the needle falling right down to 150.

He hung on grimly, still no more than fifty feet above the sea. Rudi plucked at his arm excitedly. "They've gone, Herr Hauptmann. Cleared off. I don't understand."

"That's what I was hoping for. We're just over a hundred miles from the coast. That's usually the limit of their radius on a sea chase."

Rudi was staring at the blood on his glove and touched Necker's arm again gingerly. "You're wounded."

"So I believe," Necker said. "You know at flying school they told us it was impossible to keep one of these birds in the air on one engine. Let's see if we can prove them wrong."

"What shall I do, Herr Hauptmann?"

"Take off your belt and fasten it around the left rudder pedal."

Rudi did as he was told, and with his help, it was now possible to hold the crippled Junkers on course again.

"Pull tight, Rudi, all the way home." Necker grinned, beginning to feel the pain in his shoulder now and not caring. "See how simple it is when you know how? Stick with me and you'll live forever."

When Murdoch mounted into the pulpit at St. Mungo's there were something like seventy people in the congregation, mainly women, a handful of old men, and children. It was strangely silent, the wind muted by the thickness of massive stone walls.

He stood for a moment, head bowed in prayer, then looked up. "There is a boat out there on the Washington. You all know this. And the *Morag Sinclair* is beached at South Inlet. The only question is what can be done." No one said a word. "Commander Gericke has a solution. That we haul the *Morag* from South Inlet to Mary's Town and launch her in the harbor."

There was a gasp from the congregation. Someone said clearly, "Impossible."

"Not so," Murdoch said. "Such a thing has been done before. In Northumbria, early in the war, at Newbiggin. Should we be capable of less? Or must those poor souls on the Washington perish?"

Katrina MacBrayne answered him in a clear savage voice. "Bloody Germans all. Why should we lift a finger?"

"I could say that Admiral Reeve is out there, too, and five survivors from that Yankee gunboat. I could say that there are women out there, for there are. But what would be the point? I am not here to argue. I am here to tell you. Is this all your God means? Is this what our worship together has meant? You have lost a husband to the war, Katrina MacBrayne. I have given a son—a week back some of you women wept at the graveside of German boys laid to rest in our own churchyard. Pain is the same both sides. Everyone loses. But what does that prove? That there is no

God in this life? No, by heavens, for he gives us choice in our actions. We choose the way, not he."

The silence was intense, total. "People will die out there if we do nothing, and who they are doesn't matter. You see the state I'm in. Not fit to handle a wheel. But when the *Morag* leaves harbor, Commander Gericke stands in my place and I, by God, will be at his right hand." He slammed his fist down hard on the lectern. "There has been enough of talking. I am going to South Inlet to get that boat. Those who will can follow. As for the rest—to hell with you."

He came down out of the pulpit and marched up the aisle like a strong wind.

Barkentine Deutschland, *25 September 1944. At four bells in the forenoon watch, in winds of hurricane strength, we struck on the Washington Reef three miles northwest of Fhada in the Outer Hebrides. We are in the hands of the Almighty now, and although help is promised, I fear there is little hope for us.*

Fifteen

The *Deutschland* lay hard on the reef, her back broken, the fore topmast swinging down in a tangle of rigging, the sea breaking over her, one wave after another. Her stern jutted high into the air. Those who had been able to make their way aft in time clustered on the quarterdeck. There were still several men forward, some tied to the mainmast, others high in the rigging.

Berger, Reeve, and Jago huddled together at the quarterdeck rail. Sturmm hauled himself up the ladder, crouched beside them, and spoke to Berger, shouting to make himself heard.

Berger's English, though far from perfect, was good enough to get by. He turned to Reeve, his mouth close to the admiral's ear. "The women seem safe enough for the moment in my cabin. Sturmm says the bulkhead's breached but it's mainly holding together."

"Not for long," Reeve said as the *Deutschland* lifted, then crunched down onto the reef again.

"Gericke will come. He said he would."

For a moment Reeve saw again the *Morag Sinclair* on the beach at South Inlet and wanted to tell the German the truth. But what would be the point? At least the end, when it came, would be quick.

Berger leaned over the rail, in spite of the breaking waves, and tried to count the men in the rigging and on the deck by the mainmast. "Not good. It looks like we lost five when we struck."

Lloyd, the telegraphist, was forty feet up in the ratlines, where he had climbed to avoid the worst of the waves. Jago saw him plainly. The little Welshman waved and actually managed a smile. A mountain of water curled in. When it subsided, he was gone.

"We've got to get those men out of there," Jago shouted.

Reeve plucked at his sleeve. "Don't be crazy. You won't last two minutes on that open deck."

Jago shook him off, crawled to the quarterdeck ladder, and descended cautiously. He hung on at the bottom as another wave washed in, holding his breath, refusing to let go. As it subsided, Richter dropped down beside him.

He carried a coil of rope over one shoulder and tied one end quickly about Jago's waist, then looped the rest around the ladder. Jago started forward and Richter paid the rope out gradually.

Jago struggled desperately alone in a world of cold, green water. He lost his footing at one point, fetching up in the scuppers, but braced himself hard against the rope, and carried on, sometimes on hands and knees, until he was almost within touching distance of Petersen, tethered to the mainmast. Another wave bounced Petersen toward him on the end of his line, and Jago grabbed him by the leg, then the belt, hauling himself over Petersen's prostrate body until he reached the mainmast and was able to stand.

He unfastened the rope from around his waist and tied it to the mast, then waved to Richter. The German lashed the other end securely to the ladder so that there was now a lifeline stretching to the mast three feet above deck level.

Jago gestured to the men in the rigging and they started to descend. Petersen and the others, who had been tethered to the mast, had already untied themselves and were making their way across one by one; the rest followed. Jago waited until last, made a final check to make absolutely certain the deck and rigging were clear and went after them.

In Berger's cabin, Prager and the nuns were still reasonably protected from the full fury of the storm, in spite of breaches in the bulkhead. Prager crouched against the bunk, the rum bottle in both hands. He had almost emptied it, had ceased to feel the cold.

"Not long now, Gertrude," he whispered. "Not long."

Sister Angela prayed aloud at one end of the desk, hands clasped. "Save Lord, or else we perish. The living, the living shall praise thee. O send thy word of command to rebuke the raging winds and the roaring sea, that we, being delivered from this distress, may live to serve thee, and to glorify thy name all the days of our life."

The door opened and Richter entered, slamming it behind him. He looked around the cabin, frowning. Sister Angela said, "Mister Richter."

"Where's Lotte?"

She was very cold and when she unclasped her hands, she found, to her surprise, that they were shaking. "Lotte?" She looked around, a dazed expression on her face. "Has anyone seen Lotte?"

Sister Brigitte was sobbing. No one seemed to have anything to say. Richter crossed to Prager and hauled him to his feet. "You were supposed to bring them up from the saloon just before we struck. Didn't Lotte come with you?"

"Definitely," Prager said. "I was right behind her."

Sister Kathë said, "She went back."

Richter started violently. "That's not possible."

"I heard her say she'd forgotten something," Sister Kathë said vacantly. "Then she went out."

Richter wrenched open the door and plunged outside. He started down the companionway, but the deck and entire superstructure were buckled and twisted, the way into the saloon blocked by a tangle of wreckage.

"Lotte?" he cried. "Lotte?" But there was no reply.

It was Jago who saw him first, crossing the deck below, using the lifeline they had rigged. He tugged at Berger's sleeve. "What's he up to?"

"God knows," Berger replied.

As they watched, Richter took out his gutting knife, sprang the blade, slashed at the ropes securing the cargo hatch, surprisingly still intact, and disappeared into the forward hold.

The *Morag Sinclair* was almost at the top of the track leading up from the lifeboat station. She sat on a trolley with enormous broad iron wheels, not used since the time of the pulling lifeboat, when muscle and oars provided the power. Gericke had thought it impossible to lift her into position. But the solution was simple. They had pushed her out into the surf, as in the old days, floated her onto the trolley, and hauled them in together.

Now, close to the crest of the hill, the lines were hauled by eleven farm horses, forty-one women, eighteen children, and eleven men.

Gericke and Lachlan moved behind, blocking the

wheels every few yards with balks of timber. Sleet mingled with the rain, cutting cruelly into the flesh.

Someone in a long oilskin coat fell down a yard or two ahead of Janet. She left her place on the line and ran to help, discovering, to her horror, that it was a frail, white-haired woman of seventy at least. There was blood on her hands. She looked down at it, a dazed expression on her face, then raised her long skirt and tore strips from her petticoat.

She started to wind them around her hands and Janet tried to pull her over to the side of the track. "You must sit down."

The old woman pushed her away. "Leave me be." She staggered up the track and resumed her place.

"Oh, God, this is madness," Janet said to herself.

Murdoch was beside her, pulling her to her feet. "Are you all right, girl?"

"Yes—yes, I'm fine."

"Then why have you left your place?"

He glared at her like some Old Testament prophet about to invoke the wrath of God and smite the wrongdoer. She turned from his anger and, slipping and stumbling, ran forward along the column to resume her place beside Jean.

Time was meaningless now, a long agony as she strained, and voices swelled around her, women urging each other on, reaching beyond the agony to another place. Then, quite suddenly and to a ragged cheer, they went over the crest and started to move faster, following the path beside the railway track.

There were five to ten feet of water in the forward hold, depending on where he stood, for it was inclined sharply to starboard. The storm lantern hung from a hook in the bulkhead, its light playing across the dark water, which erupted suddenly as Richter surfaced.

But there was no route through there. The communicating hatchway was hopelessly jammed. And even if it hadn't been, it was debatable whether he would be able to hold his breath for long enough to get through all that wreckage under water.

So, there was only one way, it seemed. He rapped at the bulkhead with his knuckles. Still reasonably sound. It would take time. But then he didn't really have anywhere else to go. He picked up the two-handed fire ax he'd brought down with him and swung it over his head.

The *Morag Sinclair* was halfway along the track beside the railway line, high up on the spine of the island, progress slowing a little as they moved, totally exposed, into the full fury of the wind.

The scene behind was like a battlefield, people huddled beside the track at intervals where they had dropped, totally exhausted. It was a nightmare that couldn't be allowed to continue, Janet knew that, and yet still she bowed her back beside Jean, the rope biting cruelly into her shoulder and her hands dripping blood.

When she looked out over the sea, it seemed more troubled than ever, a vast wash of foam, a sky of writhing black smoke that boiled down as if it would envelop the earth.

Ahead of her, old Dougal Sinclair stumbled out of the line, crossed the railway track, and fell in the heather. Janet relinquished her grip and went after him wearily. He looked very peaceful lying there on his back, the blue eyes staring up into the dark sky. It was a moment or two before she realized how fixed that stare was and quickly unbuttoned his oilskin and jacket, reaching inside to feel for the heart.

Gericke dropped to one knee beside her. "What is it?" he demanded. "Are you all right?"

"He's dead," she said bitterly. "Are you satisfied now?"

Reeve crouched against the quarterdeck rail of the *Deutschland,* his pocket telescope raised, and looked toward Fhada. "No good," he cried to Jago. "They can probably see us from up there on *Feith na Falla,* but I can't even see the island."

"They're not coming, Admiral. Nobody's coming. We've had it."

At least in the Solomons it had been warm. He closed his eyes and a wave washed in, lifting the *Deutschland* bodily and crashing her down again.

"Christ Jesus, but I thought we were going straight over the edge of the reef that time," Reeve said.

Berger shouted in his ear. "She's breaking up now. Next time that happens, or the time after, she comes apart at the seams."

Reeve's face was bleached from the constant salt water, wrinkled like a fish's belly, and he looked a hundred years old. Jago leaned close. "You wanted action, Admiral. You've got it in spades. What a way to go."

Richter had just smashed his way through from the forward hold when the *Deutschland* lifted and started to roll. Oh, God, he thought, this is it.

She settled on the rocks again, with a nasty grating sound as more planks tore loose. He waited for the swirling water to subside. Strangely enough, he wasn't afraid, consumed totally by a passionate need to know what had happened to Lotte.

He squeezed past the mainmast mounting and the pump, found a nail on which to hang the storm lantern, and started to attack the bulkhead, which would give him access to the aft hold.

The *Morag Sinclair* was beginning to move fast now as the track sloped down to cross the railway line above Mary's Town, and suddenly the situation was totally changed. The forty or so people who were left on the lines, their roles reversed, were hanging on grimly to stop the boat from running away from them on its trolley.

Murdoch hurried alongside, shouting instructions to Gericke and Lachlan as they attempted to slow her by blocking the wheels with the same balks of timber they had used at South Inlet.

The *Morag* was really moving—rocking alarmingly on her trolley, swinging from side to side, leaving a trail of smashed windows as she coasted down the High Street. She emerged onto the front by the pier at some considerable speed, Gericke and Lachland running alongside, frantically jamming the wheels with their timber pieces, and slowly and very, very gradually she started to slide to a halt.

There was the silence of total exhaustion. Murdoch heaved himself up the ladder and over the side and nodded to Gericke. "You, too, Commander."

Gericke followed him, aware with something of a surprise that his arms were having difficulty in holding the weight of his body.

Murdoch looked out over the crowd. "What is wrong with you, then? She's only fifteen tons. One more heave now."

No one made a sound, and then, somehow, women who had collapsed were on their feet again, reaching wearily for their lines. They dragged the lifeboat forward to the top of the stone slipway at the head of the pier and ran her down into the harbor.

Watching her there, grinding against the pier, Janet couldn't quite take it all in. She was aware of Jean crying helplessly beside her, tears pouring down her cheeks, heard Gericke say, "Get those petrol drums along here quickly now," for they had emptied the tanks at South Inlet to lighten her.

Murdoch, in the aft cockpit, was calling up to the pier. "Lachlan, are you there, boy? No time for your sick belly now. I need you—and you, Hamish, and Francis Patterson. Are you still game?"

They went forward, those old men, even James

Sinclair, whose brother lay dead back beside the track. Janet turned, started to run back up the High Street, finding a new strength in her purpose, never stopping until she reached the cottage. She went inside, snatched her medical bag, and ran back down the hill to the harbor.

She pushed her way onto the pier through the crowd and saw them on deck below, fastening their life jackets, each man in yellow oilskins, even Gericke. She went down the stone steps to the lower landing and scrambled over the rail.

Murdoch turned to confront her. "And what is this, girl?"

"There are six of you, Murdoch. Five and a half if you consider that arm of yours. You should crew eight."

Gericke got between them, his hands on her shoulders. "This is no job for a woman, Janet. You must see that."

"Who got your bloody boat here for you?" She held up her medical bag. "I'm not here as a woman. I'm here as a doctor. And you might be damned glad to have me along before this is through."

Gericke opened his mouth to reply, but Murdoch pulled him out of the way. "No time to argue. You go to hell your own way, girl. Get down in the cockpit." He gave her a push. "You'll find an oilskin and life jacket. Put them on and stay out of the way."

Gericke's face was pale. He hesitated, then moved to the wheel. A second later, Lachlan, who was acting as bowman, had cast off and they were moving away from the pier out into the harbor.

At the quarterdeck rail, Jago, Reeve, and Berger still huddled together. The *Deutschland* had eased herself over a little farther to starboard and seemed to lift now with each wave.

It was Reeve who, turning to look in the direction of Fhada for the hundredth time, caught the first glimpse of the *Morag Sinclair* a mile to starboard.

"She's coming!" he cried, tugging frantically at Jago's arm. "I see her."

Jago pulled himself to his feet, holding on to the rail, and peered into the rain through swollen eyelids. "No," he said hoarsely. "You're imagining things."

But Reeve cried out again excitedly, clutching at Berger. This time the lifeboat was plain, and a sudden cheering broke out among the men assembled on the quarterdeck.

Berger waved Sturmm across. "Go down to my cabin and bring up the nuns."

Sturmm crawled away wearily. At that moment another wave thundered against the *Deutschland*, sliding her bodily across the reef. Part of the prow broke off and the storm staysail, intact all this time, fluttered away like a great bird.

"They'd better hurry," Jago said. "From the feel of that last one, I'd say we don't have too much time."

Richter had hacked his way through three bulkheads and scrambled into the aft hold as the men on deck started to cheer. He hesitated, put down the ax, turned and crawled back through the hole he had just made. He clung on to the base of the mainmast as the ship moved again on the reef, but emerged from the forward hatch a few moments later in time to catch a glimpse of the *Morag Sinclair* on the crest of a wave some distance away.

How much time did he have? Impossible to know. He dropped down into the hold, forced his way back through the water, negotiating the holes he had made in the bulkheads, until he stood again in the aft hold.

At some time in the *Deutschland*'s earlier history, the hold had been halved to make room for the additional cabin accommodation. The intervening bulkhead having been added at a later date, it had nothing like the strength of construction of the ones he had already negotiated. He picked up his ax, waded toward it, and started to attack it furiously.

The *Morag Sinclair* took water constantly, green sheets passing over her from stem to stern, exploding into the aft cockpit with stunning force. Janet was terrified. The waves seemed so enormous that each time they attempted to scale one the task seemed an impossibility, the *Morag* climbing in slow motion. When she swooped down the other side into the trough, it was as if she never intended to come up again.

But Gericke seemed unperturbed as he wrestled with the wheel, Murdoch at his shoulder.

Lifeboatmen, as a rule, don't wear lifelines, believing them to be too constricting in an emergency. So it was that at one moment, as Lachlan turned from beside her, reaching up to the rail, and slipped, a sea washed in, taking him out with it over the starboard rail. Janet screamed, and as Gericke glanced over his shoulder in alarm, the starboard rail dipped under and the boy miraculously floated inboard.

Murdoch reached down and shook him like a rat. "Lifeline!" he shouted. "Get a lifeline on!" He turned to Hamish Macdonald. "Lifelines for everyone. My orders—like it or not." He crouched down over Janet. "You, too, girl."

She reached for the line that was passed to her and had barely hooked herself on when disaster struck. The *Morag* hovered on the crest of a mountainous wave, broached as she went down. At the same moment, the wind gusted in fury, striking her starboard bow. She capsized.

To Janet, the world was stinking green water, washing over, filling heart and mind and brain, kicking and struggling in a desperate desire to live. The *Morag* was partially under, still pushing forward, screws turning.

Slowly, she righted herself. Janet was aware of

Gericke clinging to the wheel with one hand, reaching out to her with the other, Murdoch pulling himself up beside them. Lachlan was safe, Hamish Macdonald, Sinclair. But Francis Patterson had gone.

From then on, so vicious was the weather, so impenetrable the curtain of rain and sleet and flying spindrift, that they caught no further sight of the wreck until they lurched over the top of an enormous wave and saw her 150 yards away, the survivors clustered on the quarterdeck, waving.

"Now what?" Gericke demanded.

"Take your time, boy," Murdoch said. "And let me work this out."

Richter broke through the final bulkhead. He crawled into the saloon. It was dark in there, only the gurgle of the water, the howling of the gale outside. As with the rest of the ship, it was steeply inclined, the starboard cabins under water.

"Lotte?" he called.

There was no reply. Could be none. He had been a fool to think otherwise. He floundered through the water, crawled up the slope to where the door of her cabin swung crazily, braced himself in the entrance, and raised the lamp.

She lay trapped across the bunk, a tangle of wreckage across her stomach and legs. Her face was very pale, her eyes closed, but now she opened them slowly.

"Helmut," she whispered. "I knew you would come."

"What happened? Why did you come back?"

"Your ring, Helmut. I'd hidden it here under the mattress in the corner of my bunk. I forgot it when we were ordered on deck. Wasn't that silly of me?"

He was already heaving on the beam, straining with all his strength, but it refused to budge. "How strange," she said. "I've been so cold for days, so very cold, yet now I can't feel a thing."

The *Deutschland* shook herself and started to move, as if ready now to ease off the reef. He wrenched frantically at the beam again, then said, "I must get help, Lotte. I'll be back in a little while. I'll have to take the lantern, but don't be afraid."

"You won't leave me?"

"Never again. Remember my promise?"

He left her there and plowed back through the water, working his way from hold to hold. The *Deutschland* was in constant motion, nosing forward, slithering farther over the edge of the Washington, her prow dipping.

Richter hauled himself up the ladder in time to see the *Morag* moving in. The nuns were already making their way across from the shelter of Berger's cabin, the men on the quarterdeck crowding down the ladder.

There were cries of fear, and one of the women screamed high and shrill as the *Deutschland* moved again with a terrible rending and tearing sound.

Richter had to hang on tight to the ladder for a moment. He dropped down, waist deep in water, waded toward the hole in the bulkhead, and climbed through. The *Deutschland* was in constant motion now, water swirling all around him, but when he reached the saloon, there was that strange eerie quiet. And she was still there waiting for him when he went into the cabin. He hung up the lantern and sat down beside her.

"You came back."

"Of course."

"What's happening, Helmut?"

"They're coming for us, Lotte. They finally got here." He took her hand and held it tightly.

To Murdoch, debating on the best way to go in, that sudden tremble as the *Deutschland* slid toward the edge was enough.

"She's going, lad, she's going!" He slapped Gericke on the shoulder. "Give her everything you've got, full power and straight in over the rail. Two minutes is all we get."

Gericke boosted power, the *Morag* surged forward, catching even those on the quarterdeck by surprise, slicing in across the rail until her bows rested on the deck.

There was no need to say a word, for already the nuns were scurrying from Berger's cabin, shepherded by Sturmm, and Prager and Reeve, Jago, and the rest of them, were getting off the quarterdeck fast.

The *Deutschland* shook herself again and men cried out in fear, Sister Kathë screaming, falling across the rail. Janet reached over, dragged her bodily, pushed her down into the cockpit and the cabin.

"She'll take us with her, boy," Murdoch shouted. "Reverse those engines. Get ready!" He waved his arm and called furiously, "Come on, damn you! She's going!"

There was a final mad scramble, men vaulting over the rails in panic, Berger last of all, the ship's log and his personal journal in an oilskin wrapper under his arm. Gericke reversed the engines full power as the *Deutschland* sagged again, and the *Morag* shot away.

Sister Angela crouched in a corner of the small cabin. She tried to get up, peering at the faces crowded around her. "Lotte?" she said. "Where's Lotte?"

There was no reply—could be none. She turned, grabbed Janet's arm fiercely, and said in English, "Lotte isn't here—neither is Mister Richter. They must still be on board."

Janet scrambled out of the cabin into the cockpit. Jago was there, Reeve above him crouched beside Gericke and Murdoch. She shook Jago's arm. "There's still someone on board."

He seemed to find difficulty in speaking. "Not possible."

She reached up and pulled at Gericke's oilskin. "Paul—there's still someone on board."

He glanced down at her, startled. In the same moment, the *Deutschland* started to slide off the reef.

Berger, at the starboard rail, had tears in his eyes. As water boiled around her, his hand went up in a brief salute. For a moment, the main topmast was visible, then that, too, dropped beneath the surface and there was nothing—only the sea's leavings. A few planks, a tangle of rope, a barrel spinning.

Gericke, his face grave, turned the wheel, taking the *Morag* away from the Washington, around in a great curve, ready to start the slow and painful fight back through those mountainous seas to Fhada.

Barkentine Deutschland, *25 September 1944.
At three bells of the afternoon watch, with
the* Deutschland *sinking beneath us, the
sixteen survivors of her original complement
were snatched from the Washington Reef by
the lifeboat* Morag Sinclair, *Coxswain Murdoch Macleod and Korvettenkapitän Paul
Gericke of the* Kriegsmarine *combining in a
remarkable feat of seamanship. Afterward
they conveyed us to the neighboring island
of Fhada through heavy and mountainous
seas. I was distressed to learn that, one way
or another, seven people gave their lives to
save ours. Words, for the first time, fail me.
So ends this log.—Eric Berger, Master*

Sixteen

Reeve poured himself a large scotch and drank
it slowly. He was tired right through, more
conscious of his age than he had ever been.
The wind hammered against the roof of the cottage,
and he winced.

"No more, please," he whispered. "Enough is
enough."

He hobbled painfully across to his desk. What he needed now was sleep, but first there was work to be done. He reached for his pen and opened his journal. There was a knock at the door and Harry Jago entered, struggling to close it again against the wind. His face was swollen, the flesh split in a dozen places. Like Reeve, he seemed to find difficulty in walking.

"You don't look too good, Harry." The admiral pushed the bottle of Scotch across the desk. "Help yourself."

Jago went into the kitchen and came back with a glass. When he spoke, it was very slowly. "I feel like a dead man walking."

"I know what you mean. How's Janet?"

"Indestructible. It's like a field hospital at Fhada House, and she hasn't stopped since we got in."

"She's had plenty of practice. It's been a long war," the admiral said. "Still foul out there?"

"Nothing like as bad. Winds seven-to-eight, I'd say, and falling a little. She'll have blown herself out by morning."

He emptied his glass and Reeve filled it again. "I've been in touch with Murray on the radio. Chaotic over there apparently, but he's going to send a boat in the morning. Says he'll try and make it himself."

"What about the survivors? What will happen to them?"

"I don't know. Internment for the nuns, prison camp for Berger and his men." There was a long pause and Jago stared down into his glass. "You don't like that, do you?"

"It just doesn't have any meaning for me anymore. Not any of it."

"I know how you feel. All that bloody way and they nearly made it."

The Scotch by now was dulling the pain. "And Gericke?" Jago asked.

"What about him? There's still a war on, Harry."

"I know," Jago said. "There always is someplace. Does he go back in his cell?"

"That isn't my decision. Jean's the civil power here, you know that."

Jago emptied his glass at a swallow. "Well, I think I'll get back up to the house and see how my boys are doing."

"Then bed, Harry. Go to bed." Reeve managed a smile. "That's an order."

"Admiral." Jago drew himself up and managed a salute.

He had almost reached the door, had his hand out, when Reeve said softly, "Harry?"

Jago turned. "Yes, sir."

"All of a sudden I feel old, Harry. Too damned old. I just wanted to tell somebody that."

There was still quite a swell in the harbor as Gericke went along the pier, head down against the rain. The *Morag Sinclair* danced at her moorings, a brave sight in her blue-and-white paint. Only a closer inspection revealed the ferocious battering she had taken from the sea.

He stood there, hands thrust deep into the pockets of the reefer someone had given him, and suddenly he heard himself hailed. He turned and saw Murdoch on the lower landing farther along the pier, standing beside the *Katrina*.

As Gericke went down the stone steps, Lachlan came out of the wheelhouse. There was an oil drum on deck and he levered it over onto the landing with an ease that indicated that it was empty.

"What's this?" Gericke asked.

"Lachlan and I have been filling the *Katrina*'s tanks," the old man said. "That she may be ready for sea if wanted."

The boy nodded to Gericke. "Commander."

"I didn't have a chance to tell you before, but

you were fine out there, Lachlan." Gericke held out his hand. "I was proud to know you."

Lachlan flushed crimson, stared at the hand for a moment, grabbed it briefly, then turned and hurried away.

"There is good stuff there, I am thinking," Murdoch said. "Too good to be off to bloody war again in a few days." He started to fill his pipe, awkwardly because of his broken arm. "Have you spoken with Janet since returning?"

"She's had her hands more than full."

"Things must have eased considerably for her by now." The old man turned and looked out to sea through the driving rain. "Still rough, but not too rough."

"I suppose not."

Murdoch nodded. "Go see her now, boy."

"Yes, I believe I will."

He started to walk away and Murdoch called, "Commander."

"Yes?"

"Good luck to you."

For a long, long moment they looked at each other, then Gericke turned and hurried away along the pier.

As he went into the kitchen of Fhada House, Jean Sinclair turned from the stove with a bowl of hot water. "Hello," she said. "Are you looking for Janet?"

"Yes. Is she available?"

"Pretty busy last time I saw her. She has one of the sailors from the *Deutschland* on the table in the dining room. A broken arm."

"And the rest?"

"Mostly sleeping now. I think every bed in the house must be in use." She held up the bowl. "Sorry, I'll have to move on. Janet's waiting for this."

He opened the door. "And Captain Berger. Where is he?"

"First bedroom on the right, top of the stairs."

She went away quickly and Gericke climbed the stairs. He paused at the door she had indicated, knocked, and entered. Johann Sturmm and Leading Seaman Petersen lay on top of the bed, side by side, sleeping heavily. Berger was seated in a chair at a small table by the window, his head resting on his arms.

The log of the *Deutschland* was open before him. Gericke stood at his shoulder for a moment and read its last entry, then turned and tiptoed out.

As the door clicked behind him, Berger stirred and looked up, peering around the room through swollen eyelids. "Who's there?" he called hoarsely.

But there was no one. No one at all. His head sank down on his arms. He slept again.

Reeve was writing in his journal with care and considerable precision, mainly because he was more than a little drunk, when the door opened violently and Janet came in, Jago at her heels.

"Is Paul here?"

He laid down his pen and regarded her with drunken gravity. "Ah, Gericke, you mean. I didn't realize you two were on first-name terms."

He was mocking her and she flared angrily. "Has he been here?"

"Half an hour ago. Maybe a little longer. As a matter of fact we had a drink together, then he asked if he could leave something for you."

"What?" she demanded.

"He said it was a private matter. I think you'll find it in the bedroom, whatever it is."

She went out quickly into the hall and opened her bedroom door. The Knight's Cross with Oak Leaves lay, neatly arranged, on her pillow. She stared down at it, stupefied for a moment, then picked it up and ran back into the living room.

"Uncle Carey!" She held it out to him, her voice breaking.

Reeve nodded. "Now I understand. On his way out he said, 'Tell her she's earned it.' "

There was a knock at the door and Murdoch moved in. "Ah, there you are, Admiral."

"And what can I do for you?"

"A matter of official business only. The *Katrina* appears to be missing from her moorings."

"Is that a fact!" Reeve said. "It's a damned good thing I'm insured."

Janet ran out of the door. Jago turned to Reeve, leaning on the desk. "Are you going to notify Mallaig? They'll get to him soon enough up there in the Minch."

"Very unfortunate, Harry, but the radio appears to have packed in since I last talked to Murray. Valve gone, I think, and I don't have any spares. Just have to wait till they get here tomorrow. Nothing else to be done."

Jago took a long, long breath, then turned and went out. Murdoch said gravely, "Is that good Scotch you have there in that bottle, Carey Reeve?"

"And another in the cupboard when we've finished that. I've been holding out on you."

"Later, then, I will come back if I may. But now, I must see to my people."

He walked out. Reeve poured himself another whisky and resumed his writing.

> . . . *and so I see, when all is said and done, that this has been an old story. Murdoch, Harry Jago, and Gericke—men against the sea, who have won this time. But in the end, what is the nature of their achievement . . . ?*

God, but he was tired—more tired than he had ever been. The wind rattled the window as if trying to get in, but it could not touch him now. He pillowed his head on one arm for a moment and was instantly asleep, the pen still firm in his good hand and resting on that final entry.

ABOUT THE AUTHOR

JACK HIGGINS is the author of *The Last Place God Made*, *The Savage Day*, *A Prayer for the Dying* and *The Eagle Has Landed* (a runaway bestseller here and abroad and soon to be released as a major motion picture).

"HITLER'S WAR"

From the German point of view and secret Nazi documents never before revealed to the public, here is the whole gigantic drama of the most crucial days of World War II. Bantam now presents the books that individually capture the major personalities and events of the war.

DON'T MISS
THESE CURRENT
Bantam Bestsellers

☐	DR. ATKINS DIET REVOLUTION	(11001—$2.25)
☐	HOW TO SPEAK SOUTHERN Mitchell & Rawls	(10970—$1.25)
☐	BLACK SUNDAY Thomas Harris	(10940—$2.25)
☐	THE LAST CHANCE DIET Dr. Robert Linn	(10490—$1.95)
☐	THE LAST TYCOON F. Scott Fitzgerald	(10419—$1.95)
☐	VOTE FOR LOVE Barbara Cartland	(10341—$1.50)
☐	MAVREEN Claire Lorrimer	(10208—$1.95)
☐	LETTERS HOME Sylvia Plath	(10202—$2.50)
☐	DUBAI Robin Moore	(10099—$1.95)
☐	LIFE AFTER LIFE Raymond Moody, Jr.	(10080—$1.95)
☐	DORIS DAY: HER OWN STORY A. E. Hotchner	(2888—$1.95)
☐	LINDA GOODMAN'S SUN SIGNS	(2777—$1.95)
☐	MEMOIRS Tennessee Williams	(2768—$1.95)
☐	THE GAMBLING MAN Catherine Cookson	(2749—$1.75)
☐	RAGTIME E. L. Doctorow	(2600—$2.25)
☐	THE EAGLE HAS LANDED Jack Higgins	(2500—$1.95)
☐	ASPEN Burt Hirschfeld	(2491—$1.95)
☐	THE MAGIC OF FINDHORN Paul Hawken	(2463—$2.25)
☐	THE MONEYCHANGERS Arthur Hailey	(2300—$1.95)
☐	HELTER SKELTER Vincent Bugliosi	(2222—$1.95)

Buy them at your local bookstore or use this handy coupon for ordering:

Bantam Book Catalog

Here's your up-to-the-minute listing of every book currently available from Bantam.

This easy-to-use catalog is divided into categories and contains over 1400 titles by your favorite authors.

So don't delay—take advantage of this special opportunity to increase your reading pleasure.

Just send us your name and address and 25¢ (to help defray postage and handling costs).